TRIBURBIA

ALSO BY KARL TARO GREENFELD

Boy Alone

NowTrends

China Syndrome

Standard Deviations

Speed Tribes

TRIBURBIA

A Novel

Karl Taro Greenfeld

HARPER

An Imprint of HarperCollins*Publishers*
www.harpercollins.com

HarperCollins books may be purchased for educational, business, or sales promotional use. For information, please write: Special Markets Department, HarperCollins Publishers, 10 East 53rd Street, New York, NY 10022.

Portions of this book appeared previously, in slightly different form, in *The Paris Review, Commentary,* and *Hobart.*

FIRST EDITION

Designed by Renato Stanisic

Map by Harry Campbell

Library of Congress Cataloging-in-Publication Data has been applied for.

ISBN: 978-0-06-213239-0

12 13 14 15 16 OV/RRD 10 9 8 7 6 5 4 3 2 1

FOR MY FATHER

TRIBURBIA

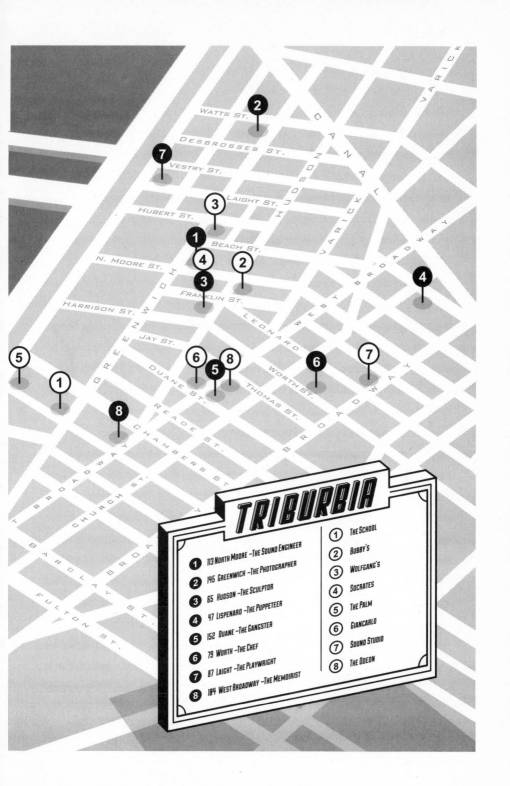

TRIBURBIA

1. 113 North Moore – The Sound Engineer
2. 145 Greenwich – The Photographer
3. 65 Hudson – The Sculptor
4. 47 Lispenard – The Puppeteer
5. 152 Duane – The Gangster
6. 79 Worth – The Chef
7. 87 Laight – The Playwright
8. 184 West Broadway – The Memoirist

1. The School
2. Bubby's
3. Wolfgang's
4. Socrates
5. The Palm
6. Giancarlo
7. Sound Studio
8. The Odeon

113 North Moore

That's me, lurking by the elementary school wrought-iron fence, standing with my hands in the pockets of my peacoat. I'm half-Chinese, half-Caucasian, shoulder-length black hair, ovoid face, epicanthic eyes, soft nose, thick lips, still boyish, I like to think, at age thirty-seven. Behind me are the children, my daughters included, a rabbling swirl of high-pitched noise, shouts piercing other shouts, aural confetti, almost impossible to reproduce in a sound studio. Around me are my fellow parents. Dutiful. Concerned about the school. But don't underestimate them. They will draw and quarter you if they think you might fuck with their kids. God help you if you happen to venture onto the playground at the wrong time. I did it once, trying to record that school-yard din for a project of mine. I walked right into the recess playground through the unlocked gate, wearing headphones, carrying an omnidirectional microphone and a digital recorder. Teachers, attendants, and parent volunteers swarmed me—they came rappelling down walls, climbing from sewer grates, materializing in clouds of smoke—before I could get close to a child. The look in their vigilante eyes, their eagerness, it was almost like they were hoping I was a pervert, some sicko, just so all their dark fears would be justified. They were angry with me when it turned out I was a parent and *not* a sexual predator. I was sternly warned not to return to the school unless I was accompanying my daughters.

Here's what's wrong with us: there's nothing at stake. That makes us oversensitive to minor transgressions, prone to disproportionate responses, quick to counterattack.

We are a prosperous community. Our lofts and apartments are worth millions. Our wives vestigially beautiful. Our renovations as vast and grand in scale as the construction of ocean liners, yet we regularly assure ourselves that our affluence does not define us. We are better than that. Measure us by the books on our shelves, the paintings on our walls, the songs on our iTunes playlists, our children in their secure little school. We live in smug certainty that our taste is impeccable, our politics correct, our sense of outrage at the current regime totally warranted.

Our neighborhood was settled by artists so long ago the story feels apocryphal. For almost as soon as the larger world became aware of Tribeca, in rushed developers and syndicators and builders and realtors and the name turned into a synonym for a kind of urban living: a little edgy, perhaps, but ultimately safer and richer even than Scarsdale. A certain type of family arrived, drawn by that safety and the faux-bohemianism of Downtown, driving out the actual bohemians. And now, we faux-bohemians find ourselves facing the onslaught of those who don't even pretend to give a shit about books or theater.

We are cosseted, a warm little precinct, connected to the rest of the city, but for all our interaction with it, it feels as if there are drawbridges that keep out the would-be brigands and freebooters. They are among us on these sidewalks, but we don't notice them, the chubby minority girls in their sweatpants and string-strap day-packs, the boys on their way to the community college with their heavy parkas and earphones, rapping as they strut. They are local color: harmless, we tell ourselves, as unlikely to cause havoc as the pizza-delivery man or the fellow from Guatemala who works at the deli.

So it is a shock when an icy hand reaches in and ruins a life. We wake up to the news and feel that a blade has scraped against our heart. We look at our children and wonder how we let them become so exposed, but then, the sense of safety, the cordoned-off warmth, wasn't that always the aberration? An island of gentle deceit in a dark, hostile sea of truth, truth, truth?

———

I SEE MY friends across the street, fellow fathers in their late thirties, prosperous professionals in the arts. There is the sculptor, the playwright, the film producer, the memoirist, the photographer, even the "contractor"—our local thug—most of them ostensibly artists but actually businessmen. They believe their awareness of their own hypocrisies keeps them from being hypocrites. I'm not an artist qua artist, as they are. But most days I join them and we make our way in twos and threes to a steak house recently taken to serving breakfast. We convene in a large round booth, ordering coffee, eggs, toast, Cream of Wheat. We spread out newspapers and discuss films, television, political candidates, sports. You know what this bantering conversation is like. We tell ourselves that our palaver is wittier, cleverer than most, unique somehow. We are artists, writers, professional hipsters of one sort or another, and so we must be funnier than you. But then we would think that, wouldn't we? We are here, in this privileged canton, in this city, in this gilded era, so why shouldn't we be confident that our banter surpasses yours?

Yet this morning there is a rift, as an argument clouds the usual jocularity. A young girl, twelve years old, has been violated just a few blocks north of here, on a street banked by multimillion-dollar lofts. The men around this table are divided as to the threat, the appropriate level of fear, the correct response. Details are scant. She was letting herself into her building and was followed. That much is clear. Yet what happened after that is murky. The defiler joined her in the elevator, took her to the basement, and then . . . what? Nobody is sure. The newspaper accounts make clear she was not sodomized or penetrated. Did he compel her to touch him? What, exactly, happened?

Sumner, the film producer, is the most visibly concerned. He says that this is not the first time he has heard of young women being molested in the neighborhood. Why, there was the day last spring when Sumner himself was part of a group of concerned parents who chased a suspicious man with a camera from a local park.

Sumner, slightly older, graying around a shiny dome, bushy beard, handsome in an avuncular kind of way, looks around the table as if expecting huzzahs for his bravery at keeping the park free of sex offenders. He holds forth in his distinctive voice; it is throaty, almost hoarse. I have a good ear for voices and cadences, and Sumner has stretches during which he speaks in almost perfect ^{2}/$_2$ time. That rhythm makes it very hard to interrupt him.

"Within five hundred yards of where we are sitting right now," he says sternly, "there are five thousand registered sex offenders."

"Shut the fuck up, Sumner," the playwright says.

"What a big man you are, Sumner," I say, "keeping the neighborhood safe."

"You can laugh," Sumner says, "but this is a serious issue. A real issue."

"She probably knew the guy," I say. "Aren't most of these cases like that? The girl knew the guy?"

Sumner claims to know, for certain, that she didn't know him, that this was a stranger, an outsider who came into our community to molest a young girl.

I tell him he sounds hysterical. He tells me I have daughters, that I should be worried.

"Sumner," I tell him, "get over it. Not everybody wants to fuck your kids."

―――――――

I AM A noisemaker, known professionally as a sound engineer, providing the jiggle and wobble and chirp and boom that accompanies so much of our popular entertainment. Every commercial, television show, and film requires a host of effects to provide verisimilitude: a door opens, a box of cereal is poured, a phone is hung up. Each makes a sound, but if you merely record the actual noise, it won't be satisfyingly authentic. So I must amplify, distort, manufacture, repeat, substitute. I own a sound studio with a half-dozen edit bays in which filmed images can be projected and a few of us can sit behind mixers and computers to sync up the appropriate effects. I have boxes of different types of shoes, a wide range of sample floor surfaces—wood, stone, tile—a plywood board with two dozen locks and latches on it. I have gained some renown for my ability to discern and manipulate sound. I'm even asked on occasion to testify as an expert witness when prosecutors need to make an identification based on a voice-mail message or recorded conversation.

Of course, I didn't set out to become a noisemaker. I backed into it. I was a singer, a composer, a producer, a guitar player—I still have expensive electric guitars on stands in my studio; they glisten like museum pieces. I know many musicians from my generation of punk rockers in Los Angeles and New York who went on to some degree of fame in the music business. I produced and engineered albums by a few bands that never quite made it, but doing that I learned to make and control noise. The sound engineering began, in part, because I had the equipment. Friends asked me to help them on various projects; I found the work easy; they paid me well. I bought more equipment, purchased a floor in a vast old building, and became, in effect, a kind of landlord to others who work with noise. The renting of that studio space to filmmakers, sound engineers, and sound editors has turned out to be more lucrative than my own noisemaking; it actually allows me to support my family in this expensive city.

I also married well. Brooke is a tall, strapping, freckled brunette from a vast Connecticut family in which distant relatives turn to corpses at the rate of 1 every 2.5 years, leaving us generous amounts of shares, bonds, and cash.

All this has allowed me to maintain my bohemian style, my belief that I am somehow different than the bankers and attorneys who predominate in our community. I am still an artist, I tell myself, a creative person who happens to live among the bourgeoisie. This is not a small American achievement, I must tell you. The mongrel me, born in Hong Kong, raised in San Francisco, a state college graduate, joining with a prize American specimen like my wife. She could have picked anyone, yet she ended up with a halfbreed. I have traveled miles raising myself to this station. And it was an effort, a prodigious act of will. That is what those other fathers will never understand. I wasn't shown to my place. I had to scrap my way here. These were calculated decisions. These other gentlemen, they fell into it: private liberal arts colleges, internships, jobs at galleries, assisting more powerful men. For me, there was no easy path. I had no choice but to be ruthless.

And that is why, in the days that follow, as our little community is consumed by fear of the sexual predator in our midst, I find myself hoping that this man, this savage, is not an interloper but a local, a member of our tribe gone horribly awry, so that these fathers will have to blame themselves rather than simply close ranks.

"DADDY," SAYS MY eight-year-old daughter, Cooper. "That looks like you!"

We are walking past the cozy lobby entrances, the doormen standing smartly behind their stations, the bulbous fish-eye cameras protruding from above doorbell buzzers. Mornings like this, our neighborhood seems like it is made up entirely of parents taking their children to school and men and women in suits marching up the pavement to their offices.

The legal-size flyers are glued to lampposts, freebie newspaper boxes, work-site barricades. The staring face on them does look like me. He is supposed to be Caucasian, or so says the description beneath the black-and-white composite sketch, but he looks Hispanic, or, actually, as my daughter has pointed out, like me—Amer-Asian.

"Is that you?" asks Penny, our six-year-old.

"No," I tell them, a little too loudly. I try again. "No. That's a man who did something wrong."

"What did he do?" asks Penny.

Cooper, who can read, has no doubt already made out: WANTED: SEX OFFENDER. The word *sex*, I assume, has tipped her that this is an adult matter. "It's about sex," she says.

"What's sex?" asks Penny.

"When a girl and a boy kiss," Cooper says.

"Eeewww!" Penny says. "That's gross."

"But what did he do wrong?" Cooper asks me.

"He, um, kissed someone he wasn't supposed to."

"Who?"

"A girl." We're standing at the corner now, waiting for the light. The flyers are tacked up everywhere, that face gazing back dumbly. He could be lurking around every corner, right here, in front of the deli, or having coffee just inside the bakery windows. We must be vigilant, the posters insist—protective. "A young girl."

Cooper considers this. "But why are they looking for him?"

"Because kissing is bad," Penny says.

"No, kissing is not bad." As I say this, a mother and daughter walk past in the opposite direction, the woman in a fur-collared coat, the bespectacled little girl in a wool-and-shearling parka. The mother overhears me, looks at me, considers for a moment where she has seen my face—the flyers are frickin' everywhere—and seems to be momentarily confused. I feel like shouting, "I'm not him!" but that would be awkward. Instead, I unfasten my po-nytail so my long hair hangs loose.

I deposit my children in the yard, standing by Penny and hold-ing her hand until her friends join her and she seems to forget about me. There are no flyers in the school yard, thank god, and in the busy throng of parents and bundled-up children, my resem-blance to the suspect is unnoticed.

———

IN THE RESTAURANT at breakfast, I learn that Sumner is behind the campaign to wrap the neighborhood in flyers. As a member of Community Board 1, a parent deeply involved in the local PTA, a big *macher* in the Friends of Washington Market Park Associa-tion, he ordered that the flyers be printed and he led the team of volunteers that spent six hours last night stapling and pasting and taping them throughout the neighborhood. It is urgent, he stresses, to be hypervigilant.

Sumner is between projects, temporarily supported by his wife, a gallery owner and truffler of young men and women who make expensive art. She has been profiled in glossy magazines and Sumner, embarrassingly, always brings along those issues and shares them with us. His own credits, or what I can gather from Googling him and typing his name into IMDb, consist of a minor picture starring a major actor, and a television movie, both over a decade old.

"Sumner," I tell him, "if the guy is supposed to be white—"

The playwright cuts me off, smiling. "Then how come he looks like you?"

"Well," I say, "yeah."

Sumner says the police gave him that sketch, and in the photocopying the image darkened. "Why do you care?"

"It's just that, if you're looking for a white guy, why have a picture where the guy clearly doesn't look white?"

Sumner waves me off and shakes his head. "We are doing whatever we have to do, as a community."

"I'm imagining guys with pitchforks and torches marching up and down Hudson Street," says the playwright.

"If that's what it takes," Sumner says.

———

LATER, I AM at one of my studios going through the bookings with the manager when I look up and see two men in bubble parkas smiling at me through the sliding-glass window. They are doing postproduction on a pilot for a hip-hop version of *American Idol* in Studio C, which now smells strongly of marijuana smoke.

"Yo, it's fuckin' Chester the Molester." They are holding the flyer up and pointing to me.

I shake my head, smiling. "Read the fine print. It says 'Caucasian,' okay?"

They squint. "This shit's almost too small to read, but, yo, it don't say nothing about Caucasian."

They saunter down the hall, laughing.

I decide to head home. On my way back to the loft, I stop at a construction site where about three dozen of the flyers have been pasted. I notice that the line about the perpetrator's race has vanished. Now, beneath the bold WANTED: SEX OFFENDER, it only describes the whereabouts and time of the alleged attack. Below that is the sketch that might as well be of me.

I tell myself that no one is going to think I am the sex offender. Why would they? We've been living here since before Cooper was born. We are pillars of the community. I should just ignore it.

But I can't. When I go to the bank, the FedEx office, the coffee shop, I feel like I am the subject of intense scrutiny. Everyone who lives or works in the neighborhood must have seen the flyer, Sumner and his minions apparently having nothing to do but work on their campaign. The local freebie newspaper has even run a story about the effort to keep our community safe from sexual predators. The community board, according to the article, is considering hiring a guard for the local playground, additional security at the school. The tone of the article is of barely contained hysteria: quotes from mothers about spotting suspicious characters lurking near the school; a secondhand account of the man chased from the park last year (no mention of whether he was actually dangerous); and even a story about someone attempting an un-authorized recording in the playground at our elementary school. The description of this last incident is so sinister and compelling that I read the entire paragraph before realizing they are talking about me.

Then, that evening, while I'm looking through my daughters' homework folders, I find they have a sheaf of the flyers in the pocket where there is usually a list of assignments and returned classwork.

"Why do you guys have these?" I ask Cooper, who is sitting at the computer in her room, playing a game with one of her virtual pets.

Penny sits in a seat beside her, watching.

"We're supposed to take them home."

"For what?"

"I don't know," Cooper says. "To give to people?"

When I ask who told them to do this, they explain that there

was an assembly at school and a woman from the police department told them to report any suspicious-looking men and then
handed out these flyers.

"Why do you have so many?"

"I took a lot because they look like you," Cooper says.

"We're gonna draw on them," Penny adds.

I say that they shouldn't have them and that I am throwing
them away. The suddenly angry tone of my voice shocks them and
Penny starts crying, running into the dining room, where Brooke
is flipping through a Pottery Barn catalog. I can hear Penny sobbing, "Daddy yelled at me in a mean voice."

As she consoles our daughter, Brooke looks at me sternly. Her
eyes are red, veiny; she's already had her late-afternoon/early-
evening toke.

"What's wrong with you?" she asks me later.

I show her the flyer, not bothering to point out the similarity.

"Who cares?"

"How would you feel if everywhere you went there was a picture of you beneath the words *sex offender*?"

"But it's not you."

"It looks like me. Even the kids thought it was me."

Last year, when Brooke found out about my walking into the
yard with the microphone and headphones, she was furious, asking
me what the hell I had been thinking. Actually, I hadn't been
thinking. There was a crowd scene at a park in a television show
I was working on and I thought I could grab the sounds in the
playground. Brooke said I had embarrassed her, but I never really
understood what the big deal was.

Now, unspoken in our conversation, I can sense her belief
that I am guilty—not of attacking a young girl but of naive stupidity. She says, "If you didn't do anything then why would you
care?"

I don't want to answer her. "I don't know; it's embarrassing."

"Are you hiding something?" she says, half-joking, eyebrows arched.

"Of course not."

I try to remember where I was on the night in question. I have no idea. But why am I trying to come up with an alibi? In case I need it, I suppose, in case the uncanny resemblance between the perpetrator and myself leads to my being officially accused.

The next morning outside the school, after drop-off, I tap Sumner on the shoulder. He stands with a group of mothers bundled up in their parkas and wool coats. Sumner flirts shamelessly with the mothers.

"Why doesn't the flyer say the guy is white?" I ask.

"What are you talking about?"

"The flyer, of the sex offender, it doesn't mention his race anymore."

Sumner shrugs. "It got too blurry from all the copying, so we whited it out."

"But then how does anyone know who they're looking for?"

"What? It's a guy who—who looks like that. It's not confusing." Sumner shakes his head. The women behind him are all monitoring our conversation. Sumner's metronomic $2/2$ cadence is clearly audible all around us. "Why are you always questioning this project?"

"Because it seems a little hysterical."

"This is very real," Sumner says. "You have to look at your own motives here."

"What are you talking about?"

"There was the incident last year, with the microphone."

The women behind him all nod.

"Are you accusing me of something?"

"No, I'm just saying, there is the resemblance, so . . . ." He stops.

"Where were you that night?" a brunette with a short, puggish nose behind him suddenly asks. I know who she is. She is married to a guitar player in an important though not commercially successful group.

I walk away.

———————

THE COMMUNITY HAS turned against me. I was an impostor all along, they seem to have realized, ersatz, and my counterfeit composition has now been deduced. I am a fraud. A half-breed passing in this privileged sanctum for wealthy pseudo-bohemians, artists, and artist manqués. I never really belonged, and this is their way of rooting me out. But then, don't we all feel like we are on borrowed time? Like sooner or later the truth about our base natures will be revealed and we will be shown for who we really are?

I begin to run through the possibilities. What if I am arrested? What if I am found guilty? Imprisoned? We've all heard the stories: they castrate sexual offenders in prison, sodomize them, torture them, the guards condone it. Is that to be my punishment?

I am not surprised when the police arrive. They are detectives, dressed in warm-looking parkas, wearing jeans and sneakers. The taller of the two nods and looks around my office. "First Precinct," he says.

I am suddenly acutely aware of my environs. There are file cabinets behind me, an antique wooden desk in front of me, and a television next to the door. Boxes containing noise-creating artifacts are labeled and stacked along the wall beside me—SCRAPING; BANGING; RIPPING & TEARING; LEAKING & BLEEDING. There are piles of children's shoes in an opened box beside the desk, labeled CHILD & BABY STEPS. A few dozen gloves of varying sizes are piled up on a table next to me, where I have been trying them on and removing them, listening for any variation. I slide off a long, slender, up-to-the-elbow white leather woman's glove and set it down on the desk.

"Yes?"

I had been expecting men in uniform or perhaps suits and ties, like cops on television. These two gentlemen, both Hispanic, mid-thirties, look like guys who might work at the deli. They don't show me any badges. They just ask me my name, if this is my studio, if I am a sound engineer. I answer affirmatively.

I want to tell them that I have an alibi. I am almost sure I was here at the studio that night, working late. I've looked at the logs to see who was renting space that evening and have their phone numbers ready. They will remember that I was working on a series for the Military Channel. They will have seen me in Studio B. Or in the hallway. Or perhaps here, digging through the props. I can prove my innocence.

The detectives are stoic and patient. They are not in a hurry.

"We have something for you," the taller officer says.

I am wondering if I should accept anything from them without an attorney's advice.

"We have a job for you," his partner says.

Is this how they arrest people? By toying with them?

"Is that a euphemism?" I say.

"A what?" the taller officer says. "No, it's a tape. Or whatever you call these things."

He hands me a flash memory stick.

In the midst of her struggle in that basement, as she was being groped and wrestled, the violated girl accidentally made a phone call to a random stranger's voice mail.

"Some Mormon in Utah listened to this and we're lucky she didn't think it was an obscene phone call."

His partner cuts him off. "Heavy breathing, panting, some guy's voice."

They want me to work with the file, to bring up the man's voice and tamp down the rest of the sound, so that they might more easily identify the perpetrator.

"Isn't that what you do," the tall gent says, "work with sound?" I shrug. "I can try."

———————

I SIT DOWN in Studio B and slide on a pair of headphones. The recording is awash with white noise, hisses, a banging like a radiator clanging. There is the soft hum of an elevator motor. The mechanical clunk of an elevator door sliding open. They must be near the elevator. They are in a basement. Every sound is exaggerated and faintly doubled by the echo. I can clearly make out a man's voice, urging, insistent. Is the girl sobbing? It's an awful scene and I am able to project myself there all too easily. I can visualize the location. The girl is pushed against the wall. The man is facing her, his voice more clear and cutting because the sound waves are bouncing off the concrete into her phone's mouthpiece. I know how to reduce the levels of extraneous noise. The man's voice is a lower mid-register, clear when it emerges from its throaty beginning. I am stripping away the bass and treble, reducing the hiss, finding and eliminating those parts of the file containing the radiator clangs. I keep removing and excising and soon all I am left with is the man's voice, a strangely familiar voice.

No one ever comes to retrieve the file.

When I call the precinct a few weeks later, I am given a case number and passed along to a detective's voice mail. He doesn't call back. I finally e-mail an MP3 to one of the detectives who visited me.

The flyers have been replaced by other, less insistent notices: a poster for a new release by a rock band, a missing dog, Cirque du Soleil is coming back to town.

It is warmer now. The children walking to school must skirt between alfresco tables and the curb; the boys in aprons hosing down the sidewalks direct their spray away from them as they pass. After school, the parks are crowded, the nannies on benches, the less dutiful of them talking on cell phones in their native patois. I like to take my daughters there, and if I have a free afternoon, I pick them up at school and walk them over, past the ice-cream truck where the long line is no deterrent. They ask for bright red or purple confections with names like Twoball Screwball or Very-BerryBlast, which taste like frozen, crushed-up Lifesavers and have gumballs or jawbreakers at their cores. With our ice-cream novelties in hand, we find a spot among the nannies. Penny and Cooper seldom finish their treats; they dig out their gumballs and leave me to dispose of soggy cardboard cups bleeding garish red.

I have stopped joining the other fathers for coffee in the morning. And when I see Sumner now, standing by the swing with his daughters, I don't acknowledge him. He sees me and walks over, smiling, as if unaware of any change in our relationship.

He tells me he's been producing a reality show for a pay-cable station and has just returned from shooting in Vancouver.

I tell him I've been busy too.

I ask what happened to the molester. Did they ever find him? Do they have any leads?

He shakes his head. But the community, he tells me, the community learned a valuable lesson.

When I ask what that lesson is, he shrugs, suddenly uninterested, and trots after his daughter, who is shouting for him.

145 GREENWICH

I have since known many actual models, all of them skinny and adolescent-seeming. My sister Shannon, at seventeen, was already too womanly to be in the running.

Shannon had reddish hair, curled like lazy rapids, green eyes, small nose, and protuberant, exquisitely shaped lips. She was darkly pigmented for a redhead, tight-pored skin, bronzed and flawless. Shannon had been the only eighth-grader in the history of our beach town to go to the high school's senior prom. By the time she herself was a junior, she had attained a level of local fame similar to that of a star high school football quarterback. Whispers followed her. Speculation: would she be a model?

Most of our classmates didn't know she had a brother. We had never before attended the same school.

I arrived during her senior year. I was in ninth grade, finally deemed ready to transition to a mainstream school. I had been begging my parents for this for years. Whitney, the school for what were then called the handicapped, had been academically unsatisfying, in part because some of my classmates had intellectual developmental delays accompanying their physical shortcomings, but also because of an attitude, still prevalent, that those of us who suffered from some motor, muscular, or skeletal deficiencies should be made to feel good about ourselves in other areas.

I was the best student in the school—reading, writing, and doing mathematics well beyond my grade level. Even in my physical disability—Little's Disease that had slightly ameliorated so that I now had decent range of motion but with my right leg still severely limited—I was less affected than many of my classmates. I had been born with the condition, and so my body had taken on the distorted shape that results from the hypertrophying of some muscles and atrophying of others: I was thick of chest and neck, but with arms and legs like twigs barbed with tight, disobedient musculature. When I was diagnosed at fifteen months, the doctors told my parents I would likely spend my life in a wheelchair, yet by the time I was eight I was hobbling around on crutches. And soon, with new drugs (the horrible phenol injections), laborious resistance-training therapy, and braces and specially designed sneakers, I learned to walk without a crutch. It was a curious, loping sort of gait that pistoned me up and down so that if you were watching me from across the street, you would see my head periodically bobbing over the roofs of parked cars. My right leg would sweep out and around instead of bending at the knee, then my left would make a more typical step. At first, I could only walk like this for a few meters, a half-hour a day, but within a year, I could keep it up through the whole school day. I told my parents and teachers that I wanted to go to the regular high school, the real high school. I was ready.

The morning of my first day, I pushed myself out of bed—I'd had my father dismantle the pulley I'd used as a younger boy—and swung myself onto the stool I used to dress myself, hurriedly reaching for my clothes to ward off my anxiety. This would be the hardest thing I had ever done, throwing myself into the mainstream this way, eschewing forever the protection of special schools, special classes, special treatment, the ghetto-izing shelter of "special." I had been a king at Whitney, the popular boy in a school of rejects, as I saw us. And now, well, what could I be but the inverse of that?

Shannon appeared in my doorway.

"Dude, first day," she smiled. She was already dressed, in a tight-fitting T-shirt that showed off her bust and jeans that similarly advantaged her rear. Presumably, it was outfits like this, on girls other than my sister, which should have made the prospect of regular high school so attractive to me. Shannon knew I didn't like her to help me, and so she stood for a while in the threshold. I pulled on the Hang Ten T-shirt I had chosen for this morning and a pair of jeans. I had been growing my hair out so that it was down to my shoulders—where Shannon's hair was a lovely dark red, mine was a mousy, disappointing brown. I had bought a denim notebook that I had adorned with a Lightning Bolt sticker, though I wasn't sure exactly what that stood for.

———

OUR PARENTS HAD given Shannon their old Audi 100, olive green, sagging front bumper, partially scratched-out KMET 94.7 decal on the rear below the four-circle emblem.

"You nervous?" she asked as she buckled her seat belt.

I shook my head.

"You are!" she said, smiling.

I had thought I would resent her reassurance, but when it wasn't forthcoming, I was disappointed.

At school, we parked in the lot, on a gradual slope above the campus, and then, as if by prearrangement, we immediately separated; Shannon, car key-chain stuffed bear dangling from her back pocket, marched off ahead of me, joining up with one of her friends while I made my slow, oscillating walk to my first class.

I have since read about how fledglings, when they are too big for the nest but not yet ready for flight, hide in underbrush, in shadow, waiting for their parents to come back with a morsel. They are at their most vulnerable then—to cats, snakes, other birds, people—and their only hope is to stay invisible. This was what my first few days of high school were like. I was actually in shadow, seated beneath the outdoor stairwell, eating my sandwich, watching my sister and her friends, invisible to them. They occupied what seemed to be the center of the entire school, the brick retaining wall of a circular planter that got the most direct sunlight of any spot in the school. My sister was in the vortex of concentric rings of power. Around her the other pretty girls, then, around them, a larger circle, the surfers and the volleyball players, the best-looking boys, and then a larger circle around them of slightly less attractive girls, and then another circle, of boys less handsome, and so on until finally, at the outer edge of all this, was me.

I don't know why I had expected anything else. And I now wondered at my rush to go to a regular school. These were the years before mainstreaming, when it became more common for kids like me to attend a normal high school. Back then, I was expected to attempt to do everything my classmates did, which meant I had to strip for gym class, change into light-green-and-white uniform, and join my fellow freshmen on the basketball court or sports field, at least until the actual games commenced, at which time I was allowed to sit by myself on the sidelines.

But I never thought about going back to Whitney. Instead, I discovered that great panacea for all high school afflictions: marijuana. I knew that those students who socialized with me were themselves undesirable caste-mates. But I couldn't be selective and so found myself spending lunch breaks with the lowest rung of high school society. These were the kids who looked like they should be grinding through differential calculus and AP biology and getting straight As but who were instead smoking too much dope, listening to Black Sabbath, and flunking out. There were popular stoners, the good-looking surfers, but they were a different species from our crowd, interacting only for the purposes of the occasional petty drug transaction.

But in that way, I found a little group of friends. While my parents were concerned about my sudden academic decline, they excused it as part of the transition to this new school. What I didn't explain was that I was struggling in geometry and French because they were after lunch, and every day at lunch we went to chubby Doug Wirta's house across the street from the school and took bong hits and watched reruns of *The Wild Wild West*. I would then invert a Visine bottle over my eyes, and make my ridiculous lope back to school, where I'd sit, absolutely bewildered, through Mrs. Morley's explanations of the properties of lines and angles.

———————

"YOU'RE SHANNON HARRIS'S *brother?*" Brett Saucer, volleyball player, surfer, beautiful boy, said to me at Doug Wirta's house. Among Saucer's quirks was exercising his Alaskan husky dog by having him tow Saucer around on a skateboard. You would see Saucer, slaloming at the end of the leash, the black-and-white, furry dog paddling along with his tongue flapping. Because of my precociousness and his academic indifference, Saucer and I shared a biology class—Mr. Farnham's second-floor classroom crowded with amphibians, reptiles, and small mammals and smelling of decomposing vegetable matter. Saucer and I had never spoken. He had stopped by Doug Wirta's house to buy a half-ounce of mumbo. The town was dry, and Doug was holding, so the rigid hierarchy softened to accommodate the transaction.

I nodded. I was seated on a leather sofa, a bong on the glass-topped coffee table in front of me.

"She's so hot," Saucer said. He had long blond hair that fell almost to his shoulders. He had a dimple on his chin that softened his otherwise stern facial features. I wondered, as I watched him, if popular kids knew they were popular or if they wondered if they were popular and so on, all the way up to my sister. And what if all through life, this worrying about one's own status would be a constant. The prospect was terrifying. Saucer opened the baggie of marijuana and sniffed at it. "Do you even see that? 'Cause she's your sister? Can you even tell she's hot?"

I could, of course, but I just shook my head.

He looked around Doug Wirta's house, the kitchen and dining area separated by a galley, the tongue-in-groove paneling, the reproductions of what I would later realize were George Rouault clowns. His gaze settled on me, then on chubby Doug Wirta, and he paused, as if he was suddenly remembering where he was, who he was with, and then he nodded, as if surprised by his present company. "Hey, why does Mr. Farnham have all those animals in his classroom if he, like, never uses them? I mean, not once does he put them in, like, an experiment."

He had a point.

––––––––

THE NEXT DAY at school, I was traversing the quad near the planter, my backpack sliding up and down my back as I bobbed along, my sneakers scraping the pavement. By now, I had assumed my invisibility was a protective cloak that would allow me to traverse real estate at the center of the universe.

"Dude," Saucer said as I passed. He stood up from the planter, and pointed at me excitedly as if I were an elusive piece of trivia that he had been wracking his brain for. "Shannon's brother!"

I felt a dozen faces turn toward me. I had no choice: I had to materialize in this world.

"Shannon!" Saucer shouted, looking around.

I could detect her before I saw her. Her place was to our right, about four hours counterclockwise around the planter.

Beautiful girls parted and there she was, standing at the end of a tunnel of teen pulchritude.

Thankfully, the onus of conversation was on Shannon and not me, because I was at a loss. Saucer, who genuinely had no idea that he had upset a delicate balance, was grinning widely. He was, I realized, happy to see me.

"Hey Barnaby," Shannon said, and then the phalanx of lovely girls closed again and I was left with Saucer. He stood close to me, arms folded, nodding.

"Dude, this is the first time I've seen you here." He nodded. His eyes were bloodshot. "Hey, let's go up to your friend's house at lunch. Rip some hits."

———

SHANNON DROVE ME twice a week for my phenol injections, the purpose of which was to deaden the muscles in my hips and knees, supposedly to loosen them, increasing my range of motion. The shots were painful, a series of probing jabs deep into muscles and nerves around the hips and shoulders, the nurses vigorously attempting to inject as much diluted poison as deep into my body as they could. I had learned to lie quiet during this process, yet when I came to get my shots after smoking marijuana, my distorted sense of the passage of time made the pain seem elongated and horrible, and the deep stinging triggered a ringing sound in my middle ear.

Shannon and I had been closer before I became her schoolmate, I realized. Shannon had been attentive, in part because, I think, she saw me as not her equal or even of her species. I had been, perhaps, the family mascot, a great success in overcoming my worst limitations, but ultimately, just that: limited, easily categorized as not a real person. My appearance in her school, her occasional glimpses of my ridiculous gait down the outdoor halls, in the juice line at nutrition break, or mingling with my new friends and their prodigious amounts of orthodontics, had informed her that I was somehow like her, of her, was even—potentially—publicly associated with her.

She never scorned me nor avoided me, but I knew not to approach her while we were at school. There, we were strangers.

In the car, on the way to get my shots, she asked about school, about how it was going, and her tone was that of offering counsel, but when I told her that it was difficult, that I was finding the classes harder, that it was a challenge to make friends, instead of sage advice, she kept silent.

"Do you want to go back to Whitney?" she asked.

Why? I wanted to shout. Why would I want to go back? "No."

"If you're not happy. If it's hard . . . I don't know." She pulled into the parking lot, slipped the transmission knob to P, and turned to me. "Dude, it's like, I was just trying to think of what would be best for you. I mean, if it's hard."

I did my jerky version of a shrug, shoulders raised too high. I wanted to say something, tell her, Fuck you, you and your fucking friends, your fucking beautiful people! But I just got out of the car and went in for my treatment.

I'M NOT SURE that Saucer was the type to ruminate over his motivations for hanging out with me. Certainly, proximity to my sister must have been a factor, but he soon seemed to forget about that, or give it less prominence. On afternoons when the surf was flat down at State or Jetty or Sunset, he would pick me up in his beat-up Datsun B210 and drive us down to the bluffs, where we would take bong hits and listen to Pink Floyd or Ted Nugent on his car stereo.

I didn't mind walking home. I told him he could just let me off at his place. He would park, go inside and leash his dog, grab his skateboard, and the two of them, sled dog and skater, would slide down Asilomar Street and out of sight and I would begin my long walk back home.

I helped him get through Farnham's class, going through his project, a report on cheetahs, and organizing it into something like a passable piece of work. I stopped going to Doug Wirta's at lunch and hung around with Saucer near the planter. For the first time, my being Shannon Harris's brother was paying dividends: it was a simple identification, an easy answer to the question "Who are you?"

My father had given me his old Asahi Pentax 35-millimeter camera and, one afternoon, when Saucer picked me up and we went over to his house to get stoned and listen to music, I took a few photos of him, using slow-exposure, low-ASA black-and-white film—grainy, shadowy shots, as was the fashion of the time. He was the first subject I had shot besides my family—I had taken mostly pictures of Shannon, of course—and when I developed the photos, Saucer looked perfect, grinning, head tilted back, arms folded, beautiful, statuesque, seated on the white painted brick wall that set off the pool patio from an ivy embankment. "I'm totally using these for the yearbook," he said when I showed them to him at school. Two of his friends asked if I would shoot their portraits. I rode with Saucer and his crew down to Sunset one late afternoon where they were going surfing, shooting them while they were twisting into their wetsuits and waxing their boards and then following them with some difficulty, hobbling over the guardrail and down to the rocks. I propped myself onto a gray boulder above the narrow spit of high-tide sand and shot as they paddled out and then, in the late afternoon as the sun set, snapped a few shots as they surfed. I lacked the lenses or proximity for any spectacular action photos, but after they were done with their session, as they were sitting on the guardrail in the last light, just after the first streetlamps along PCH had turned on with a sizzle, I shot them in low light with a flash, the three of them in shadows, two of them leaning

against the guardrail and Saucer standing framed against the head-
lights of the oncoming traffic, his long blond hair still wet, with his
wetsuit half peeled down his glistening, sinewy chest and stomach,
the graduated U of his abdominal muscles closing in at the blond
fuzz at the tippy top of his pubes. I go back and look at that series
of photos sometimes, at Saucer, glorious, his muscled arms folded,
his self-aware smirk of perfection, his beauty.

Saucer was my first cool friend, the first boy who could have
chosen anyone but chose me, and I was grateful and delighted with
this new type of connection. He was also the first associate of mine
who my sister actually acknowledged and who, I later realized,
might have incited in her some rare jealousy toward me.

———

ON FRIDAY NIGHT, April 21, I was out with Saucer and one of
his friends. Bradley was driving his brown BMW 2002, Saucer was
shotgun, and I was in the backseat, rolling a joint. We were parked
on the bluff, overlooking the ocean near Temescal Canyon, listening, I believe—and I frequently try to reconstruct this scene—to
the Knack's first album, specifically the song "Good Girls Don't."
But that turns out to be historically impossible, since that album
came out a year later, but somehow, I am sure that we were listening to the Knack, and even recall an argument over whether this
counted as punk rock or not. Bradley believed it did; I disagreed.

Shannon's Audi pulled up next to us on the passenger side. Britt
Dawson was with her. Shannon swished her hair once and tilted
her head and made wide eyes at Saucer. I was instantly angry with
her for this. Saucer was mine, I wanted to tell her.

Shannon had been accepted by UC Santa Barbara, the school of
choice for many of her classmates as well, and was coasting through
her last semester, dating twenty-two-year-old Robby Villabianca,
basking in the final months of her reign.

She smiled at me. "What's up, Barnaby?"

I shrugged. Get away, I was thinking, get away from here.

"Hey Shannon." Saucer smiled. He passed her the joint.

From the passenger side of the Audi, Britt, who had graduated a year ago and was now at the local community college, held up a bottle of Southern Comfort.

"You want?"

Saucer nodded and Shannon relayed the bottle. We all swigged. I swigged more.

There was a rearrangement of passengers, but I can clearly recall only the beginning and then the end of it. The beginning: Saucer was with me, in Bradley's car, and we were together. Then, at the end of it, Saucer was with Shannon, in her car. Britt Dawson had relocated to the backseat. I had my camera but I only took one picture: Saucer, standing against the Audi's front door, the driver's mirror against the right side of his denim-clad butt, with Shannon's face on the other side of it, smirking at the camera.

And then they were gone.

———

I saw Shannon in the hospital, both eye sockets blackened and puffy, irises bright red, her nose a smushed relic of its former perfection, tubes shoved up and through blackened nostrils, stitches thick like the laces on a football running from a point above her right eye all the way down and into her shaved hairline below the ear. There was no reassuring beeping or pinging, as I had seen on hospital dramas on television. I looked for the little squiggly lines that are supposed to indicate the beating of the heart, the human pulse, but instead I saw a read-out of numbers, meaningless numbers.

Shannon had been pried from the vehicle and transported by ambulance to Saint John's, where she was quickly stabilized. She needed twenty-nine stitches on her forehead, rhinoplasty to repair her severely broken nose, several rounds of orthodontia to restore her smile, and skin grafts where her canines had torn through her lower lip. She suffered four broken ribs, a dislocated shoulder, and would contend with back pain for years. Britt Dawson emerged badly bruised with a fractured tibia and torn ligaments in both knees.

Brett Saucer had been thrown through the windshield, his carotid artery cut by broken glass. He was almost certainly knocked unconscious by the fall on hard pavement, and probably never woke as he bled out. It happened on Highland Drive, a stretch of road where kids like to drive fast, and Shannon was driving fast, and she was drunk and stoned, but who or what she was swerving to avoid would remain unknown, as her memory of the few hours before the accident would never return.

I knew then only that my sister was badly injured. The news of Brett Saucer's death didn't spread through our town until the next morning.

Shannon wouldn't return to school. She instead went through a long and laborious rehabilitation, recovering from her literal and figurative loss of face. When she came home from the hospital, she was ensconced in her room, curtailed in a back-brace, her appearance ghastly with her shaved head, stitches, and facial bruises. But her fine features would win out, and over time, just a few months, she regained her former good looks, although not all of her beauty. Shannon completed her schoolwork by correspondence, and stayed on track for UCSB.

She didn't last long up there and dropped out after a quarter and a half. She moved back to Los Angeles, and moved in for a while with the drummer from a local new wave band.

I would occasionally see Saucer's father, who had taken up skateboarding, his urethane wheels making a mournful growl, towed by his still-happy hound on a leash.

I LIVE IN Tribeca, in a loft near the entrance to the Holland Tunnel, a large, open live/work space that we have lavishly decorated. I have done well, my career as a fashion photographer—a snapper of celebrities, models, beautiful women, and, of course, advertising campaigns—making me wealthy, lending me confidence, and winning for me the love of my handsome partner, Oliver. We have adopted a son, Miro, a boy almost as handsome as Saucer.

I have shown Oliver the photographs of Saucer; they now seem embarrassing and melodramatic to me, but I still insist that the boy in them, the subject Saucer, is beautiful. I don't know if Oliver agrees with me only because he knows what happened to Saucer, or if he really sees Saucer's beauty. I still do.

Shannon has had a difficult life, the mother of two girls by two separate men, neither of them her husband. She endured a slew of lingering medical issues, some stemming from the accident— scoliosis, painkiller addiction, migraines. She never completed college and has, in some ways, lived off her good looks, winning over men with ease, though that is, as we all know, a diminishing return.

From time to time, with gathering frequency, she calls me and asks for money. Though these are not small sums, a few thousand here for rent, a few thousand there for a new car, I could easily afford them. But instead, I give her a maddening fraction of the amount she needs. If she asks for two thousand, I give her six hundred.

We never talk about Saucer.

113 NORTH MOORE

———

You should see who my friends married in the Nineties. It wasn't like now, when girls are marrying, like, handsome, mixed-race guys with good hair who ride bicycles. Do you know what men were like in New York in the Nineties? White and boring. They had real jobs—lawyers, architects, doctors. And they were DULL. I had girlfriends I used to get stoned with every night and do blow with at Limelight and who would even suck off some guy with dreadlocks at Robots, but who ended up marrying, like, an IT guy from Boston. Pretty girls who would go from dating an English junkie to a Long Island accountant. Those seemed like the only choices back then. Now, you have these hybrids. I don't know what guys do anymore, but it seems like when I meet a man in his twenties or thirties, he does something in advertising or marketing, but is more defined by his hobby of riding fixed-gear bicycles or some intense and very particular food enthusiasm.

So in a way I was lucky that I met Mark. It could have been much worse.

Mark later told me that when we met, he suspected I had never paid for a drink in my life. He was almost right. I was working as a mid-level staffer at a Condé Nast title that didn't survive very long in the digital age. My parents had bought me an alcove studio on Eleventh and Fifth that I had successfully traded up for a one-bedroom farther downtown. I remember the fashion editor at that job, Marni Saltzwell, who had been prominent socially in her twenties, and who had been presented in *Vogue* magazine, and who eventually married a very successful mortgage broker—after leaving her first husband, a writer briefly notorious for faking his memoir. Anyway, she told me that if you couldn't figure out if you were wealthy or not, that meant you weren't. But there was money in my family's past, pots of it hard-won in New England mills before those businesses went off-shore. My father had done nothing to increase any of this wealth, but despite his lifelong adolescence and his fondness for marijuana—which he passed down to me—he also didn't spend much of it, keeping the vast house in Stonington, the acreage in Maine, and enough liquid assets for remarkable acts of generosity like buying me that studio apartment.

I remember one time after he'd lit up a big joint and cracked open a biography of LBJ, I asked him point-blank—rich or not? But he shook his head and said, "Don't ask me this kind of stuff when I'm stoned."

But I didn't get far, did I? Just a few miles south to Manhattan, an okay editorial job at a magazine. This was when you could still dream of being a writer, when writing for magazines, and then writing books, and all of that, added up to a good life. I was part of a crowd of pretty girls who made their living from the media: profiling actresses, writing in angsty detail about our dating lives, reviewing books, makeup, plays. (This was before it became culturally normal to write about the smell of your vulva on your blog.) Rebecca Johnson, Christina Kelly, Anka Radakovitch, Jeannette Walls—I had issued checks to each of them when $1 a word was almost enough for a writer to live on. Looking back, I wonder, was

I always the promiscuous one? I thought we were all fucking lots of guys; it couldn't have been only me.

Then all of them, the writers too, they went and married boring guys.

———

THE THREE OF us, my younger brother Ed, my dad, and me, we all smoke plenty of dope. Mom abstained from the marijuana and from our family life, spending even the frigid winters alone in Maine.

Ed was visiting from California, where he was in Year Six of an education that would finally culminate with his successfully dropping out of a community college near Stonington. He had brought back East with him a quarter-pound of seedless marijuana, which in most families would probably sound like a lot but in our household could get whacked up in a weekend. He was crashing at my apartment, and he came up to meet me near 350 Madison for lunch, but instead of eating we took a walk down Madison and smoked a joint. It was a sunny, mid-winter day.

"Dad's been calling," Ed said.

"He can probably smell your stash from Stonington," I said. I looked around at the men in suits and trench coats, a pretty young girl in a leather jacket, a black guy wearing headphones leaking tinny-sounding music. "I'm too high for work."

Ed, who had never held a job, didn't really understand the issue.

"I have to go back," I said. Or did I? Would anyone even notice? We were like twelve days from the close of that month's issue and there was nothing to do today that couldn't be put off until tomorrow. "I'm going to go back and get my stuff and go home."

Ed said he would go with me, and we rode up in the elevator and then walked down the halls to my office. I didn't even have a window office. The old Condé Nast offices were tiny, even for executive editors and fashion editors, but their small, well-appointed rooms at least had windows. Ed was sitting on my little couch when Marni walked in to ask me about a photo shoot that I had nothing to do with.

"Um, photo editor." I pointed down the hall. "Senior editor." I pointed to my chest. "Different."

She smiled at Ed.

I introduced them. "Marni is famous," I said. "Her name gets me in everywhere for free."

Marni laughed. "That's why whenever I show up they tell me I'm already inside."

Ed was flipping through *Details*. "Man, I wanna go to Prague."

His eyes were blazingly red.

Marni looked at his eyes, and then at mine. "You guys!"

"What?"

"Stoned!"

"Shhhh!" I looked around.

"I want some," Marni said. "Prague?"

"It's like, look at that!" Ed said, holding up a full-page spread of blond girls in a bar. "And beer is like fifteen cents a pint."

"Can we really smoke here?" I asked. Marni was strictly a school friend, not an after-school friend. Whenever I ran into her when we were out, it was weird, and she kind of acted like a bitch. But at the office, she was great, really funny. You wouldn't even have known that she had just had lunch with Jackie Onassis or someone like that.

Marni nodded. "Just light a cigarette."

We did, and then I gave Marni the rest of the joint. She lit up.

While she was holding it in, she said, "IwenttoPragueonce. Fashionshoot. Scaffoldingseverywhere. Wenccellassquare."

Ed nodded. "Maybe I'm too late."

Marni exhaled. "Ohmygod."

I needed to get out of there. Suddenly I was terrified that our managing editor would come looking for me and find us all stoned and giggling. Marni wouldn't get in trouble, but I might. "Quick!" I collected my bag.

Marni nodded. "I'll be right back. I'm going to discreetly go to my office and get my stuff. Oh god, I don't want to see Klara." Klara was her assistant. She turned to me. "You go."

"No way," I said.

"It won't be weird for you."

"It will."

"What's the new Prague?" Ed asked, flipping through a British *Vogue*.

"Berlin?"

"Tokyo?"

"Any non-Axis capitals?" Ed said.

"Just go," Marni said. "Just tell Klara I sent you to get it."

I took a deep breath, opened my office door, and walked out into the hall, past an empty researcher's cubicle, and down the corridor, past the managing editor's office and the assistants' cubicles and then past Klara and into Marni's office.

"Brooke?" Klara shouted as I tried to blur past her.

"Klara! Marni wanted me to get her stuff. We're outie." I smiled at her.

She was holding a bunch of pink message slips in her hand. "Can you give these to her?"

"I can totally do that."

I walked back to my office and gave the messages to Marni.

"These are weird. Look at this." Marni handed me one that said JPG. "Jean-Paul Gaultier."

I could vividly picture him at that moment.

"Oh my god, I can't call him back," Marni said. "That accent."

"Call him tomorrow."

"I have to call him," Marni said. "Can I use your phone?"

"I'm leaving."

"Okay, I'll come with."

The three of us walked down the hall and waited at the elevator in dead silence. We rode down without saying a word and then passed the lobby newsstand and found a black car. When we were inside with the door closed, we all exhaled and sort of collapsed into each other, laughing.

———

WHEN I HAD moved in, Leroy Street actually seemed a little bit remote to me, slightly farther south than I would have liked, but it was a beautiful block and the living room of my brownstone floor-through had an open and airy view of the gingko trees and ball fields across the street and my rear bedroom window had a view of the back garden, to which I had access down a rickety stairwell. Ed's duffel bag was in the living room, his suit valise hung from a hook on the front of a closet door.

Marni sat down on my sofa, an auburn Byrd mid-century, and then began flipping through her Filofax.

Ed opened a beer for himself and then offered to mix cocktails. He brought us gin and tonics. "Call Jean-Paul Gaultier!" he said.

Marni nodded. I handed her the cordless phone. She dialed. "Hi, it's Marni for Jean-Paul."

She waited.

"Hi! Yes, I have them. I have to show them to Amanda but I am stricken. I want them to keep! . . . You will, oh my god, thank you. I'm the luckiest girl . . . Yes! . . . We'll get them in. We have to! . . . I'm so happy . . . I'm the happiest girl in the world . . . Because of you . . . huge kisses . . . and tell Marcel hi . . . and, okay, okay, okay, okay . . . so happy!"

She hung up.

Ed and I burst out laughing.

"What?" Marni said.

"You just sounded completely insane," Ed said. He was rolling another joint. He had placed a one-gallon-capacity Ziploc bag of marijuana on the table. The whole room was saturated with dope.

"Oh my god," Marni said, picking it up. "You're like a preppy Pablo Escobar."

Ed lit up.

This was before everyone had access to high-grade marijuana, before haze and bubblegum and kush and strawberry cough, before vaporizers and medical marijuana. This was the end of the era during which marijuana still seemed vaguely illegal, before it became a prescription for everything from autism to chemotherapy side effects. And even in the era of dope with a doctor's note, you'd have to actually go into a dispensary to see a stash like the one Ed had just casually dropped on the table.

I'd always taken it for granted that my brother would have huge amounts of marijuana. When I had left for Sarah Lawrence, I was scoring from Ed, and he was in tenth grade. But for a moment, I caught a glimpse of him through a stranger's eyes, through Marni's: handsome, brown curly hair, skinny with good shoulders, and with access to such a weighty amount of marijuana that it made him seem almost glamorous.

Marni sipped her drink. "Wow, I am so high. Okay, we have a dinner and then we're dropping in on a recording session."

"*We?*" I said.

"All of us. You guys can't leave me. Not if I'm this stoned."

I felt powerless to resist her.

But Marni needed her clothes. She called Klara and asked her to take a black car to Marni's apartment, pick up a skirt, a blouse, a jacket, and shoes, and then come down to where we were.

"That's like slavery," Ed said. "She should quit."

"Oh, she loves it," Marni said.

"Doubt that," said Ed.

Ed began explaining to us his plan to gradually sell off this marijuana—before my father was aware of its existence, or perhaps sell it TO my father—and then fly back to California.

"Shouldn't you be in school right now?" Marni asked.

"That's fraught," I said.

"I'm only going part-time," Ed said.

"To a community college in Santa Barbara," I said. "He was kicked out of UC Santa Barbara." I wasn't sure why I was undermining him.

"You go all the way across country to go to a community college?" Marni said.

"I'm really committed to my ultimate Frisbee team," said Ed.

"Seriously?"

"No. It's that the credits are easier to transfer back to UC." He was flipping through an issue of *Condé Nast Traveler*.

"And my dad doesn't know he flunked out."

"And it's that, too," Ed admitted. He was looking at a spread photo of a beach in Africa. "Maybe Mozambique is the new Prague. The Bique. I hear dope is like ten dollars a pound."

"Like getting large amounts of marijuana is really a problem for you," Marni said.

GORDON CALLED. NOW, I could have married Gordon. He was handsome, in a narrow-faced, prematurely balding sort of way. He was funny, obviously gifted with a knack for making money while simultaneously seeming to not care very much about it; he was an architect who had stopped designing and now put together real estate syndicates, LLCs that converted old buildings to condos. But he was charming and funny; and he was a voracious reader, which was rare among the boys we dated, the sort of boring guys who my friends would all soon end up marrying.

Was Gordon boring? Short-term, no. But long-term, I had my doubts.

"Can I buy some pot?" Marni asked Ed.

"Who is that?" Gordon asked as soon as I picked up the phone.

"Marni Saltzwell."

Marni shook her head and stage-whispered, "No, no, oh my god. Who are you talking to? Did they hear me?"

"It's Gordon," I said. "You guys have met."

"Oh." She turned her attention back to Ed. "This is really good pot."

Gordon was talking about a building he was considering. He periodically suggested that I, or my father, join one of his syndicates. As he explained them to me, you put in a few hundred thousand dollars and ended up with thousands of square feet of Lower Manhattan real estate. You just had to be willing to wait until Gordon finished the building, which could take anywhere from six months to a decade. He was always getting sued.

We agreed to meet Gordon at the restaurant in SoHo. He said he didn't want to go anywhere that was too loud. I told him Marni was in charge.

My buzzer sounded. I let in Klara, who came upstairs carrying two garment bags and two pairs of shoes.

"This place reeks." She noticed Ed's bag of marijuana. "Oh my god."

"You want?" Ed asked, holding out a joint.

"No!" Marni shouted. "I will not get stoned with my assistant!"

"God, that sounds so hippie patrician," Ed said.

Klara had taken the joint but was now unsure what to do. "Um, this is weird."

We were all silent save for Marni, who was unzipping the garment bags. In the presence of beautiful clothes, she would lose focus on anything else, and as she pulled out a Prada jacket and skirt, Chanel blouse, Jimmy Choo shoes, and a Gucci belt, she fell completely silent.

I made a toking gesture toward Klara. She quietly took a hit.

Marni stood up and withdrew to my bedroom. She emerged a few minutes later completely topless, her plum-size, firm breasts swaying happily as she asked for a pair of scissors. Ed, momentarily stirred from his stupor by her breasts, said, "Whoa."

———————

THE COLD AIR slapped us sober for a moment or two, un-gauzed our minds as we walked southeast into SoHo. Being with Marni in Manhattan at night was probably what it felt like to be in the claque of a capricious soprano. As long as you remained in her favor—or she remembered that you existed—life was good; you were permitted beyond velvet ropes and offered seats at good tables and free drinks. But she was also in the habit of sliding past velvet ropes and not looking back to see exactly who had been allowed to follow. She would gesture vaguely behind her, and the door-men would arbitrarily reconnect rope to stanchion and an unlucky member or two of Marni's party would be stranded outside Spa or Lotus, and that would be especially exasperating because you didn't really even want to go to a club in the first place.

God I hated Marni.

But tonight I loved her. Or maybe I always did. She had been and forever would be the cool girl in every place she went: Gstaad, St. Barths, East Hampton. That idea had a powerful hold on me, made me grateful when she deigned to be around me. But, like being stuck outside a club you didn't even want to go into, it infuriated me how much I liked being liked by Marni. It is a fact seldom commented upon that New York's club culture, in all its various strata of tree-ringed history dating back to Studio 54, or, if you prefer, Max's Kansas City, has always been as class-conscious and socially stratified as that class outline in *Debrett's Peerage*. Good-looking or rich always mattered, at least in New York, no matter how punk-rock the venue, and Marni was at the top of every hierarchy.

And even years later, when that scandal engulfed her first

husband, she would emerge from it unscathed, even more famous, and would write a successful book about his downfall.

Maybe it was Ed's dope, but Marni was solicitous and friendly and when we got to the restaurant, the new Italian place on West Broadway opened by Giuseppe Cipriani, she made sure to introduce each of us to Giuseppe and Giancarlo, his chef with the long curly hair, who would later become famous for his own restaurant empire—and that hair. Gordon was standing by the bar and seemed relieved to no longer be alone. Giuseppe squeezed us into a great table just inside the open facade to the street, and Marni made sure, I noticed, to put Ed next to her. And coming over to greet Marni was Naomi Campbell, who was so physically intimidating, with such surprisingly muscular arms, that she reminded me of a panther. Her presence was oddly powerful, like a force field of cruel, angry beauty that silenced us.

Marni introduced us all.

Naomi smiled.

I could feel Gordon barely resisting the urge to lure Naomi into one of his building syndicates.

When Naomi left, I realized I had been holding my breath.

The restaurant had a roar: excited voices coalescing into something like a jet taking off. I had experienced this before, this new hot-spot roar, and the Ciprianis excelled at producing it. Marni knew how to project her voice over the din so that it sounded as if she was speaking at a conversational pitch, while I had to shout to be heard. Whenever I am as stoned as I was then, I can never find a level for my voice that is comfortable or doesn't make me sound like a harridan. Ed had a huge grin on his face and was talking conspiratorially with Marni. Klara seemed stunned at her good fortune at being in a place like this with a crowd like this. Gordon was massaging my thigh beneath the table.

Then we all had to slide over so that a photographer with a weird limp could join us.

"Is he wearing pajama pants?" I asked Gordon.

Gordon nodded.

The photographer immediately raised a glass as if toasting Marni.

I had never seen Marni so happy, nor had I seen Ed quite so smitten. She was at least eight years older than he was, but they settled into an easy rapport, smugly and jocularly dismissing each other so that it seemed as if they had known each other for years.

We were all famished.

Giancarlo came over, had a hushed conversation with Marni, and then returned with a plate covered in cheesecloth, which he pulled back to reveal a fist-size truffle.

"What is that?" Klara said.

"Gold," Marni said.

Six plates of egg-noodle pasta with a light sauce of cream and caviar were brought over, and Giancarlo shaved generous slices of truffle onto each of our plates. Our table became absolutely silent as the six of us began twirling up the best stoner munchie in the history of the world: pasta with caviar and truffles. Two bottles of twelve-year-old Barbaresco appeared, and then another two, and once we had eaten, whatever anxiety or incipient paranoia I had felt seemed miraculously lifted.

Ed had a crooked smile on his face. He sat back from the table and threw his arm over the back of Marni's chair. "Do you think everything will be incredibly fun all the time?"

Marni looked at him and laughed.

"I mean, for us," he added.

"Who's us?" I asked.

"Like, I mean, *this*." He pointed to the empty plates before us, the wine bottles, the stemware, all of it making a happy glisten in the soft yellow light.

"I think so," Marni said, as if she had really mulled it over.

Gordon nodded. "Do you mean, like, basics? Food, shelter,

warmth? Will we be fine all the time? Yes. Is that what you mean by fun?"

"No, I mean actual fun. Great food. Naomi Campbell coming over. A table in a place like—"

"A huge bag of grass," Marni added.

The gimpy photographer suddenly seemed interested. "Wait, wait," he said, "who's got that?"

"Oh, Ed has this obscene bag of marijuana," Marni told him.

"Marni, you can't just—"

"It's okay, Barnaby is the reason we can expense this dinner," she said. "*Fun*, remember?"

Ed nodded. "Okay. But I mean, think about it globally. We have plenty of everything, resources, all that. Oil is like ten dollars a barrel. You can fly everywhere you want. There're practically no wars anymore. They can bring truffles over from Tuscany."

"You mean like an end-of-history kind of thing?" Gordon asked.

"Sort of," Ed said. "But I'm tweaking it to be 'fun forever.'"

"Something will fuck it up," I said. "The ozone layer or something. Something will ruin the fun."

"What?" Ed said. "What could ruin the fun?"

We were all quiet for a few seconds.

"Kids," Klara said in a small voice. "When people have kids, they seem to have less fun."

————

THEN I MET the man with whom I would have kids.

Marni wanted us to go by the studio where a college friend of hers was recording her second album. I was tired after dinner and Gordon begged off, saying he wanted to head home. "Come by after," he urged me. I told him I might, but not to wait up.

The recording studio was on 28th Street. We shared a joint on the sidewalk and then were buzzed up. We never took off our coats and carried with us the smell of smoke and winter. Mark was sitting next to the producer, and I didn't know enough to perceive that this was a hierarchy and Mark, the engineer, was a level down from the producer. The two of them sitting behind the mixing boards and LED lights and meters and computer screens and talking in technical terms about levels and settings held my interest for about fifteen seconds before I became impatient waiting for the singer to do another take.

Marni had gone in to greet her friend and I sat down on the sofa behind the console. Mark turned around and smiled.

"Cold out?" he said.

I nodded. "Cold."

"You get to feel cut off when you're in here," he said. "You lose touch with the outside world."

"The Cold War ended," I told him.

"Thank god!" Mark said. "Who won?"

"Fun," I said. "Fun won."

We shook hands, Mark asked me what I did, and I told him I worked at a magazine. His work seemed almost glamorous to me, collaborating with quasi-famous musicians making songs. But more pleasing to me was his air of knowing how to do something, how to operate this equipment, this software, to manipulate and control. He was as close to blue-collar as any boy I had ever known. We dated bankers, artists with trust funds, editors and writers, but nobody who knew how to do anything. Back then, if I had met a carpenter instead of Mark, I wonder what would have become of me.

Still, when I left the studio a few hours later, I never thought we would see each other again.

———

WHEN I RETURNED to my apartment the next morning, the bedroom looked like a murder scene. My sheets were stained colors

I had never previously considered as part of the sexual palette. Ed had brought Marni back and the two of them had engaged in some very creative, and evidently violent, lovemaking, and neglected to clean up after themselves. They obviously shared a similarly over-developed sense of entitlement.

I stripped off the sheets, pillowcases, and duvet cover and loaded them into a bag to be trashed (they couldn't be cleaned) and then set out new sheets and made some coffee before beginning my morning walk across town to the F to 42nd Street.

We didn't really have staff meetings; our editor in chief pre-ferred to keep us all off-balance by relaying her conflicting in-structions privately. The Darwinian logic to this, apparently, was that the best of us would thrive through cattiness and undercutting our colleagues to rise up the masthead, those attributes being what made the perfect Condé Nast EIC. This was particularly brutal for the beauty and fashion editors; determining what styles or looks were in or out was utterly subjective, and the ultimate arbiter of those decisions, namely Marni, could be pathologically cruel.

"So," I said when I ran into Marni. "My brother?"

She smiled sheepishly. "I know. At my age. But he's such a sweetheart!"

It was then that I noticed I was jealous of Ed. He had captured Marni in a manner that I never could. A socialite, a genuine It Girl—the status to which all young New York girls of a certain demographic aspired—and my brother had succeeded where I had failed. She sort of tolerated me; but she had chosen Ed.

I was even more surprised by how angry I was at Ed when I finally saw him back at the apartment that night.

"What the fuck? Leaving my bed like that?"

Ed looked taken aback. "I was going to clean it up. I went for a run."

"It was gross. I'm so pissed."

"Brooke," Ed said. "I'm sorry, but what's the big deal, seriously?"

Shouldn't Ed have been embarrassed about this? His semen and who knows what other bodily fluids on his older sister's bed?

But he wasn't. "I'll pay for the laundry."

"I trashed the sheets. But that's not the point—it's just rude."

"I said I'm sorry."

Why Ed? I wondered. What had she seen in him? He was handsome, but Marni could have had any man in New York. I wanted to ask Ed, to ask Marni, but I couldn't. I just had to sit there and feel jealous and hate myself for feeling jealous of my brother.

I told Ed he had to go. And he did: he went to crash at Marni's for a few days before heading up to Stonington.

———

I RAN INTO Mark again at the release party for the CD he had been recording the night we met. He was cuter than I remembered, and looked slinky and glamorous in pegged leather jeans and a white shirt. I had finally broken up with Gordon and his suits and handmade loafers and real estate syndicates and was looking for a boy instead of a man. Not literally a boy, but someone fun and youthful. Men were boring and serious. I knew we weren't supposed to date musicians, but Mark technically wasn't a musician—okay, he played guitar, but he made his living as an engineer and sound editor. And nothing about him seemed serious, I told myself. He was nothing but a giggle, a cute, half-Asian, dissolute boulevardier who was ultimately disposable.

He was living down on John Street when nobody lived that far downtown, and would drive up and meet me after his sessions—which always ran late—in his kidded-up Volkswagen GTI with Yokohama tires, stiffened suspension, and this ridiculous metallic paint job. It was the kind of car Chinese kids in Chinatown gazed at with envy but that looked preposterous in the West Village. But I loved riding around in that little fake Porsche, smoking a joint, listening to Mark's latest project, and feeling the throaty accelera-tion of the souped-up engine.

I watched more television than he did (I also smoked more dope); if he watched, it was to catch a game. I was a more avid film buff; he knew much more about music. We had a wide spectrum of conversations, and were able to enjoyably while away drives up to my family's beach compound in Stonington, a monstrous old church that had been converted to accommodate the whole clan in almost martial barracks arrangement. There was a vast lawn, as smooth as pool-table felt, that extended from the rear of the main house to the narrow cliff and then to the rocky little beach with its tiny spit of sand barely big enough for two towels laid side by side. A little finger of a wharf extended into the gray sound, where my brother kept an old beater of a motor boat tied up, an aged and splintering Chris-Craft with a busted ladder that made it a struggle to climb out of the water. The first time Ed took Mark out tubing, he dunked Mark into the sound at least a half-dozen times. Mark stoically accepted this beating as part of the cost of admission.

On that earliest visit to the house, Mark hadn't inquired be-forehand about sleeping arrangements but I could tell he hadn't ex-pected to be sharing a bed with me. Ed slept in a bunk bed across the huge former rectory loft. Despite the proximity, Mark and I did manage to make love; I was biting into a corner of a pillow to keep quiet.

Ed had finally moved back East from California, and he'd brought with him another prodigious bag of dope. He dutifully enrolled at Gateway Community College in New Haven, where he achieved perfect attendance. His fling with Marni had been brief, and at the end of it I was angrier with Marni than with Ed. I doubt she had thought much about Ed, and I suspected the only lingering effect of their multi-night stand was the awkwardness between us at the office.

Ed's latest plan was the Bique—Mozambique. He was obsessed with the East African country, believing the coastline was an undiscovered hedonistic paradise—Tahiti before Gauguin, Bali before the Australians. He sold the half-pound he had brought back from California and took off.

———

MARK SNUCK UP on me. We were practically living together before I figured out how serious I was about the relationship. My father liked him. Dad was the slightly sleepy patriarch who liked to stay up late and talk about music and books. He was a soothing conversationalist until his dope-induced mellow began to make him stupid; Mark would sit there for a few awkward minutes, trying to think of a way to extricate himself from the dialogue that had long since turned to monologue. I knew to avoid my father after nine p.m. He would sit in front of the television with a biography open in his lap, some massive volume on Teddy Roosevelt or Bismark, and half-watch baseball and read history. Mark's ability to hang in there through some of his circuitous conversations—Dad would explain why we needed another Bretton Woods or how his grandfather had invented the first loom that allowed wool to be blended with synthetic fibers—may have persuaded other members of the clan to accept this weird Amer-Asian kid. (Why do I say *kid*? Because I still feel like a kid, that's why, barely wiser or smarter than our babysitter or even our daughters. I still want to go out, snort coke, pick up boys. I can't, of course, grown up on the outside as I am, responsible, holder of a mortgage, mother, wife. I try to never ask myself how did I get here, I ask myself why.)

———

MARK HAD RENTED his own studio space a few months prior, already thinking of going into business for himself. Because of digital technology and cheaper software, the barriers to entry were

so low that for a few tens of thousands of dollars he could assemble
what just five years earlier would have cost hundreds of thousands.
The older man who rented him his studio on Broadway no longer
wanted to make the journey in from Bayshore to his second-floor
management office where he and two Chinese women wrote up
leases and rented space. He had decided to sell the building, then
in a run-down part of town that I had thought of as the Futon
District because of all the cut-rate furniture sellers who sold beds
and sofas made from these stiff cotton tablets. The building had six
floors; there was a bike messenger dispatcher on the ground floor,
and there were always bike messengers standing around outside the
front door, smoking and leaving empty Snapple bottles under the
awning. Various tradesmen vaguely affiliated with the arts occupied the other floors: filmmakers, film editors, musicians, producers; and one floor was a vestigial sweatshop. Mark was on the top
floor and a tenant of some standing, having rented the front two
offices, which he had combined to create studio space. He paid his
rent in person, something like $800 for all that space, and he told
me the two Chinese girls who sat facing each other across metal
desks seemed to have taken a liking to him, giggling and making
small talk whenever he stopped by. It was through them that he
heard about the building being for sale.

This was before the whole area—a dead spot between Chinatown, Tribeca, and the Financial District—was reconsidered to
actually be *in* Tribeca. I didn't know this then, but that whole re-
appraisal had to do with the fact that the area was zoned for a very
good public school. At that moment, it was still the Futon District
and the entire building could be had for $975,000. When Mark
told me that, I sat up.

He had used that number to illustrate the impossibility of ever
buying the building. You might as well have quoted a price of a
billion, because he had no interest in the property, nor the means
to come up with that kind of money. But I suggested he talk to my

friend Gordon, a syndicator who bought buildings. "Own, don't rent," I told him.

That, too, was my bloodline talking. We were owners, going back hundreds of years. Mark's people? They probably rented their shoes by the hour.

I called Gordon, asked him out for a drink, and told him about the property; he promptly went down and had a look and quickly decided to make an offer. The building was vast and zoned exclusively for commercial use. Gordon called me and said a few partners would come in and form an LLC that would borrow the money as one entity and buy the building. It was a simple way to leverage up and get much better deals than the individual investor or borrower could ever get. Did I want in?

I told him I didn't, but that Mark wanted in. "My boyfriend."

"Oh," Gordon said. He still carried a little torch for me.

"He *did* find the place," I reminded him.

Gordon's deals were exclusive. When Mark was offered a sixth of the deal, the whole floor, for $108,000, he was being offered a ticket into our crowd. Gordon wanted just 40 percent of that in cash and he, or the syndicate, would arrange the bank loan. I wish I could say that Mark jumped at the deal, saw the plain wisdom of putting down $41,000 for 6,500 square feet in what would become, at least nominally, Tribeca. But even then, he hesitated: the building was in terrible condition, the floors creaked, the elevator was always broken, the hallways stank, there were rats, there was no heating system, no air conditioner, and it was a block from a homeless shelter. "Plus, there are bike messengers out front all day," he told me. "They smell like sweat."

"It's just a hundred thousand dollars," I said.

"Hundred and eight," Mark countered.

That wasn't a great deal of money even back then. But he had just paid off his consoles and multi-tracks and work-stations and would still have to invest a few thousand more to make the place state-of-the-art so that a union production would consider using it. But I was so resolute that it was easier for him to go through with the purchase than try to talk himself out of it. Within forty-five days he was the owner of a huge amount of studio space on lower Broadway. Within ten months Gordon had cleared out the undesirable tenants, including the bike messenger service, reno-vated every floor save Mark's, and was renting the space out to Internet start-ups and second-rate financial services firms. Just like that, Mark had become, at least on paper, a landlord.

I remember the day the syndicate closed on the building. A half-dozen of us were standing in the vast and abandoned third floor, atop the splintered, uneven maple floors. Gordon had a bottle of champagne, which he carried by the neck as he paced off walls and rooms—there would be a bathroom here, a run of offices there. He was even envisioning getting COOs and turning the whole place condo. We passed around the bottle of champagne, and I noticed Mark looking around as if perplexed at having become an owner. Yet what I thought as I watched him, handsome, soft-spoken, and communicating a hip sort of reliability, was that I had somehow steered Mark to a place where he would be wealthy enough to marry me.

———

MARNI ENDED UP living a few blocks from us, up on West Broadway. I saw her around the neighborhood, at Bazzini's, down at the Amish Market, and I always dutifully said hello. But the sight of her now angered me. It wasn't her fault; it was just that she had been the last and only thing to come between my brother and me.

I had seen the footage of villagers huddled atop mounds sur-rounded by swamp. The UN estimated twenty thousand dead, many thousands more missing. The Bique hadn't turned out to be the bacchanal Ed had been searching for. Oh, he had e-mailed me: the beaches were beautiful, the dope was plentiful, and there were German and Swedish and Israeli girls. But it was so poor, shockingly so, he said, and when he went just a kilometer in from the coasts, what he saw made him wonder about a life of searching for fun all the time. Ed had been staying in the interior when the monsoon came, and was last seen wading into a torrent, trying to rescue a Mengitsu boy who was clutching at a branch.

The boy made it.

Sometimes, after the kids have gone to bed, when I'm vaporizing a few hits, I'll think about how much one life is worth, and how certain lives are worth more than others, and I will curse that boy. I would trade his life for Ed's. I would trade a thousand lives.

65 HUDSON

I t had become a source of mounting disappointment to Brick that the woman he was having an affair with looked so much like his wife. Why, he sometimes wondered, of all the females in this neighborhood, this borough, this city, did he end up having afternoon sex with a woman so similar to Ava? Her feet, her calves, her thighs, the hang of her buttocks, the stiffness of her pubic hair, the softness of her stomach, the half-dollar-size areola (the half-cigarette-butt protrusion of the nipples), the freckles on her cleavage, the length of her neck, the flatness of her larynx, curve of her chin, pout of her lips (the same smug dissatisfaction communicated by that pout), dimples in her cheeks, narrowness of her nose, blue-gray of her eyes, the crow's feet radiating from those eyes, the hairline at her temple, the squareness of her brow, the sweep of her blond hair (same few stray wisps), the way she wore it tied back in a ponytail (just like his wife) with the straw-colored hair hanging down (of course) to the middle of her back. All of it! When Beatrice was undressed, it might as well have been Ava. Was his being here due to wandering male libido, to the pathetic randomness of male urges, was her only virtue, if he was honest about it, that her vagina, similarly responsive clitoris aside, was not his wife's vagina?

A few of his friends, the guys he had breakfast with some mornings after they dropped their kids off at school, had commented on the similarities between his wife and Beatrice, recently separated from her husband, who had twin daughters in the school. They hadn't known he was fucking Beatrice, and he had not really believed his wife and mistress were so congruent until he began taking careful inventory of Bea's properties. They were even, he discovered when he asked Bea, the exact same height. In no way did that dissuade him from continuing the affair; but it did cause him to work through torturous interpretations of it. Was he more or less of a philanderer for cheating with a woman who looked like his wife? Was he more or less guilty? Dishonest? Duplicitous? He sometimes wondered if that physical similarity could be used as a defense in the event Ava discovered the affair. Or would his cheating with a woman so physically similar be more condemning, as if the only thing wrong with Ava were her character, intelligence, personality—her *insides*.

Now as he sat at the edge of the bed in Bea's darkened loft—her daughters were with their father, Giancarlo, a flamboyant Italian chef who seemed to open a new restaurant every few months—he felt around for his socks and managed to find just one. Bea's apartment was large but belied by a too-low ceiling so that you never really felt like you were in a grand space. She let her daughters sleep in the vast living room with her, their beds in a distant corner, each beneath a narrow window. There was another bank of windows facing east, but a new hotel across the street blocked out the afternoon sun. It was one of those apartments charming on paper (large, in Tribeca, on a good block, plenty of windows) but disappointing in real life. And Bea was one of those women, Brick was now concluding, who were charming on paper, but . . . no, he didn't want to compile that list right now. (Okay, okay: French, separated from her husband, pretty—but sad—worried about her daughters, her finances, angry with her ex, probably drinks a little too much.)

And where was she anyway? He slipped on his sock, pulled up his jeans, the same jeans he wore every day, then his black work boots, and stood up, his left foot sockless inside its boot, shirtless, his stomach pale in the dark room. He heard a toilet flush and then she came back, wearing jeans and a tank top—Aha! Ava never wore tank tops—and looking at something on her phone.

She told him the latest rumor: that the police suspected the molester had been a local, a relative of the girl. That she had known him all along.

Brick nodded. "That's good. Or, I mean, not good, but better."

"Better than what?" Bea asked.

"Better than, I don't know, a random stranger coming here to fondle children?"

Bea shrugged.

"Are you going to go to Math Night?" she asked.

Though their children attended the same school, thankfully they weren't in the same class. It unnerved Brick whenever Bea would talk about the school.

He didn't know. About Math Night. That was Ava's area.

"Your wife, she knows about these things? The school?"

He nodded.

"Giancarlo, he doesn't go," she said of her soon-to-be ex-husband, "or if he goes, he gets in a fight about something. With the teachers. About how to do math. I tell him, shut the fuck up, but he can't. He always says he knows the right way."

"It's been a long time since I've had that kind of conviction," Brick said.

"Well, but it's stupid." She pronounced it *stoop-eed*. Bea had walked over to the kitchen island and taken a seat on a stool, one elbow leaning on the granite top and the other against the back of the stool. They didn't swivel, Brick remembered. Who gets counter stools that don't swivel?

"You don't go to meetings with the teacher to show you know more than her," Bea said.

Now he was listening to another woman complain about her future ex-husband. Instead of his own wife complain about him. That was an improvement.

———

IT WAS OFTEN remarked among Brick's friends that he was the least likely of them to cheat on his wife.

Tall Brick (rectangular, closely shorn head with a crown shaped like the blunt end of an egg you break if you want to peel it, wide eyes, metal-gray irises, long nose and thin lips) had a knack for keeping his mouth shut. Essential to pulling off this stolid persona was his size: he was a large dude. And he had been throughout elementary, junior high, and high school, always dogged by Erie, Pennsylvania, basketball and football coaches who saw in the well-built, quiet kid a power forward or tight end. He ended up playing baseball, and was starting pitcher for his high school team with a fastball clocked in the high eighties—low nineties, if you asked Brick. He was promising, almost a prospect, yet his quiet, indifferent demeanor was viewed by the few college scouts who came to see him pitch as a drawback. He lacked competitive fire.

His own son, Jason, two years older than his daughter, Georgina, was developing into a very good athlete. He was already the fastest kid in fourth grade, or so he told his father, and Brick could discern that he was athletically precocious for a nine-year-old. He had a good arm, so when Brick took him to Roosevelt Park to play catch, he showed Jason how to grip the two seams on the baseball with his tiny hand. Brick would trot over, bend down, and let Jason hurl away, enjoying the satisfying smack of the ball hitting his mitt.

Jason was going to pitch this year, he told his dad, in Downtown Little League. The Rangers pitcher from last year was moving up to high minors, which meant they needed a new arm. It made sense to Brick. He had been the best pitcher throughout his Little League career. He had been imposing even then, a giant compared to other ten-year-olds, and already so quiet that opposing hitters mistook his silence for anger. He had excelled at each level of youth baseball and was playing for the varsity at McDowell by the end of his freshman year of high school.

It was his high school baseball coach who pulled him aside and told him that he had great stuff, but if he wanted a college scholarship, he would have to choose between baseball and drugs. Brick wondered how his coach knew he pitched most games on LSD, but now that he was ordered to choose, he picked drugs. No, that's not right. He hadn't *consciously* selected drugs; he actually believed he had been choosing art, culture, painting, poetry, philosophy, all of that, the path that led him, eventually, via the University of Wisconsin's fine-arts department, to New York.

He was a sculptor, a hulking man working with vast sacks of concrete, capacious vats of poured cement, and bulky piles of cinder blocks, swinging the weight around his studio with a one-ton pulley crane, the resulting objects looking a little like, well, sacks of concrete. If the almost imperceptible uphill gradient of his career path bothered Brick, he never showed it. He reported to his sculpture studio every morning after dropping off the kids at school and having coffee with the guys, then muscled his large objects around for a few hours, mixing, molding, pouring, setting, drying, head-scratching, until he took off in the afternoon to go fuck the French lady.

Ava, however, did occasionally voice impatience at Brick's career-long digression. She was, after all, effectively subsidizing his sculpting, his studio, their loft up near Canal Street, the house out in Peconic, all of it paid for by her work as the head of her own public relations firm. She had achieved a small measure of fame, partnering with a powerhouse gay male associate in Los Angeles and working on behalf of a host of celebrities, specializing in young, troubled actors and musicians. When she had embarked on this career, which in New York came easily to an attractive woman in her early twenties, it had seemed an ideal way to make a living and go out a lot, yet she had always sworn, to Brick at least, that she was contemptuous of its vacuousness and found the adulatory small-talk laborious. But she was good at it, and as she grew toward middle age, she took on a gaggle of subordinate publicists whom she could dispatch to hand-hold "the talent" while she conceived strategy and made lucrative alliances with various designers, producers, and executives on behalf of her clients. Brick had long ago figured out that Ava, her protestations and her genuine desire to keep her children away from her glamorous world of vagina-flashing starlets and sex-tape-making actors notwithstanding, loved her work and her milieu. She traveled frequently, woke most mornings before Brick, returned many evenings after dinner, and at least once a week ordered Brick to don his Armani tuxedo and escort her to the Met or the Museum of Natural History for a benefit or celebration of some kind, where they would invariably share a table with a client of hers, which meant that Brick, despite his indifference to pop culture, was on a first-name basis with Tinsley and Blake and now Diablo.

It frustrated her that the one area of public life over which she exerted absolutely no influence was the art world. She hated Brick's artistic anonymity and periodically said as much. Why couldn't he be as successful as so many in their circle? He sold sculptures occasionally—small pieces to colleagues—and he showed a few pieces in group shows that were curated by other friends. But if others were charmed by Brick's unwillingness to let his lack of recognition get him down, Ava despised her husband's calmness in the face of rejection. How could he possibly not be bitter? It was almost unmanly, so different from the toughness that she had initially found attractive. But nothing got to him. Not even, she would concede after an evening berating him, her.

————————

THE IRONY OF everyone supposing that Brick wasn't the type to have an affair was that he was exactly the type. A more voluble man, a talkative fellow, would never have been able to pull this off. No one expected conversation from Brick, so he could go wordlessly from Bea to Ava, unchanging, unflinching, unmoved. The same metronomic nods as he listened, occasionally a tilt of the head or, and both women loved this, he would open those blank, big eyes even wider, like he was redoubling his attention. (He didn't even know he did this.) But keeping your trap shut around two women isn't much harder than maintaining radio silence around one.

Even around the guys, at breakfast or when they met some evenings at the bar across from the hotel, he didn't say much, though there he was more prone to observational comments, about a woman's hair or bust, or the state of his testicles—"that one makes my ballsack tighten up"—which never really made sense to the other guys but which generally sounded like manly banter, so they let it slide.

Brick liked to talk about baseball, and in his studio he would listen to the occasional day game and had come, over the years, to switch his allegiance from the Pirates to the Yankees. It was during one morning conversation with the other fathers that one of them said that a Yankee pitcher seemed to be losing velocity, and was now, probably, throwing in the high eighties, to which Brick replied, "I can throw faster than that."

The conversation stopped, and one of the fathers, the sound engineer, called bullshit.

"I can throw ninety miles an hour," Brick said. "Used to throw in the low nineties. Still could."

"Bullshit."

"Bring it on."

"How?" said the playwright. "You could pitch while I'm driving ninety right past you, and see if my car gets to the stop sign before you hit it?"

Brick shrugged. "Get a fucking radar gun."

Then he went quiet. Again.

———

BEATRICE'S SOON-TO-BE EX-HUSBAND, Giancarlo, had become omnipresent in the neighborhood with his famous flagship French restaurant; a second restaurant, which served German food; a third joint, which served slightly cheaper versions of the same dishes as the first two; and now a bakery that sat at a prominent intersection and that was therefore almost impossible to avoid as Brick made his way from his studio to Bea's. There were tables set up on the sidewalk, forcing pedestrians nearly to the curb. Giancarlo had complained to the city that the stretch of the boulevard next to his new bakery was being used as a kind of highway by drivers looking to cut across town, so the sidewalk was further congested by the cables powering an LED sign that displayed the speeds of passing motorists to chide them if they were driving too fast.

Giancarlo's culinary expanse was now threatening to cross this avenue and take over the restaurant across the street, where he planned to open a sushi bar. The whole operation struck Brick as overly ambitious, almost imperial in its Xerxes-like expansion. But who would stop him? Brick had been regaled by Beatrice with stories of her ex-husband's tireless industriousness. Their marriage had floundered, in part, because he simply never slept and accused Beatrice, who could win sleep medals if that ever became an Olympic sport, of sloth as he built his spaetzle-and-yellowtail Reich.

She professed to hate Giancarlo, but in her steady denouncement there was something else. Longing. Regret. Bitterness at what she had lost.

He found listening to the accounts of Giancarlo's parsimony, his spiteful withholding of their agreed-upon monthly payments, his removal of Beatrice's name from his corporate health insurance roll, to be tiring and, frankly, whenever he walked by Giancarlo's various bustling venues, infuriating. Giancarlo was inflicting upon Tribeca a gastronomic blight, making millions slinging overpriced baguettes, rabbit stew, and bottles of Pinot Noir marked up 400 percent. And he still withheld from his own flesh and blood their due? What kind of man was this?

Brick had watched him, tall, skinny, with beautifully coiffed curly brown hair that he wore to the middle of his neck. He had a German shepherd that he would tether to one of the wrought-iron garden dividers outside the school when it was his turn to drop off his daughters. He looked, Brick thought, like an asshole. He was predictably handsome in an Italianate sort of way, and because of his local celebrity status and rising national profile, he was used to being looked at and spoken about and so didn't notice Brick glaring at him most mornings. Brick doubted Giancarlo even knew who he was.

Jealousy was an uncommon and novel emotion for Brick. At first he had trouble identifying it, positing the sharp tug as a kind of general outrage, before realizing this was different. Giancarlo could rouse in Beatrice the kind of raw hatred that could only mean she still loved him.

Brick hadn't thought much of it before, but now he asked himself if he roused that kind of passion in anyone? His son, Jason, and his vegetarian daughter, Georgia, perhaps, loved watching spy movies with him. But if he really thought about it, he saw they took after Brick in their quiescence. Neither was prone to great bursts of affection and both clung to Ava more than to him. Not that he really measured such things, but the harsh truth of every relationship, even between those who love each other, like fathers and sons and daughters, or husbands and wives, is that the love is always unequal. One party always loves the other more. That this inequality is never commented upon is the deception mutually agreed upon in every relationship.

Brick arrived at Bea's, rang the intercom, and was let in without a word.

She said they had to fuck quickly, her girls were due back from ballet in just half an hour and the helper had the keys, so someone could walk in on them. He had previously enjoyed their quick sex, in some ways more than those occasions when they took their time. He relished the hasty strip-down, then approaching her from behind, rubbing himself against her lips through her panties. They both liked it rough, with her bent over the bed.

But today he was disappointed that they would be rushed. He had wanted to spend an hour or so talking, listening to Beatrice.

She was all business, pulling down her jeans but only removing one leg from them as she spread.

When they were done, she started in again with Giancarlo and his new bakery, how he hadn't made the girls' birthday cake on time, claiming the bakers were busy with multiple upcoming wedding cakes. She said he was demanding that they sell the boring Fujita cityscape that hung next to the dining table, to help fund his ongoing expansion.

"He is such a bastard," she said. "So petty. So small."

On his way home, Brick stopped at the bakery. He figured he would buy some treats for the family, a few fruit tarts and some elaborate-looking chocolate-and-meringue confections. A mere forty-eight dollars for dessert.

———

AVA KNEW GIANCARLO. She had brought many of her clients to his restaurants over the years, and had the insider phone numbers

that allowed a person to jump to the top of the month-long reservation list. She wasn't surprised that Brick had brought home a
white-and-red box filled with novelties. What caught her, and the
kids, off guard was the vehemence with which he reacted upon
tasting those pastries. As soon as the meringue hit his tongue he
stood up, walked over to the kitchen sink, and spit the gooey rem-
nants into the garbage disposal, quickly pouring a glass of water
and then rinsing his mouth and spitting again.

Ava and the kids looked at each other and shrugged. The desserts tasted fine to them but Brick quickly removed all their plates,
saying that he believed the tarts were rancid. "He is trying to
poison the neighborhood," he half-joked.

Ava shook her head. "What's wrong with you? My god, the
desserts are delicious."

"They're disgusting." Brick shook his head. He had drunk
nearly the whole bottle of Lambrusco but he believed that what
he said was true. They were vile, as if filled with the venom and
bitterness of Giancarlo's dealings with Bea. It was irrational, he
knew, to believe that everything Giancarlo touched, presided over,
or that even just bore his name was somehow tainted, but that
was how it tasted to Brick. And this scoundrel was able to inflict
his terrible flavors and essences upon this whole community. The
thought of it infuriated Brick, who was rarely roused to anger.
As he sat there, at the head of their Jean Prouve dining table, his
children and wife silent in uneasy concern at his sudden darken-
ing mood, he felt his rage unfold into a precise cartography of his
newfound angers—at Giancarlo's fucking restaurants, his fucking
dog, and his fucking precious brown locks; at how he treated Bea,
at how Bea still seemed obsessed by him, at how it all left him feeling upset and pathetically vulnerable to his family's concern.

"What's wrong?" Ava said.

Brick told her nothing and stumbled to the bedroom, where he
lay down on the bed and closed his eyes. The first thing that came

to mind was him standing on the mound, his right hand dangling by his side as he looked in to get the sign. He really only had two pitches—the fastball and the change—but the fastball was wicked and when he two-seamed it to right-handed batters they would chase it down and in right out of the strike zone. He had such wonderful focus then. The LSD seemed to give him clarity; it allowed him to relax and slow down his movements until throwing the ball seemed effortless. What if Beatrice had seen him pitch? That was a strange notion, the French woman turning up at his Erie high school, and why did it matter? She would admire him, then, for the magnificent young man he had been, for his potential, for how he could have been a great figure—a Giancarlo of the diamond!—if he had wanted.

But he had never cared that much about baseball, and so when he gave it up as a seventeen-year-old it was with a shrug and hardly a regret. Recently, he had begun to reassess that period of his life, and to wonder at how lightly he had taken his talent. At the time, because it had come so easily, he had thought pitching would be the first of many activities that he would similarly master. Yet never again, he now realized with sorrow, had he done anything as well as he had thrown a baseball. Perhaps Jason had inherited his father's small gift and would take it further. Brick found that a satisfying fantasy.

Then, for an instant, in the dark, he saw Beatrice, walking toward him, in a bra and panties, and he sat up, eager, until he realized, of course, that it was Ava getting ready for bed.

———

THEY WERE DRUNK, the four of them, the playwright, the sound engineer, and the photographer, standing with Brick near the curb on West Broadway, just down the block from Giancarlo's bakery. The playwright held in his hand, as if it were a box of pastries, a cardboard container with a dozen new Rawlings baseballs, each in its own little compartment and wrapped in tissue. In the street-light's soft glare, the baseballs looked like precious objects, over-grown pearls. Brick was loosening his arm, rotating it vigorously, four times forward and then three times back, then stretching his right arm by pulling it down behind his back with two fingers of his left hand. Then bending backward, to the right and to the left, doing some version of the stretches he used to do in high school.

The sound engineer had a bottle of single-malt scotch in a white plastic bag, which he swigged from before handing it to the playwright.

The genesis of this project had been the sound engineer men-tioning again that Brick could not throw as fast as he claimed, a challenge that for some reason roused in Brick an immediate and ardent "Fuck you."

"They got that radar speed check thing at the bakery," said the photographer, "you could just throw past that."

That had been at breakfast a few days ago, and the topic, which should have been dropped, had again come up while the guys were drinking at an Italian restaurant in the neighborhood. The box of baseballs had been procured by the playwright, comman-deered from his son Ely's Little League team. He also had a first baseman's glove that he held pinned under one arm as he sipped the scotch.

Brick had actually considered trying to find a hit of LSD, as that would loosen him up, but instead settled for a few glasses of wine and then a Red Bull.

Holding the ball, as he did now, felt natural, comfortable, as familiar as his daughter slipping her hand into his while they were walking to school. He flipped it from hand to hand, scuffing it a little with his palms as he did so. He no longer had the calluses, the stiff skin on his index, middle, and ring fingers, the hardness at the fat part of the palm, but he now noticed that his hands were rougher in other ways, more weathered, perhaps even stronger.

From moving his sculptures around, from all the lifting, hauling, pouring, bending, he was fit, his shoulders still broad, his upper arms muscular, his legs in shape. He felt limber, his shoulder relaxed and arm dangling the way he liked it before he threw. When was the last time he had pitched a baseball at full strength? He couldn't remember. He'd played catch with Jason plenty of times, but that was different. But he still felt that old power, that dispersed musculature that he had always been able to gather, the energy smoothly transferring from legs to ass to back to shoulder to arm to hand and finally to the baseball.

"I need a glove," he said.

They only had one, and the playwright pointed out that he needed it to catch the ball.

Brick shrugged. He felt a little unbalanced without the glove but he could still throw.

The playwright was to crouch down about sixty feet away, just beyond the orange speed check sign, which was now showing 0. Brick tossed an easy one down to the playwright; the sign flashed 68.

In the warm evening, the guys didn't feel self-conscious about the curious stares coming from pedestrians passing on either side of the street. Just a bunch of guys with a box of baseballs, taking advantage of a warm evening to play a little catch. Nothing to see here.

Brick began warming up, throwing the ball with more velocity, so that by the time the sign was flashing 76, 79, 80, 82, the playwright was no longer even trying to catch the pitches, but was rather jumping out of the way as baseballs skittered past, making sharp thumping noises as they bounced off the pavement into the undersides of parked cars, denting fenders and oil pans. The sound engineer ran back, gathering up the baseballs, collecting nine of the dozen, and brought them back to Brick.

Brick turned the ball over in his hand. He reared back, fired.

"Holy shit!" shouted the playwright, bailing out again. The ball made a nasty hiss as it passed the sign.

88.

And Brick knew he could throw harder.

Okay.

"This is for real," Brick said.

The playwright nodded, and reluctantly took up a catcher's crouch beyond the sign and held up a mitt to give Brick a target.

————

THE WIND WAS slight, a gentle breeze that carried with it a hint of the summer to come, the hot afternoons, the Friday rush to collect the car from the garage and then pick up his wife and kids and head out to Peconic, the long nights out on the front patio there, the ocean down the steep bluff, the children inside watching a DVD, the gay neighbors over for a visit and a glass of wine, the swordfish on the grill. His wife in a muumuu or khakis, seated in the wooden recliner, texting or e-mailing on her iPhone, and Brick could see himself, beer in hand, counting the hours until, until . . . what? (He thinks this: You stay in the marriage because you believe this false front is convincing the world but it isn't fooling a soul. They all know that your family is a mess, that you hate your wife, that she hates you, that your children fall asleep every night worrying that when they wake up, you will be gone.)

Ava would look up from the phone, scrunch her nose up, and say, if Brick did venture a rare attempt at a joke, "Don't quit your day job, honey. Oh, that's right, you don't have one."

Brick was now standing, leaning forward slightly, his arm loose by his side as he looked at the playwright's glove. He should have been a better husband, a more talkative father, a more reliable friend, a more successful sculptor. Instead, what was he? A philanderer, and failing even at that.

He started his wind-up, his sneakers finding traction on the rough concrete, swept his arm up in his three-quarters delivery, followed through, the ball leaving his hand feeling pleasantly empty, then that familiar hiss. But instead of throwing to the playwright, he had pivoted so that he was throwing at the window of the bakery. The empty round display trays that during the day proffered lemon tarts and *fraîcheur acidulés* and Montebellos were suddenly covered with shards of window glass. He picked up another ball and fired it, blasting another large hole, this one down and in, so that the bottom part of the window gave way completely, falling out on the sidewalk and shattering with a horrific crash. Strangely, the top part of the window stayed in place for a moment, so Brick hurled another fastball through that portion, which then seemed to explode.

The playwright, sound engineer, and photographer stared at each other in shock. They all ran, at the sound of breaking glass, scattering uptown, downtown, or across town, adolescent survival instincts kicking in. But Brick stood there, managing to throw six more balls, knocking over serving trays and cake plates and then smashing through some interior display cases as well. He took up the bottle of scotch and listened to the sirens approaching, two squad cars making their way down West Broadway in a pool of flickering candy-pink light. He smiled for a second, because his first thought was to wonder at their urgent errand—maybe they were going to arrest the molester—until he remembered—of course, they were coming for him.

———

HE SLEPT FOR a few hours, handcuffed to a bench, and woke with a headache. He was told that bail had been posted. As he wobbled down the First Precinct main stairwell, he spotted Ava wearing a tank top in the hot early morning, standing with her back to the building, killing time scanning wanted posters. He knew she would lay into him, for his juvenile behavior, for his stupidity, ask him why, of all the fucking stupid totally fucking retarded things to do, would he go and throw baseballs through a bakery window? The window, she would note, of an important chef. Brick was not only the father to their children, he was her husband, and she was an important publicist, so . . . how did this make Ava look? She turned around to face him. It was not Ava.

It was Beatrice.

"I love it," she shouted. "When I heard this I was laughing. That cheap bastard." She embraced him and as he drank in her soapy, morning smell, he did what he always did.

He said nothing.

47 LISPENARD

I was wiry, strong with ropey muscles that had surprised me
when they appeared in my early twenties when I began working with saws, lathes, hammers, nails, building first my puppets
and then their stages. I called it folk art for kids for grown-ups. Everything about me—my size, my strength, my ideas, my work—
was suddenly boundless.

I had outgrown the three-bedroom Second Avenue tenement
flat I shared with two roommates and found this long and skinny
loft, windows on both ends, a toilet in the middle, no kitchen.
At $280 a month I almost passed on the deal, but I found another
artist, a Puerto Rican named Rael who made these fake street
signs, like instead of STOP the red hexagon would say THINK. He
would pound and snip the sheet metal, and then paint it, in a
vacant lot near Avenue D. The owners of the lot finally ran him off
and so he was looking for a space too. I told him about my find one
night when we were drinking in a basement on Avenue B, next to
a scrap metal yard. I couldn't even tell if he was listening but the
next evening he was shouting my name from Second Avenue and
when I opened my window he said, "I'm in. Let's take it."

But moving day, he never turned up, and I never saw him again.

I piled my trunks and suitcases and books in milk crates into Keith's white Econoline and Keith drove down Broadway saying with every block farther south we went, "You're actually going to live down here?" Then we hauled all that up three flights to the loft. This was before there were wheels on luggage; you carried your stuff around, by handles, on your back, jerking it up stairways and dragging it down halls.

By the time I figured out that Rael was never going to show, it was three days later and I had already reassembled two of my puppet stages and was nailing some scrap pieces and a plywood plank into a bed frame. There was an open-flame DuraJet heater on the street side of the apartment, which was fitted into an opening in the wall, so that when the gas was lit, the blue flames would blow into the loft. You couldn't put anything within about four feet of that window. It was mid-winter, so I set my sleeping bag on my mattress, turned on the gas, and slept that night for the first time in Tribeca. I was the only person in the building, one of just a dozen people living on this block.

During the day the streets were clotted with double-parked panel trucks and idling semis, the drivers asleep inside their cabs, the carbon monoxide fumes wafting up to my loft. There were still a few factories and sweatshops, and suppliers and subcontractors for the small manufacturers who had persevered in their storefronts after the closing down of the West Side piers. There was a store selling radio parts down on Murray, a guy who serviced and sold spare letters for printing presses over on Broadway, and downstairs in my building were three Italians who fixed sewing machines. I could find a full set of rasps or chisels within a block of my new apartment, but if I wanted a bagel I had to walk twenty-five blocks north.

I came to know my neighbors. There was short, fat Max, who opened a gallery around the corner, who I drank with at El Teddy's or Nancy's Whiskey but who still wouldn't give me a show. Mike Hatch moved in down the block; he was the first painter I knew who had a family—a skinny, tough-looking little wife and two sons. He was also the first artist I knew who had a proper kitchen: countertops, stove, oven, fridge, sink. It was inspiring to go up to his loft and see what he had done: it was civilized.

I went over to the Bowery, bought a slab of butcher's block, a steel restaurant sink and fixtures, and hauled it back to my place—three round trips with a grocery cart—and then set to work building my own kitchen. I had taken a roommate, a hairy Jewish guy named Karp, who biked everywhere and supported himself messengering. He always stank of sweat and exhaust and I saw him as strictly temporary.

He lent me a hand and over the course of three weeks, we built a kitchen, complete with a gas hookup for a stove (for when I procured one) and a slot with outlets for the fridge (in case I got one of those). I was preparing, without being conscious of it, for having a family. The same transition, from artist to family, often within the same loft, was ongoing all over Tribeca. I don't know what Karp thought we were doing. He slept on a futon in the back of the place, amid his bicycles and chains and inner tubes, and didn't have much use for a kitchen; he ate the same Cuban takeout I did, or he boiled ramen in a pot and tossed a few hot dogs in with the broth. He barely used the bathtub I had set up next to the toilet, separated from the rest of the flat by sheets clipped to sprinkler heads. I wasn't disappointed when he told me he was moving to California. The last I heard, he opened a bike shop in Santa Barbara.

———

I WAS HAVING my first (and only) period of success. My puppets and stages had been dubbed "installations" by a gallerist a few blocks north of Tribeca, in SoHo. Using the then-nascent format of Beta cassettes, I had filmed a few of my "installations," the wooden puppets appearing eerie and starkly modern in the grainy video footage. I wasn't the most able storyteller, so I made a virtue of my inability to structure a narrative and cut the dialogue and scenes up so that it was intentionally dyspeptic. My tall, tin-can robot puppet with rolled-up sardine-can-top hair would show up while my hero, the monkey-wrench fairy, was at his most needy—and then sodomize him. I didn't know what I was doing, but it had, I was surprised to discover, a horror movie vibe, as if my puppets and puppet stages were the preferred entertainment of monsters or zombies, as if Dracula and the flesh-eaters from *Dawn of the Dead* would knock off after a night of drinking blood and eating brains and watch my puppet theater.

I had inadvertently created punk puppetry. They were showing my videos between bands at CBGBs, then at the Pyramid Club, and even the Ritz. My next gallery show was a success. Though not in the manner I had hoped. Instead of selling my installations and puppets, the gallery was selling videotapes of my puppet shows for $7 each. My most widely reviewed and attended show netted me a grand total of $330. Later I heard the term "monetize" used in the sense of converting audience, interest, power, whatever, into cash. I had utterly failed at that.

At the time, it didn't seem that much of a concern. Nobody was monetizing their work. I knew plenty of artists who were having shows, maybe even selling their work, but we all maintained a similar lifestyle. Of course, a few guys were getting rich. But the successes of Basquiat and Haring seemed to have nothing to do with me. I didn't know them. I had never met Warhol or his crowd.

What I didn't know was that even the guys down in my neighborhood, artists no more famous than I was, were quietly transitioning from renting their lofts to owning them. They were not only installing kitchens and proper bathrooms, they were also, in some cases, buying the buildings they lived in. My rent never rose, so why would I buy my loft, even if I had the money? Anyway, it didn't seem to make much difference if Max down the street owned his place and I rented mine. A home, a loft, is just a machine for living.

To that end, along with my new roommate, Gallagher, a freelance writer whom I never saw type a word, I built a proper bathroom, and at a bathroom supply place I found a fancy Jacuzzi bath that was supposed to shoot out jets of hot water while I lounged in the spacious tub. It had been ordered but never picked up by a contractor, so the merchant gave me a good deal. Gallagher and I installed the bath, built a countertop, and mounted the tiles around an oval sink. I was slowly getting better at rudimentary carpentry and masonry, though there were still some flaws in my work, among them, the floor tile I laid down didn't quite reach the wall in one corner, so that you could see the loft below through the crack in the floor.

Still, having a proper bathroom was a great improvement. I excitedly drew the hot water for a bath in my new whirlpool, climbed in, switched on the jets, and enjoyed a full fifteen seconds of soothing hydrotherapy, then heard a loud, coughing noise and the jets stopped. Because our building was only rated at 80 amps—and the whirlpool required 120—the jets had malfunctioned, causing the water to flow backward into the system and choke the pipes. It never worked again.

———

MY VIDEOS HAD made their way to the studio of Teri Ann, a woman whose children's puppet characters were beloved all over the world. I despised her work with an intensity that came out in obscene tirades when I was drunk. I had spent years reading about and studying Japanese *bunraku* masters, Javanese shadow puppeteers, Milanese marionette makers; had I the money, I would have traveled the world to watch these artists at work. But when you asked Americans about puppets, they inevitably mentioned Teri Ann's Teddy Turtle or Missus Possum. They were glorified sock puppets with ping-pong-ball eyes. An insult to true puppeteering.

When I received a call from the assistant to Teri Ann's master puppeteer, who had watched my videos, I showed considerable restraint in not telling him off on the phone. He told me they had all been enjoying my videos and were wondering if I wanted to come in and maybe kick some ideas around. It's embarrassing to say this, but instantly, my thoughts jumped to how much money I might make if one of my characters would turn up on *Miss Possum's Playhouse*. I had no hope, nor was it even conceivable, that Seman the Sodomizing Robot could end up on a children's show, but I was stricken by the damaging dream of instant and rapid riches.

I even told myself I would like to buy a Jacuzzi bath that works.

Teri Ann's production company, the American Children's Workshop, was on Broadway between 8th Street and Houston. I was immediately assaulted in the foyer by posters of Teddy Turtle and actual Missus Possum show puppets. The only time I had ever seen these puppets was on television and at toy stores and notion shops in their many licensed variations. They put me in a foul mood for my meeting with the master puppeteer, a balding man with thin strips of hair around a shiny crown. He wore a T-shirt and loose-fitting slacks and drank tea from a mug. By the time we met, I had decided I wanted nothing to do with this fascistic sanitizing of the great, potentially subversive art form of puppetry.

"I'm Benny," he said. "Want some tea?"

I nodded. "Before we start, I just want to tell you, I can't stand what you do. I despise this condescending, lowest-common-denominator approach to puppetry. You are debasing an art form, and creating a generation of Americans who expect nothing more from their puppets than squeaky animal voices and the recitation of simple arithmetic problems. You are everything that is wrong with puppetry today. You are my enemy."

Benny laughed and started clapping. "Wonderful, wonderful."

They were looking for someone like me, he explained, someone who could help the American Children's Workshop develop more mature material. They had seen my videos and enjoyed them. *That* wasn't exactly what they were looking for, of course, but something with an edge, something with some bite.

Benny had done puppet shows for tripping hippies at Dead concerts before joining Teri Ann and helping her come up with the staging that allowed the characters to work so well on television interacting with real actors and celebrities. Astronauts, starlets, and baseball players appeared on the show alongside Teddy Turtle.

Now, Benny said, they wanted to develop another prime-time show, this one aimed exclusively at adults. New characters, new concepts.

"No more Missus Possum?" I said.

Benny nodded.

His office was upstairs over a vast workshop where young people in loose-fitting clothing glued eyes and stitched foam rubber. It was like a factory, I thought, and a cult. It reminded me, actually, of a pamphlet Gallagher had shown me of the cult in upstate New York he later would join after moving out of our loft.

"What did you have in mind?" I asked.

"Teri Ann sees herself as a patron of all puppetry, of the form," Benny explained. "She wants to support the art."

"So?"

"So be free, man, be wild. Take on big subjects: peace, freedom, anarchy."

I gazed around the room at the young attentive apprentices and the bright green and pink and orange and blue puppets, the shag and velvet and shiny polyester, the ping-pong-ball eyes, the red bulbous noses, the semicircle flap mouths. Anarchy? This was Adam Smith's pin factory rendered in the most inoffensive manner possible, but it was still the dark heart of capitalism.

Benny stood up. "I want you to meet Teri Ann. You need to hear where she is coming from on this stuff."

THAT SATURDAY, THEY sent a limousine to pick me up. When my new roommate, Dmitri, a Russian artist who worked with neon, saw the car waiting downstairs at the curb, he denounced me as a "capitalist bastard." (Dmitri's denouncement of capitalism would extend to his insistence that we refuse to pay our "capitalist bastard" landlord our rent, by which he meant his share of the rent, which meant he lived rent-free until I kicked him out.)

Teri Ann lived on an estate in Bedford, a vast stone manse with stables, swimming pool, and a stream burbling through the back garden. As we drove up the long access road and into the circular drive, I saw the paisley Rolls-Royce that Teri Ann had been famously photographed next to for a *Time* magazine cover story about her puppets. There was a stone staircase up to vast oak double doors with lion's-head knockers. The doors opened as I approached and there she was, the grande dame of American puppetry and the embodiment of everything I hated.

"Well howdy!" she said. Even though she was a Jewish girl from the Bronx, Teri Ann affected a Southern drawl. Her voice was familiar, and it took me a second before I realized, of course: Missus Possum's voice.

She was pretty in person; in that famous *Time* photograph she had shorter hair, which gave her face a rectangular shape, like Sandy Duncan. Her eyes were more pronounced in real life than in photos, and she had let her hair grow out so that her face seemed more ovoid. Her eyebrows were surprisingly lush, and her lashes were almost caterpillar-thick. Her facial skin was smooth and shiny tan with reddened triangles at the cheeks. Teri Ann was slender, with very upright posture, and naturally toned.

She gave me a hug and led me down the hall, past a cabinet full of antique *bunraku* puppet heads. I recognized them as eighteenth-century Sansebo and Tonda heads, rare and valuable. The faces were perfect examples of the intricacy of expression possible in puppetry. The white lacquered skin, the black-lined eyes, red lips, thick black hair. In *bunraku* each puppet was operated by three puppeteers, one for the head and right hand, another for the left hand, and an apprentice for the legs. The emotional range made possible by this combination of appendages and face, when handled by masters, was perhaps the highest form of our art.

Then we passed a gigantic mockup of Teddy Turtle, his vast green stomach vulgar after the delicacy of the *bunraku* faces.

"Benny isn't here yet. We're going to barbecue later. Can I get you anything to drink?"

Bloody Mary in my clenched fist, I carefully settled into an outdoor beanbag chair. There were about fifty of them scattered around the back lawn and patio, red, blue, orange, and yellow dots on the verdant green grass. Teri Ann had disappeared somewhere, and I found myself struggling to make conversation with the other guests, a few of whom I recognized from the workshop on Broadway.

I wandered back into the house. As I went, I kept hearing Dmitri's "capitalist bastard!" every time I saw a David Salle painting or a Lutyens dollhouse or a Botero sculpture. I wasn't accustomed to wealth, to truly fine things, and it was disorienting to stand amid this kind of opulence, the wood-paneled den with a John Singer Sargent portrait over a fireplace larger than a van. Even while I was denouncing all this, I found myself feeling jealous, and then somehow guilty because of my jealousy. It would have been better for me, I felt, had I never laid eyes on all this wealth, derived from puppets, of all things.

"There you are!" Teri Ann said.

She had changed into white jeans and a silk blouse, with a simple pearl necklace dangling into the V of flesh visible in the open collar.

"Benny is running late, and before it gets too hectic, I thought we should talk. He raves about you!"

"Thanks, I guess."

"And I've seen your work!" She made a huge smile, teeth everywhere. "Wild!"

"Um—"

"So Benny told you what we're doing: grown-ups!"

"Right, I'm not really—"

"Adults!" Teri Ann flopped onto a generously stuffed Chesterfield leather sofa. "You could become one of us at the Workshop."

I wanted to tell her: *That* I will never be. I want to make my art my way—uncompromising, subversive puppetry. But something about the mansion, this room, and even Teri Ann, stretched out, her shirt pulling a little more open, her freckled chest coming into view, the intertwining of desires for money, luxury, sex—it muddled me so that I only said, "Okay."

"Great!" She sat up. "And Benny said you would be tough to convince."

What had I done?

"Wait, wait," I told her. "No ping-pong-ball eyes. No red noses. No fluffy animals."

"Darlin', we don't want any of that. We want you to take the Workshop in a totally new direction. When Benny gets here, you put him in touch with your agent and we've got plenty of space at the Workshop. I could wet my britches I'm so excited!"

———

I DIDN'T HAVE an agent, so I had my friend Max, who owned the gallery around the corner, act as my manager. We had no idea how much to ask for but when Max suggested a number that we considered generous, he told me that Benny reacted with such extended silence that he was sure we had overshot. Instead, Benny came back with, "Is that per day?"

The deal we finally signed said that I would come join the Workshop, developing puppets and concepts for a new televised puppet show for grown-ups. If we developed a show from my puppets or concepts, I was to come on board as an executive producer—master puppeteer—and at that point, some of those apprentices and junior puppeteers building puppets down in the vast workspace area would come and work for me. In exchange, I was to be paid as much in a week as I had ever made in a year.

My office was along a balcony of offices that looked down upon the workspace and the various puppet stages, flats, and scrims at the far end of the cavernous space. Directly beneath my offices was a sound stage and production studio where some ACW productions were mounted, and where puppets and puppeteers came and went all day. As I sat at my drafting table and watched the green Teddy Turtles and orange Missus Possums gliding in and out, I felt as if I were living through an endless rehearsal for the Macy's Thanksgiving Day Parade.

"Benny, man, I don't know," I said one afternoon as I was looking through some felt fabric swaths he kept in his office. They were all bright colors, neons and Day-Glos, stuff that popped through the muting of cathode-ray televisions.

"Hey man, we're all just winging it," he said. "Look, do you care about puppetry? Do you love it?"

"Yeah, of course."

"Then this is your chance. Use Teri Ann, use the Workshop to make something great."

Teri Ann only came into the workshop for shoots. She would change into a blue-screen body suit that I found disturbingly erotic and then urge the cast and crew to "Light this firecracker up!" She would go to work behind and slightly below Missus Possum, just off-camera, operating the puppet with her right arm and a control rod, and saying the dialogue into a headset microphone. I had to admit it was a mesmerizing performance. She could improvise seamlessly; she knew exactly when to scrunch the puppet up into the famous Possum-face and when to bob Missus Possum's head in a laugh. Teri Ann was as fine a puppeteer as I had ever seen, so deft with manipulation of the hands and the delicate maneuvering of Missus Possum's mouth that she reminded me of a *bunraku* master. It was remarkable, but for what? So that an anthropomorphic possum could flirt with Bo Jackson? So that millions more Missus Possum dolls could sell throughout the world and Teri Ann could live in baronial splendor—and subsidize the selling-out of an avant-garde puppeteer?

Teri Ann kept a place in the city, a high-floor modern apartment on Fifth Avenue in the Eighties, and she called me up there for a meeting in the middle of one afternoon. I pulled together a few sketches, stuffed them in a valise, and took the subway uptown. She greeted me at the foyer and led me into her office, a room with floor-to-ceiling windows and a dazzling view of the park. She didn't go behind her glass-topped desk but leaned her ass against it.

I showed her some sketches, rough outlines for my vague ideas about a show built around the *Divine Comedy*, complete with Beatrice and Cicero, Inferno, Purgatorio, and Paradiso. I had ideas about doing it with cut-outs so that we would need side views, three-quarter views, and front views of each puppet, and the backgrounds and stages would be as elaborate. I didn't believe anyone had ever attempted anything on this scale.

Teri Ann flipped through the sketches, nodding, and said, "Gosh, I sure wouldn't mind getting my beak wet. How about you?"

She led me out of the room to a vast living/dining room where an elevated, carpeted area with various plush risers made up the primary seating. I cautiously took my place on the shag, with my back against a yellow throw pillow, and sipped my gin and tonic.

"Did you always know you were a puppeteer?"

"Oh no, when I was younger, I wanted to be an actress. I went to Juilliard." She told me that she developed her signature-style puppets, the furry foam-rubber sock puppets with ping-pong-ball eyes, when she needed a way to fill the time during complicated set changes for an undergraduate review. The quirky puppet characters brought down the house.

"So you had no training?"

"Gosh no. It was just . . . filler."

She soon created her first TV show, a five-minute children's show for a local TV station, while she was still at Juilliard, and soon was producing her show for the Public Broadcasting System. The prime-time show, the Broadway show, the movies, and the licensing deals all followed quickly. George Lucas was now asking her to work with him on the next installment of the *Star Wars* franchise. She had met every living president.

"Why do you need me?" I asked.

She shrugged. "How much more can we do with felt and foam rubber and ping-pong balls? This ranch needs new breeding stock."

We had a few more drinks and she suggested we go downtown for some sushi, to a place she liked on the East Side in the Twenties. We could tell when we got there, without leaving the limousine, that it was closed, and so we decided to go to the Chinese restaurant next door. We sat at the bar, sharing shrimp toast, moo shu pork, and fried dumplings. I was surprised by how much we had to talk about: the other folks at the Workshop, Benny, puppetry. She had an irreverent sense of humor; no surprise that she was the person behind the sly, sassy sarcasm that made Missus Possum so popular. When we left, it seemed natural that I would climb into the limousine with her; she never even asked if I wanted to be dropped off at home. I had been attracted to Teri Ann from our first meeting, but I wasn't aware of making any particular play to seduce her. Yet now it seemed so effortless. We held hands riding back uptown, that first tight grasp giving me an almost adolescent thrill, a stable and steady hardening.

Back at her apartment, we climbed onto that carpeted seating proscenium and snuggled up and slowly disrobed. She never turned on the lights, and next to us, outside her large windows, the whole city was shining, Central Park lit by the dots of streetlamps. In the reflected light, Teri Ann was all narrow planes aglow, long arms and legs, flat stomach, smooth cheeks, wide, un-notched forehead, her creamy white skin taking on the city sheen. Her blond pubic hair invisible, lost in the light.

When I was actually inside her, I found myself imagining her in the blue bodysuit she used when she was filming. Her moans were the only sounds she made that didn't remind me of Missus Possum. During a languor, while I was reloading, so to speak, I went to the bathroom, not the small half-bath near the living room but the distant master, and rummaged through cabinets until I found what I was looking for, lubrication. I came back, already tumescent, applied the ointment, turned her over, and, finally, we had our subversive adult puppet show, Seman the Sodomizing Robot having anal intercourse with Missus Possum.

At dawn, I asked her about my *Divine Comedy*. She said, "Let's do it."

I ENVISIONED THE South Bronx in the Seventies, a black Cicero, Nixon and Reagan and Ollie North in the ninth circle of hell. This was going to be austere but powerful puppetry, the art would be in the figures themselves, the backgrounds, the sets, it would all be hand-rendered. I went up to the Strand and bought a shopping cart full of schematic engineering books and coffee-table art books. I had a print shop over on Fourth Avenue blow up Brueghel's *Tower of Babel* and Bosch's *The Temptation of Saint Anthony* and tacked them to my office walls, along with a Dead Kennedys *Plastic Surgery Disasters* album cover.

At night, I would show Teri Ann my creations. There would

be three layers of sets, I told her, hence three depths of field. The puppeteers would operate in the traditional manner, beneath the stage, but the sets could also move and transform, and as the camera panned from, say, three-quarter view to frontal on a character, the set behind would also be shifting, and at a different rate than the one or two layers farther from the camera. This would be continuous motion, done without special effects, and while it would not require the kind of hand-in-puppet virtuosic performance that Teri Ann excelled at, it did require immense resources in terms of rendering, painting, and crafting the sets, backgrounds, and puppets. The result would be something unique in the history of puppetry and television: a sixty-four-episode, slide-puppet interpretation of the *Divine Comedy*.

She would smile and give me a kiss. "Oh darlin', you're a real maverick. This is just what I needed." She would tell me about her next big project, a road picture with Missus Possum, Teddy Turtle, Ferguson the Bear, Diana Ross, and Kenny Rogers in search of a magical crystal. It would be shot primarily in LA to accommodate Diana Ross.

And then we would go out to dinner or order in and make love.

———

DMITRI MOVED TO Berlin. With my income from the Workshop I no longer needed a roommate. The neighborhood had for some time been transforming, entire loft buildings now going coop. The sweatshops were gone. The Italians and their sewing-machine repair shop vanished overnight, and were replaced by an art gallery. I had to go all the way over to Ace hardware store twelve blocks away to buy chisels, handsaws, or bits. The elementary school over on Chambers and Greenwich opened; at the time I hardly noticed. Celebrities began moving in, movie stars, sons of presidents. Absentee landlords reemerged to develop their properties, drive up their rents. The Mudd Club, Area, then Wetlands came and went. Odeon was joined by Chanterelle, Giancarlo's, and newer restaurants even more expensive, but my bloated Workshop wages made me believe I was part of this gentrification.

When Caroline called me (a friend of a friend, she had heard my roommate had moved out) I almost told her, forget it, I'm not looking. But old habits prevail and I told her the rent, which had by then risen to just $380 a month, and explained the improvised living situation. I had put up drywall to demarcate a back bedroom, but there was still just the one bathroom with its broken Jacuzzi; a jerry-rigged hand spout allowed it to serve as a vast, treacherous shower.

She said she was interested, came by, and gave me a deposit. She was a recent graduate of the nonprofit program at Columbia's School of International and Public Affairs and was the first person I had seen in years wearing sandals. She had short black hair, wore round-framed glasses set on a small nose over thin lips. There was a compactness to her that made me think she would be a good roommate. Quiet. Contained.

I wasn't home much. Between the Workshop and nights with Teri Ann, I returned mainly to change clothes or crash for a few hours. Caroline would often be there, reading one of her policy books with bands of primary colors for covers, or talking quietly on the phone with a food bank in Brooklyn or a public housing assistance agency in the Bronx. I came to enjoy falling asleep to her steady, soothing, reasonable voice—the opposite of Teri Ann's twang.

Teri Ann was soon spending more time on the West Coast, and her film work became a bigger and bigger part of the Workshop. I saw her on weekends when she was back; we'd spend an hour at the apartment, entwined. During the first few months of our affair, we had worked up to my fucking her in the ass at the crescendo of each session. Now, she was no longer allowing me to sodomize her, saying that all the careful preparation, the stops and starts, it all tired her out.

When I showed my *Divine Comedy* sketches to Benny, who would soon be decamping for the Coast, he smiled and said, "Fantastic, man, this is so fucking out there." I was at the point where I needed a few artists and illustrators, some hands to help me start fabricating some puppets so I could see what would work, how this would actually play. Maybe even a carpenter to help with some backgrounds. I had an evolved idea of the kinds of modern-day purgatory and inferno I wanted for the settings, but I couldn't draw, paint, and build them myself. But Benny said he couldn't spare the bodies. Between the shows and the movie, "Every oar is in the water, man."

During one of the weeks when Teri Ann was in LA, I was drinking coffee at the Square Diner and looking through the *Daily News* when I saw a photo of her and Bob Evans. The caption below said the two had been canoodling at Chasen's, where they were also talking about her next picture. I guessed it was true. He was a handsome, successful, very wealthy man, so why wouldn't Teri Ann sleep with him? I was the aberration. I went home and was about to call her, but Caroline was on the phone with one of her clients, some agency that brought food to AIDS patients who couldn't speak English. Instead of waiting for her, I headed up to the Workshop, where I saw Benny getting ready to head to the airport.

He was in his office, going through some run sheets.

"We're never doing *Divine Comedy*, are we?"

"Hey man, I'm glad you caught me," Benny said. "We, Teri Ann, feel the grown-up TV stuff—the vibe isn't right for the Workshop. She wants to keep it real simple and like family, you know?"

Teri Ann didn't even call me to tell me we were finished. I got a call three days later from the Workshop accountant, who informed me my next check would be my last. The hurt was three-fold: the art, the money, the girl.

———

I WAS RETURNED to my rightful place. I took to smoking a lot of pot and watching television and eating pints of Häagen-Dazs ice cream, which you could now purchase from any of the many neighborhood delis that had opened. When I headed out to buy more weed or Jamocha Almond Fudge, wearing sunglasses, hooded sweatshirt, jeans, I felt like I no longer belonged in my new neighborhood. Yuppies had taken over and even my fellow artists started to look and talk like them. Around the corner, Max's gallery had expanded and he had openings for shows of photographs taken by Michael Stipe and people like that. Stuff yuppies liked. My fellow artists and the other early arrivals here in Tribeca were all getting rich, their lofts appreciating, and soon they all seemed to drive SUVs and own summer houses. I wanted to hide; without my big paycheck and big project, what was I? The scene I had come out of, a subculture that might pay attention to punk puppetry, was long dead, and I mean that literally: many of my fans, or at least people who had heard of me, were dying of AIDS.

I kept my front curtains closed. I had an old La-Z-Boy lounger that I had scavenged on the street and set it up facing the TV, and a blue plastic bong, and while I watched a lot of MTV, I avoided watching any Workshop productions. I was also getting fat. Inactivity and ice cream making me that least attractive of figures: the chubby starving artist.

Caroline had started out that winter as a distant, immobile form, squatting, observing, a vaguely soothing presence at the edges of my consciousness. She wore dark clothes, black jeans, blue T-shirts, a black wool peacoat. She had taken a permanent position, at a Brooklyn nonprofit where she oversaw business development. When she was gone, I posited the absence as you might the removal of a salad fork from a place setting.

We must have spoken, figured out our shares of utility and telephone bills, relayed schedules, solicited requests before we went for deli runs, but I don't recall a single conversation.

How many hours of television did we watch together? How many *Real Worlds* and *MTV Beach Houses* and Pauly Shores? How much Jamocha Almond Fudge did we share? How often did she hear me defecate through that cheap drywall barrier I had built? Had any woman ever seen me in such an unattractive state before?

Yet, by that spring, we were sharing my bed. After the most intense love affair of my life, I met the mother of my daughter literally under my own roof. Did I ever find her attractive? Maybe, but it was more a matter of proximity. She was here and I was in no condition to seduce anyone who wasn't.

She was a fine roommate; she consumed few resources, was tidy, quiet. And in her steady, stoic way, she was restoring me. How pathetic was I? In my late thirties, to have my heart broken like some adolescent Romeo, showing my hurt everywhere on my body, in my fat stomach, my stoned eyes, my bloated cheeks and double chin. Only Caroline could stand me, and with the addition of quiet, steady sex, my routine became like some teenager's vision of the good life: weed, TV, pussy.

One day Caroline brought home a bicycle she had bought for $5 with the idea that instead of taking the subway, she could ride over the Brooklyn Bridge every day. The bike was a mess; it needed a new rear tire, chain, chain ring, spokes, tubes, crank case, and stays, but while she was at work, I took a look at the old Huffman and found myself admiring the graceful curve of the frame, the antler-like jauntiness of the handlebars. I turned off the television, rolled the bike over to my workshop area, and began to see what I could do with the machine. By the time Caroline had returned home, I had the Huffman in fine working order. Caroline and I took it down to the street and she rode it up and down the wide sidewalks of Lispenard Street.

I asked if she could get me a bike, and she said she would return to the East Village church rummage sale where she had found this one. She came back that night with a red Western Flyer that I spent the better part of two days working on until it, too, was restored to fine fettle. I didn't beautify these machines, or paint them; I was simply making them run.

By the time Caroline told me she was pregnant, I had posted handbills, advertising my services, on the sides of newspaper boxes and lampposts, and soon had to shift my puppet stages over against the west wall to make room for all the bikes. This wasn't an ideal location to repair bikes—we didn't have an elevator—but porting them up and down three flights was working me back into shape.

I had never imagined when I moved into this loft—back when I had felt like I was a pioneer—that I would end up raising a child here. I dutifully joined Caroline for the birthing classes, where we watched the videos, practiced massages that might soothe her natal pains, and planned our birthing strategies. When the time came, Caroline gave birth with a midwife at Roosevelt Hospital and revealed to me a frightening resilience when she eschewed pain medication and epidural and pushed baby Sadie out *au naturel.*

WE LOOKED, TO the untrained eye, like just another yuppie Tribeca family. Here we were, mother, father, baby, loft. Yet I knew we were unlike the multitude that had moved in. Our presence here was completely dependent on rent control; we were the aboriginals who were slowly being driven out by the wealthier, colonizing settlers.

Everything was changed. I a father. A repairman. What happened?
It wasn't the life I had dreamed of, it wasn't even the life I

wanted now, but it was a life I could live. My dreams had receded into the quotidian banality of feeding and clothing a child. Into paying bills. Into trying to keep a marriage going.

But they occasionally surface. I see myself reflected in the store windows as I walk down these streets. Out of the corner of my eye, for an instant, I am twenty-nine, thirty-two tops. And for a moment I am confused and my old conceits about myself, about art, about puppets—the frank sexual excitement that I had felt with Teri Ann—come geysering up and it takes almost a physical effort to keep them in. I put my head down. I hold my daughter more tightly. I keep walking.

———

TERI ANN DIED just a few years after Sadie was born. She had received Emmys, an Oscar, and along with Missus Possum and Teddy the Turtle had been feted at one of those Kennedy Center Honors events, yet she couldn't beat cancer of the uterus. Poor girl. I watched the story on the evening news, Dan Rather earnestly explaining that we had lost a great American, someone who had brought joy to millions. Caroline was at work, and Sadie was playing with some of my old *Divine Comedy* prototypes on the floor. She looked up and recognized some of Teri Ann's characters in the short tribute CBS had assembled. Missus Possum, Teddy Turtle. I had banned those toys from the house, but Sadie had seen plenty of Workshop productions on television. How could she miss them?

"Missus Possum!" she shouted, looking at me.

She noticed I was crying.

"Why are you crying? What's wrong?"

"Nothing, someone died."

"Who? Missus Possum?" Sadie asked.

I nodded. "No, not Missus Possum, er, kind of, yes."

Then Sadie began blubbering, sad that Missus Possum was dead.

152 DUANE

In the long afternoon light, the yellow glow extending down the west-east thoroughfares from river to river, casting business-men and bums and wives and bike messengers all, for a moment, in a halo-like glow, so that the most repugnant and repulsive among us looked, for an instant, exalted and beatific, how easy it was to imagine that we had found our own blessed plot. Sure, Rankin thought, there had been 9/11, Ground Zero just a few blocks away, but it was already ancient history, a subject his son came home from school asking about—bad guys flew planes into the Twin Towers. We could see them from the roof, Rankin had told him. And somehow, the boy found that answer satisfactory.

He wasn't the type to marvel at how they had all put that behind them, the whole neighborhood, displaced for a few months, sent to hotels and relatives uptown while they waited for the all-clear. Oh, he felt the appropriate horror and fear; his children were too young to understand what was happening, they were sitting in their car seats holding their sippy cups full of green juice (*gee-goo*, Jeremy called it), but he still found himself comforting them. It was not in his nature to succumb to his emotions. His intellectual response to seeing the buildings aflame from his roof, to watching those falling bodies (they hadn't seemed human to Rankin, or he had managed to convince himself, while he was standing there, that they weren't), was to buy. Later, he would realize what he had seen. But his first impulse, and it was as deeply felt as any feeling he would ever have, was, remarkably: buy now. Buy property. Buy Tribeca.

Where did such pragmatic instincts come from? He didn't know. But as Sydney loaded the Escalade and made sure Jeremy was strapped into his car seat—Amber had just been born—he found himself wondering if any brokers were open that day.

That had been a universe ago. And that stream trickling out of Tribeca that morning had been more than offset by the vast tidal inflow looking to move in. The downward blip in prices had been momentary, and since Rankin had been buying immediately, as the city had reveled through this almost onanistic celebration of itself and its prosperity, he had felt as deserving of positive strokes as anyone else in the neighborhood.

Now it was ebbing again, the trickle outward, bankers and money-runners pulling up, selling short, bailing. Rankin was not subject to herd pessimism. Unleveraged, he bided. Soon, it would be time again.

He had become an upstanding member of the community, an early pillar of the Lower Manhattan Hebrew School and major donor to its community center. He sponsored the planting of maples along his block and gave scores of Yankee Stadium boxes to the PTA auction. He had become, by necessity and intention, dependable, reliable, yet still regarded, by anyone who spoke with him, with a certain degree of fear.

———

WAS RANKIN CONNECTED? Who, exactly, did he know? Rankin himself couldn't tell you—*connected* was such a freighted word. Yet even the new rebbe consulted with him when he heard that a young shiksa had been molested and was worried about security at the Hebrew School. Could Rankin have one of his guys keep an eye on the community center?

Rankin did know an awful lot of guys. Guys he grew up with in Flatbush. Guys he worked with at nightclubs. Guys he paid to get him cut-rate booze and other guys he bribed to leave his clubs alone. Guys he hired to work his doors. Guys he trusted to run his betting rooms and guys he knew who collected debts. Just some guys. That's all. Hardly any of them lived in the neighborhood, but you would sometimes see a couple of guys parked outside Rankin's building. Sometimes, Sydney would send the maid down with sandwiches for the guys, or the guys would order from the Mexican on the corner.

When Rankin went out to breakfast with the other fathers from the school, he found their conversation boring. Movies. Books. Sports. Rankin once paid a great deal of attention to point spreads but now he preferred to simply collect rents from the local clubs and bars where his bookie friends congregated, and provide—for a huge price—some of the operating capital. He still had his baseball tickets, boxes at Yankee Stadium and Citi, tickets he gave to clients and partners. (Guys loved the free tickets.) So he didn't add much to the conversation, but the funny thing was, whenever he did speak, all the other dads buttoned. And not out of fear. But because they were really listening to him. When Rankin would mention whatever he was doing that day, going up to look at a space in Chelsea for a club or that he was putting together a syndicate for this credit card debt consolidation business, they would pay attention in a way they didn't with each other.

As if they knew that Rankin was real. Real real. And the rest of them, rich fucks, were full of shit.

———

SO WHILE THE neighborhood had smugly appreciated, dollars per square foot increasing like vigorish on a loan, Rankin found himself assuming certain airs. He liked these other fathers, the window they provided onto the finer things. No, he wasn't about to start reading novels or whatever the fuck they were talking about, but he liked the sense he was part of a community where guys did more than work angles and collect. He hadn't left Flatbush just to find another bunch of fathers sweating over their schmaltz and the fifth at Aqueduct. Who even played the horses anymore? Old people and Chinks, that's who. He remembered his father talking to the rest of the fathers outside the Greek's, degenerate horseplayers all of them. His father, a huge man with hands like catchers' mitts and a big, round face like the Mr. Clean logo—Rankin, with his thick black hair, now cut short, took more after his mother, Zeidy—had taken horse and sports bets, and Rankin had run the slips for him and had gotten to know a few guys. But even then, so much of the horse action was Chinese. The Chinks would bet on anything. Trotters. Dogs. Fronton. This was before buses parked three-deep under the bridge to take them to Atlantic City or an Indian reservation. The only action was the underground clubs in Chinatown and the track. Even old Chinese ladies learned enough English to check off their sucker trifecta bets.

Rankin wasn't the type who you just casually asked, "So what do you do?" At potluck dinners for class parents, over brisket or cheese plates, occasionally an innocent father making small talk would inquire, and Rankin would shrug, shovel broiled beef onto his paper plate, and say, "I'm a contractor." He never in his life had picked up a hammer except when he was nineteen and that was to smash in a windshield.

Having never done anything that he could really explain in polite society, he struggled to figure out if it was normal for men to go around asking each other what they did. The guys he knew, they took the measure of each other without a word. But most of the parents in Jeremy's and Amber's classes would practically be asking for your social security number and zodiac sign a few days after back-to-school. Bankers, lawyers, admen, dentists—all chirping away and expressing pleasant surprise at mutual acquaintances. Sharing all this information and data about themselves so casually that Rankin could figure a fella's net worth from just a few minutes of morning chitchat. Rankin, meanwhile, didn't even have a fucking e-mail address; he had no need for communication that sat in electronic limbo after he sent it, waiting for someone to find it and fuck him over. He rarely made it to school for drop-off anyway, relying on the nanny to get the kids to school while he slept off a late one. When he did make it, he fell into the company of the guys who went out to get coffee, only because they didn't seem particularly interested in what anyone else did, self-centered fucks that they were, but Rankin found their lack of interest comforting.

He loomed over them. There was only one guy even near his size, some sculptor or something. Wife-supported, no doubt, because who can make a living from that shit? But Rankin could sit and listen for a while, eat his eggs and chicken livers, drink coffee. He found the gossip about the neighborhood useful, which restaurant was closing, which kids store was going out of business, who was foreclosed in 200 Chambers or selling over at 111 Greenwich, who was divorced, who was fucking around, who was taking over the downtown Little League, what the new rabbi had said last Saturday, whether or not the cops had caught the kid who threw eggs from the roof of a building during the Jewish Community Festival or the rapist who looked like the sound guy. That data was useful. Half the action in this neighborhood probably flowed through his betting shops. If a punter's slips started outpacing his mortgage, Rankin needed to know. And then he could move on a guy's condo.

———

THE COFFEE GUYS were thrilled to have a maybe-connected guy like Rankin among them. Though ever-vigilant never to mention the subject, they did occasionally turn to Rankin when they needed a crime-related question cleared up, especially as it pertained to a plot twist in a film or television show they had seen. Rankin would shrug and say, "What the fuck do I know?"

For most of the men, Rankin also served as the living embodiment of warning. Of whom you never want to turn to. Of a desperation you hope you will never feel. It was understood, by those who came to know Rankin a little, that he possessed great powers and a web of the kind of unseen connections that order a good portion of this city. Cops and robbers, as it were. That he had the power to transform your problem into a bluntly simple affair. But there would be a cost to that, a terrible cost. They speculated among themselves, when Rankin wasn't around, what that cost might be. He would own you, said an attorney who knew a little about such things, he would *own* you.

———

RANKIN WAS UP early, having stayed in last night rather than dropping in on the clubs. Sydney usually handled dawn patrol, but today it was his turn. Rankin had been pleasantly surprised that Sydney, a cocktail waitress turned mother and wife, was mothering and wifing like the outer-borough Jewess she was supposed to be, albeit one with artificially enhanced cleavage. Baked brisket and roast chicken and her sweet-and-sour stuffed cabbage and she never failed to collect the kids at 2:50 p.m. and deposit them as required at Little League or Hebrew school or soccer practice. He originally thought he had been marrying down but actually he had married up. The woman was a warrior mother, as efficient at cajoling broccoli into Jeremy's gullet as she had been wheedling bills out of the wallets of lap-dance bar patrons.

He tried to get up with the kids to take them to school once a week. He'd tell the nanny to go tidy up somewhere else in the house and he would prepare eggs and lox and rye toast, pour the orange juice, and sit down for a few minutes while Jeremy and Amber ate their breakfasts. He would ask them about school and do his best to stay interested in their long-winded, half-baked descriptions.

He had been lucky when it came to their kids, Rankin knew enough to know. No retards. No little gimps. Two healthy little kids, neither of whom needed Adderall prescriptions or even, so far, eyeglasses. And Jeremy was already a little gangsta. Big-boned, thick-forearmed, already menacing, in his little fifth-grade way. Rankin had him enrolled in every stick-and-ball league going and thank god the kid had that. He had trouble sitting still in class and had more than once been sentenced to those extended-day pro-grams where they send the slow kids to read or count. But Rankin didn't worry about that. Jeremy was happy in the way that a boy who every other boy in the class knows is the fastest and strongest will always be happy. That was more important than knowing how to spell.

Amber, he wasn't so sure about. Looks are for girls what sports are for boys, and Amber wasn't blessed in that regard. She wasn't ugly; she was dull-looking, but at an age where the girls were starting to segregate according to looks and status. She dealt with it, Rankin saw, by retreating a little. Sydney said don't worry about it, don't focus on her looks. But that was easy for her to say; Sydney had always had the easy self-confidence that comes with hotness. Amber, Rankin knew, wouldn't have that. He told Sydney that she needed to arrange more playdates for the girl.

Now, as Amber was pushing eggs and lox around in a greasy puddle, she asked if she had to go to school.

"Of course you have to," Rankin said. "What? You don't like school?"

Amber didn't peep.

But then, on the way to school, as Jeremy was pulling at Rankin's arm to make him walk faster, he could see Amber's face—freckled, slightly too-large nose, blue eyes—she would be like an uglier version of Sydney, he thought—clouded by concern. What did she have to worry about? he wondered.

Then she told him, tears welling, snot dripping, drool cascading, her whole face turning shiny like it was covered in Crisco. (Where did kids get all this fluid?) Another girl was picking on her. Cooper, another girl in her class, told her she was ugly and wouldn't let Amber play with Cooper's gang in the yard.

Jeremy was tugging at him. "Let's go."

"Shut the fuck up," he snapped. "Show some respect for your sister."

Jeremy quieted.

Rankin was torn between downplaying Amber's concerns as just another fourth-grade spat and going to her classroom, grabbing this Cooper by her ponytail, and throwing the little bitch out the third-floor window. Cooper was a pretty little brunette, big round eyes, perfect nose that if it wasn't god-given you would have said came from Park Avenue, big lips, a gorgeous smile, slender, the kind of kid you saw in Gap ads or in brochures for new condominiums that wanted to appear family-friendly. Rankin had seen enough of her to know she was a killer—he knew that an eight-year-old who is aware of her looks and social magnetism, and is willing to use them to take down other girls, can be harder to fight than cancer.

———

AFTER DROP-OFF HE milled around by the gate, waiting as the guys ambled up. "What's up, you faggots?" asked the playwright. Cooper, he knew, was the daughter of that long-haired music producer or whatever he did, the one with the hot shiksa wife. Rankin hadn't exchanged much more conversation with him than to suggest a contractor when the guy was thinking about renovating one of his studio spaces.

But there was a code among the fathers, Rankin knew—you didn't mention to another of the dads if his daughter or son was being a little prick. The kids were supposed to work it out for themselves, and Rankin had been a firm believer in this law of the urban jungle when it was Jeremy terrorizing another child. Now, however, he wanted to violate the code. But Rankin was not one to transgress established male boundaries. That seemed so queer, to be the father who whines that your kid is picking on my kid. But Amber was shrinking right before his eyes. The kid didn't want to go to school. And she was a sweet kid—Jeremy, hell, he was a different type. If Rankin found out some kid was picking on Jeremy, he would show Jeremy a move or two, then force him to slug it out on his own. No way was he incubating those pussy habits.

Amber was a little girl and had no clue how to fight back.

At breakfast, he sat with his usual frown, sipping his coffee and listening to conversational crap about property values and new restaurants. They were like women, these guys, in every way but the "Don't call out my kid" rule.

He had done terrible damage to men. It was clear from taking a look at him that he knew a great deal about such hurting. He was in the gym every morning; his shoulders were broad and thick and muscled. He could bench-press four hundred, could do three sets of ten reps at three hundred, yet he couldn't come up with a way to mention to another dad, Hey, your kid is fucking with my kid.

He thought about the dilemma all morning, even as he sat in on a meeting where the president of the Lower Manhattan Jewish Community Center was interviewing a new teacher for the Hebrew school. The old one, a hippie lady, had been deemed too loosey-goosey, the kids barely learning how to say Shana Tova or ask the four questions, much less read the Torah. As far as Rankin could tell, all they did was eat popcorn and play a Hebrew edition of Monopoly. Not that he gave a shit, but if his money was going into that community center, then his kids might as well learn some Hebrew. The new guy, a junior rebbe from some uptown synagogue who was looking to move down here, promised to be more strict and traditional than his predecessor, but was this really the direction they wanted to go in? To end up with a rebbe who was a slightly better-dressed version of the guys Rankin remembered hating when he had gone to Hebrew school back in Flatbush? The neighborhood really was changing, and for the better, he guessed. Jews were moving in by the hundreds, into the new condominiums at 200 Chambers or 156 Murray. These were bankers, doctors, a more conservative breed than those who had first settled down here, and Rankin had to say he wasn't unhappy to watch his neighborhood take on these sorts of bourgeoisie airs. But these families wanted a real Hebrew school, with a tough rebbe mumbling over his texts while their children suffered in modern, brightly painted rooms. Why, in all other areas of their lives, were these families progressive but when it came to their children's Hebrew school, they wanted Stone Age? They had been planning an actual school, a K through 5 for families who wanted local, traditional Jewish education. Some parents urged immediate action. They had the space, or at least enough to start up. Once they had the new rebbe, then they could find the teachers.

Not that he gave a fuck. He couldn't stand that hippie lady and her Israel- and America-bashing. You know what? He hadn't put a quarter-million dollars into the Lower Manhattan Jewish Community Center so that his kids could be told the Zionists are oppressing the fucking Palestinians.

And now, the community center was saying they might have to start with just pre-K and K, delay 1 through 5 for a few terms. Some of the committed money had welshed, bankers pleading bonus-deprivation. The community center would be a few hundred thousand behind where they thought they would be. That's the salaries for a half-dozen teachers. The space had already been leased; Rankin had helped negotiate the terms. Now the community center was wondering if they could sublease.

Rankin shrugged. There was a lot of retail space out there in this market. Tough.

RANKIN DIDN'T SEE the irony of going from the Jewish center to the Pakistani *masjid* but that was his destination now. He had partnered with a Pakistani gentleman to provide bridge financing to a host of beleaguered small businesses. His deal was he would take over and consolidate all the struggling ventures' debt, adding 20 percent on top and then a heavy monthly interest. To repay the debt plus interest, the Pakistani would send a percentage of every credit card transaction directly into Rankin's accounts. It was a simple, risky, highly volatile, and remarkably lucrative business that a few other guys he knew had gotten into. Rankin, though, was the first to partner with a member of the merchants' own ethnic group. It's amazing how hard a small businessman is willing to work, Rankin had observed, Bangladeshi and Pakistani kebab shops open twenty-four hours a day and giving 25 percent of everything they sold over to him.

Not that Rankin was willing to wander up and down Church Street or Broadway, collecting money from loser cell-phone distributors or newsstands. That's why his partnership with the owner of the *masjid* was genius. The *masjid* was somehow holding out in the middle of Jewifying Tribeca. At dusk, a hundred or so brown-skinned, mustachioed gents in kufis or taqiyahs would be shuffling down the concrete stairs to the vast basement prayer hall. Right here, in between mothers walking their daughters to the orthodontist or fathers walking their boys still in cleats back from soccer practice, a lot of them Jews like him no less.

Rankin's man was Gulam, a wiry, bespectacled fellow who

sat behind a desk in a sweet-smelling room off to the side of the entryway, next to the prayer hall. He had the lease on this space, decades long, he told Rankin, as well as the three floors above him, a fact that both amused and annoyed Rankin, the value of this building having long ago reached into the eight figures, an opportunity Rankin would have eagerly exploited if it weren't for this studious-looking Karachi-ite seated behind his old, Art Deco–style steel desk.

But Rankin was a pragmatic man, and while he understood that he would never be able to profitably expunge the Muslim element from this neighborhood, he realized that Gulam was a valuable associate, an entrée into a whole new needy class of entrepreneur. He was well aware of the stereotype of the money-lending Jew, but, he thought, let's face it, which ethnic group now labors under a blacker cloud of bigotry: Jews or these sad, Allah-worshipping kebab makers? At least here in Tribeca, Jews had it easy. The Pakistanis were barely tolerated, moving as they did like invisible men, pushing their wagons down Church filled with cut-rate goods or hunks of ground goat meat shaped like beehives to be delivered to their kin operating out of undesirable ground-floor retail stores shaken down by their own—and now funded by the Jews.

No one had it tougher than these brown-skinned fellows. Rankin had no sympathy for them, but he knew hard work when he saw it. His own son would never put in a day like these humps, and wasn't that the point? Rankin labored and schemed so that his offspring wouldn't have to. They could live the latest version of the American dream, as it was expressed in these fancy New York neighborhoods, some mixture of drinking in bottle-service night-clubs and pursuing a creative career as a video producer or painter or performance artist. He was sure not one of these Pakistani gentlemen had ever for a second considered the possibility of a career in anything that didn't require you to either break your back or get in someone's face and sell the shit out of something. While the

Lower Manhattan Jewish Community Center was wringing its hands about not being Jewish enough, these ochnods were Allah to their skinny frickin' bones.

So his children were soft, what was wrong with that? He somehow found himself mentioning his daughter to Gulam. The middle-aged Pakistani sat behind his Art Deco desk, chewing Nicorette gum and looking at a printed-out list through his reading glasses. He had a light beard and mustache; long, narrow nose; wide, veiny eyes; and a broad, arched forehead beneath a little woven cap he wore that looked like a yarmulke. He was a slender man, surprisingly tall, and reminded Rankin of a less-wrinkled Abraham Lincoln.

"This is a successful program," Gulam was saying, nodding. "Satisfactory participation. A boon for the *masjid*—"

"You have kids, right?" Rankin asked. He had to restrain himself from putting his feet up on Gulam's desk.

Gulam nodded. "Praise be to god. Two girls."

"How old?"

"Twelve and fourteen."

"They happy at school?"

They attended a Muslim girls' school, Gulam told him, a private school, the best in the city. Expensive.

"My daughter is getting picked on," Rankin said. "By another girl. She's eight. She comes home crying. It's making her sick."

"Children are cruel. And females are the most cruel."

"I don't know what to do."

"Talk to the father of the girl," Gulam advised. "Tell him his daughter is behaving negatively."

"We don't do that," Rankin said. "You don't complain to another father about his kid. Not when the kid is eight."

"Then perhaps your wife should talk to the mother," Gulam suggested.

Rankin considered that as he took the printed sheet from

Gulam. He looked it over and then tore it up into tiny pieces, leaving a few scraps in the wastebasket and taking the rest with him. Damn if he was going to leave a paper trail. "Don't ever print this stuff out," he said.

Gulam nodded. *"Inshallah."*

———

A MONG THE PETTY gripes Sydney had regarding her husband's muscular earning power was that despite his vast holdings he still pissed away most of his day meandering to his various ventures to ensure their continued progress. They were rich, and Sydney appreciated that as she folded *kreplach.* But the motherfucker could be home more than once in a while. And now he was telling her to call this shiksa bitch a few blocks away to tell her to control her children.

"You have breakfast with her father all the time," she said. Her voice could be all nose, so that when she said *father* she almost sounded like a Kennedy.

"I can't mention it to the guys," he said, standing in the kitchen. His shaved head shone beneath the skylight.

"What's wrong with you retards? What do you talk about?"

"Not that."

"Fine," Sydney said, sliding the dumplings into the pot of boiling water.

He went downstairs to the middle floor of the apartment. Rankin had three floors of a twenty-five-by-hundred-foot building, a monstrous space filled with more flat-screen televisions than he had bothered to count. Just the other day, using the bathroom near the rear of the bottom floor, the building's third, he had been surprised to find a flat-screen TV mounted in front of the toilet. Amber had her own, of course, across from her bed. Rankin had wondered about the wisdom of giving his children their own televisions, but as long as he was renovating the place, he realized, they might as well get installed now.

Amber was sitting on her bed playing with a heart-shaped cardboard box full of buttons.

"How's your stomach, kiddo?"

"Fine."

"Not bothering you?"

"It only bothers me at school."

"Where does it hurt?"

"I don't know. All over."

Rankin sat down on the bed. "That girl is still bothering you?"

She nodded. Little face, tiny eyes welling up, sniffling starting. "Idon'twannagotoschool."

"Mommy's gonna talk to Cooper's mommy."

"NOOOOOO!" Amber seemed terrified.

His daughter was afraid of being a rat. Even kids hate rats. But what choice did Rankin have? His daughter was having psychosomatic pains and always on the verge of tears. It was up to his wife to confront that WASPy Connecticut bitch and tell her to tell her kid to knock it off.

———

THE ANSWER SYDNEY relayed back was disappointing. Let little girls be little girls was Cooper's mother's response. They need to learn how to socialize. We can't be there every minute for them.

What the fuck? Amber was practically doubled over with pain as she walked to school and this bitch is saying she won't get involved? Sydney had to be restrained from walking up North Moore and attacking the woman. Every parent of a bully says the same thing, said Sydney. When it's their kid who's the monster, suddenly they're laissez-faire to the fucking max.

"I'm going to slap that fucking WASPy cunt around."

Rankin shook his head and smiled. It felt like she was back in the dressing room at the Stopless Topless again arguing with the strippers. "You can't."

"I know that." Sydney laid her head on his hard slab of shoulder. "I know that."

On the way to school Rankin saw the smug bastard and his cute little kids. With his long hair, the expensive-looking coat, the fancy sneakers, the father looked like an overgrown little boy. What happened to grown-ups? Rankin wondered. When did every mom and dad start to look like an oversize version of the shorties they were dropping off in the yard?

He watched how Cooper interacted with Amber in the yard before school. She was too smart to do anything while parents were around, but he noticed his daughter sneaking wary glances at her. Amber stood right next to Rankin, unwilling to let go of him while Cooper stood in the center of a cluster of four girls, with two more girls at the periphery of this inner group. Beyond them a few boys were watching this cluster. Rankin was an astute observer of power and it was clear that Cooper ruled here. She had a pleasing mixture of Asian and Caucasian features, had the unmistakable makings of a future beauty. It would be fun to take a seat and watch her for the next ten years just to see and appreciate each lovely stage of her development. Unless you were Amber.

And here was the dad, Rankin's nominal buddy, sliding over for morning bullshit.

"Wassup, playa?"

"G'morning." Rankin offered nothing more. Rankin towered over the music producer. He wanted to place his hand on the guy's head and push him down, just press him into the earth so that he would be on his stomach, his face ground into the school-yard asphalt.

Amber was by now marching into the building with the other children. The teacher, the parents, everyone unaware of her torment.

HOW DO YOU silence a little girl? It had been years since Rankin
had even thought about having to get rid of someone. His real
estate empire was worth somewhere in the eight figures, his off-
the-books income enough to fund another empire; he was a more
legit businessman than some guy whacking up, reassembling, and
then peddling mortgages in securitized tranches of bullshit. But
he had no idea what to do with this little bitch. Hire a bunch of
nine-year-olds to rough her up? That was one idea, but kids, even
Jeremy, can't keep their mouths shut. Or could they? Say a bigger
kid approached her, in the yard or the park, threatened her, told
her to knock it off, to leave Amber alone, how would that play out?

Or another kid, a big brown-skinned boy, from another neighborhood entirely, a kid nobody knew or knew where to find?

Or . . .

THE CONFLAGRATION VISIBLE from his roof was to the north
this time, a burning building up Broadway, toward SoHo, the small
glow orange in the misty and smoky sky, a reassuring hue like the
inside of a jack-o'-lantern that projected its warmth into Rankin's
heart. He'd had to go outside his usual network of guys for this
job, to hire a few of Gulam's connections through the *masjid*, to set
the fire to the music producer's studio. Rankin watched the flame
with some satisfaction. See what you get when you fuck with my
daughter? I am different than you. Stronger. A man of action.

He snapped out of his reverie and with a sinking feeling came
to the truth: he would never burn down the building. How would
that save his daughter?

No, he realized, now he would have to write a big check to the
Lower Manhattan Jewish Community Center and urge them to
hurry up and start that new school. Because he and Sydney would
soon be taking Amber out of this one.

113 NORTH MOORE

T here was among the little girls a desperate yearning to please her, which felt to Cooper as familiar and nurturing as her mother's embrace. She lived as the object of anxious looks and careful appraisal of her moods and desires; her reaction to every comment or joke or suggestion or observation was carefully studied and analyzed by her peers, lest she should appear displeased by the offering. How she had arrived at this position would have been a subject of some conjecture if the other little girls were capable of such analyses. But as it was, they inhabited a fixed universe, a clock set in motion by a malevolent god who made Cooper in her own image, if god were a beautiful nine-year-old girl who wore Abercrombie every day, had white skin smoother and softer than the flesh on a kitten's paws and hair that was three different browns and two reds, all shining.

Cooper's dominance over the entire fourth grade was the subject of conjecture among teachers and administrators, but virtually impossible to confirm and awkward to bring up in discussion with her parents. It had been noted that girls often came to the office crying after encounters with her, but Cooper's composure was such that these cases ended up as hard-to-parse "she said/she said"s, and Cooper had already deduced that adults much preferred to avoid entanglement in these spats. Cooper herself did not recall when she began to take pleasure in shows of dominance over her classmates; it came about as soon as she became aware that she was indeed dominant. She never wondered where this power came from. One day in second grade, it was simply there. A few of the girls she had played with in first grade, girls less cute than her, slower readers, less gifted on the monkey bars, kept trying to play with her during yard and she would shake her head and inform them without any malice in her voice, "I'm not playing with you." And Cooper would turn to those she had chosen, and they would feel blessed, and those she had rejected would feel cursed. They would try to compel her with platitudes recalled from books and teachers who believed all children should be friends in a vast continuum around the earth—make new friends but keep the old—but Cooper dismissed that idea. She could never put words to it, but she had already formulated her dictum: no ugly friends, no fat friends, no dumb friends. How, exactly, did it benefit the species for prepubescent girls to be making each other cry? Nobody could answer that, but in the years since Cooper's first assertions of dominance, her behavior had transformed the school so much that some children were terrified of attending, others were moved to private schools, and still others attended expensive and ultimately fruitless child psychiatry sessions, which invariably resulted in the prescription of antidepressants. If there had been a meeting of parents, therapists, administrators, and girls with tear-stained faces, then perhaps Cooper's role as catalyzing agent in this cycle of fear and intimidation would have been revealed. But Cooper, observed in the school yard by the untrained eye, was just another very pretty little girl. There were small signs: the body language of defeat after a dismissive wave from Cooper; the glances freighted with hope and desire; the way every little clique in the school yard seemed to radiate in descending order of attractiveness and/

or popularity from Cooper's position just inside and to the right of the gate; her back to the school yard, her hoodie draped on her shoulder beneath that lustrous hair. Her disapproval was as imperious and cutting as a dauphin's waving away of an insufficiently delicious pastry.

———————

COOPER'S PARENTS BARELY registered their daughter's status, only noting to each other with some satisfaction that she seemed popular and to have many friends. There had been the occasional phone call from another mother, reporting their daughter was upset with something Cooper had said or done, but most parents adhered strictly to the "let the kids work it out for themselves" rule, which made sense to Brooke and Mark, particularly since that meant they didn't have to intervene. And when occasionally they mentioned such matters to Cooper, she easily persuaded them that the conflict was more the fault of her peer rather than herself, that the insult and the hurt had been at the very least mutual if not, in fact, directed at Cooper. She had merely retaliated, and was, indeed, a victim herself. No parent was equipped to objectively adjudicate such matters and so the conversations ended with imprecations to behave, be good, be nice, and how could any parent gazing at this adorable nine-year-old not believe her? Cooper had been among the top academic performers throughout her elementary school career, and even occasional absences because of modeling go-sees had not impeded her mastery of times tables, division, or her reading of the required Junie B. Jones books. Though her teachers had noted that Cooper's modeling, her appearance in ads for Benetton, Gap, and even Apple, had caused among the girls a fervent wish to also be models, and some had taken to stating that as their career ambition.

Brooke was aware that promoting her daughter's modeling career could be seen as tacky and not in line with contemporary

parenting ideals—the child should choose her own path—yet it
was clear that Cooper not only enjoyed the photo sessions but
also thrived on the competitive aspects of go-sees and casting. She
took pleasure in meeting with photographers and art directors and
playing the cute little girl. So how could Brooke deny her this?
Though she limited her daughter to just one day of castings a
week—for actual jobs, Cooper was, of course, allowed to take as
many days as the shoot required—Cooper had been late to school
eleven times this semester because of morning castings. A note
had been sent home warning the parents that any more tardies
and they would have to attend a special program for the parents of
chronically late children. But Cooper wouldn't consider skipping
work for school and the money was being deposited in a 529 account, so both parents felt there was ultimately some virtue to all
this commerce.

And didn't all parents harbor the wish that their daughter
would be pretty, popular, and smart? This was a neighborhood of
winners—attractive, bright women, MAs, JDs, PhDs, or IMGs,
WMGs, Fords—who had married successful men so that they
could live in expansive apartments in an exclusive part of town.
So wouldn't the matriarchs be adept at spotting their offspring's
prospects, even as mere nine-year-olds? There was such emphasis
placed on beauty, on fame, on being famously beautiful, that a
little girl who seemed particularly gifted in these areas was a source
of some secret pride to her parents. And so it was for Brooke, who
could see in her daughter's sometimes haughty mien (she had to
admit, Cooper occasionally could be sort of a bitch to other little
girls), the makings of an alpha female, the type who could have
a featured-in-*Vogue* run through New York society—the kind of
run usually reserved for pretty, well-born English girls, the kind
of run that Marni Saltzwell had had—that so many women who
came to Tribeca from the suburbs instead of from the Upper East
Side still secretly believed was the truest form of making it.

————

THERE WAS A pleasing rhythm to Cooper's life. From the walk with her sister and father down Greenwich, past the security guard who always wished them a good day, alongside the restaurants still shuttered, to the market where her father would buy her an avocado sushi roll for lunch, and finally to drop-off, where she would take up her position by the gate and wait with a few select peers for Heather, their teacher, to gather them for class.

Cooper carefully curated her friends. There were the girls she found physically appealing, there were those whose families had elaborate summer houses, and others whose parents occupied glamorous perches. On what, Cooper couldn't even say, but she already knew that connections mattered.

It had been a while since she had organized an ostracism; such bullying no longer held out much fun for her since it was too easily accomplished. But she did recall with some smug satisfaction when she had made Amber cry, when she had made Sophie cry, when she had made Juliette cry, and so on. It had all been so easily achieved, unthinking even, just a snub, a refusal at jump rope, a disinvitation to play tag, and then the careful informing of her more elite friends that the girl in question was no longer welcome. There were always unreliable allies, Cooper had noticed, girls who would continue to play in secret with the ostracized one, but she could usually forge a solid alliance among these girls. Particularly the ones who had more looks than brains. All this calculation, for Cooper, came as naturally, easily, and instinctively as choosing an outfit. It was who she was.

————

THE ARRIVAL OF boys as an object of interest, and the end-less online chat that accompanied this new dimension, was the first change of the established school order that had occurred on Cooper's watch, and before she had time to react, she noticed that her hold on some of her best friends was slipping. The other cute girls were paying more attention to their various crushes, boys who seemed stupid and diffident but were nonetheless the fervent object of their desires, than they were to Cooper's latest drama. She understood, immediately, that this important change in the power dynamic meant that she had been displaced. A girl who was liked by many boys could survive—even thrive—without Cooper's blessing. This turn of events was surprising but Cooper felt it was manageable. She was the prettiest girl—professionally pretty, even—and so why wouldn't the boys see her as the most prized? So, she adjusted. (Years later, when Cooper would learn algebra, she would quickly grasp the concept of variables, of a number changing value depending on the equation around it.)

First, she took note of the boys who seemed to inspire the most erratic behavior among her peers. There were two, Jason and Jake. (Jake was one of a pair of identical twins, yet strangely his brother, Jagger, was largely ignored.) Both Jason and Jake were of average height and size, prone to the same boisterous shouting and frequent shoving as their peers. Yet, by some quirk, they had emerged as the most prized. They were both tasseled-haired, their locks descending in wisps over their blue eyes, slight freckles dotting pink cheeks, gapped teeth, pink lips; both were athletic, both were successful participants in Downtown Little League, both had, at one point or another, been the fastest boy in the fourth grade, that title passed back and forth like a scepter among monarchs in a line afflicted by regicide.

It was easy enough for Cooper to persuade the 2Js, as they were called, that they should focus all their boisterous attention-seeking, their clamoring look-at-me antics of skirting up the wrought-iron gate, sliding down the hallways on lunchroom trays, and walking on their hands up the stairs, toward Cooper. All it took was an indication, by giggling, by pausing to gape, by teasing, that she had noticed and was interested in their antics. It succeeded so completely that when Cooper deigned to speak to them, about pop songs or movies, they could only answer with default "totally" in response to everything Cooper said. She had reestablished her position. And though Brooke was perplexed when Cooper suggested she would like a playdate with Jason, it seemed harmless enough and she arranged one over many awkward laughs with his mother, Ava, a publicist she had dealt with a few times during her magazine career.

But Cooper found the playdate disappointing. What were you supposed to do with a boy? She had no idea. Immediately upon his arrival, deposited in their loft by a Jamaican helper and received by Sadie, her babysitter, it was apparent that the squawking, clucking little rooster of the yard was here much diminished and maddeningly shy. Boys were terrible bores, Cooper realized. They didn't express any interest in drawing or painting or dressing up or looking for music clips on YouTube or going through her modeling book. Jason seemed interested only in playing tennis and baseball on the Wii, and so Cooper went along with that. It was a dull afternoon that she vowed she wouldn't repeat. The boy was sufficiently transfixed by Cooper that he would continue to badger his mother for another playdate but Cooper indicated to her mother, with a quick, even shake of the head, that she was not interested. Her status secured by her having a playdate with the more desirable of the Js, she felt she could afford to now take a break from laborious and torpid boys.

———

MOST OF HER go-sees took her out of Tribeca, to lofts and studios in Chelsea or Dumbo, but there were still a few photographers in Tribeca, those who were successful enough or who had bought in early enough. As Cooper's career progressed, babysitter Sadie was increasingly delegated by a sometimes-stoned Brooke with the task of depositing Cooper at castings and go-sees and hanging around and making sure the little girl wasn't fondled, ignored, or made to feel ugly. The photographers who worked with children tended to be women and, if at first they were excessively sensitive about hurting a child's feelings, over the years expediency necessitated less hand-holding and more curtness. It was impossible to look at a hundred kids in one day without making a few feel bad that they weren't cute enough, and certainly the mothers who so often accompanied these kids would glower at the photographer and art director when they felt their child wasn't receiving the love he or she deserved, but the parents were generally so supplicating at the possibility of the next job they hesitated to voice their displeasure, or, more frequently, they would turn their anger not inward but toward their son or daughter, for not being beautiful enough or being diffident or shy or fat.

This photographer, Barnaby, in his Hudson Street loft, wore the vintage tortoiseshell-rimmed glasses, artisanal T-shirt, and skinny jeans of a fashion photographer. He was more accustomed to dealing with an entirely different type of child, the gamine pubescent girl, fifteen to eighteen, who increasingly was the type the magazines wanted for their editorial. Advertisers, on the other hand, still wanted grown-up girls in their campaigns, and in this particular luxury campaign he needed a glamorous child who could serve as a lovely prop for a statuesque model in an ad for some beautiful alligator-skin luggage laid out on the backseat of a Maybach sedan. Yet while most fashion photographers would quickly flip through the comp, look at the girl, and then snap a few test shots, this photographer had a mellower, calmer, sweeter manner. He asked Cooper about herself, how she got into modeling and whether or not she liked it, and he seemed genuinely surprised that she lived just a few blocks away and even more shocked when she told him where she went to school.

This was one of the most beautiful lofts Cooper had ever seen, and she had seen plenty. Though she didn't know how to express size in terms of square footage, she guessed that this loft was three times the size of her family's loft, and twice the size of her richest

friend Cameron's, so that meant this photographer was money-
bags. There were floor-to-ceiling windows facing east and south,
columns in a row down the middle with leaves carved in at the
top, and even a DJ station in the corner with twin turntables.
There was a pod that looked like a giant mushroom cap, the exte-
rior to the coolest kid's room she had ever seen. When she asked
who lived there, she was told, "Miro. He goes to your school."

Miro? She didn't know him.

"Is he in fourth grade?"

"Fifth."

Ah, an older boy. His appearance in the loft, blond-haired,
sleepy-eyed, in button-up blue shirt, slim-cut selvage denim, and
Converse sneakers, seemed to Cooper a manifestation. Had he
been here all along?

"Miro—Cooper goes to school with you," Miro was told by
the photographer.

Cooper looked at the photographer, with his crazy gyrating
limp, his somewhat effeminate manner; he didn't seem to her like
other dads, but she guessed he was Miro's dad.

Miro nodded, uninterested.

Cooper gazed at him hoping he would recognize her: surely even
the fifth-grade boys must have noticed her. Miro, though, merely
flopped on another of the many sofas in the room and started doing
something on his phone. But when they were finished with her
test shots, Miro asked her if she wanted to draw, and Cooper loved
drawing. She looked at Sadie, who looked at the photographer, who
shrugged and said sure, though he wondered if it might be weird
for Cooper to see the other girls coming in for their go-sees. Sadie
assured him that Cooper wasn't the type to be bothered by that.

Cooper and Miro went to draw inside the mushroom cap. He
had the coolest stuff: a huge round bed, a flat-panel TV, a new
Apple computer, and iPods and iPads casually tossed around like
throw pillows. And for painting and drawing he had easels and

tons of colors, craypons, crayons, paints, and clean brushes in every thickness. He pulled over an orange stool and told Cooper to sit down at one of the easels and asked her what she wanted to draw. She suggested, how about Kidrobots, and Miro shrugged, said "Whatever," and so they drew and painted their own designs for Kidrobots. A barefoot Burmese man brought them cookies and soy milk and while they were working in the warm afternoon sun, Cooper snuck glances at Miro and thought he was the perfect-looking boy, not all trying to be cool or tough but just the way he sat there concentrating on his drawing gave her a pleasant but unfamiliar feeling. And then, when they showed each other their designs, Cooper saw that Miro was definitely the best drawer in the whole school and she thought that was so awesome. He even let her keep some of his designs, which she folded up and put in her leather valise where she kept her modeling book.

She found herself hoping more than usual that she would get this job, and that she would be allowed to return to this apartment. She admitted to herself that it had something to do with Miro.

SHE SAW MIRO at school the next day, and he barely acknowl-edged her. He was in double-file line with his class, waiting at the library entrance, and he just bobbed his head slightly when he saw her and she couldn't figure out why he didn't start fighting with his neighbor or walking on his hands the way fourth-grade boys did when they saw her. For the first time, Cooper felt snubbed, and the unfamiliar ache of it ruined even her usual mean-girl enjoyment. So that day at lunch she would even have let ugly girls play with her if they had asked, because she was so preoccupied trying to figure out why Miro didn't seem as excited about her as she was about him.

She broke school rules four times that day—she used her cell phone at school to call and text her mother to ask if she had gotten that job. Both calls went to voice mail and neither text was returned. They heard nothing that evening, and when Sadie took Cooper and her sister to get dinner at Bubby's, Cooper was so distracted she didn't even think to tell Sadie there was no way she wanted to sit with another girl from her class who happened to be there with her helper, so she ended up having her mac and cheese with Evie, the kind of girl who she would never, ever sit down with under normal circumstances.

———————

DID SHE GET it? Did she? Did she? Brooke was tired of fielding this question from Cooper, who was jumping up and down and pulling at her wrist.

Finally, two days later, she said, Yes, okay, yes, you got it. Next Tuesday, she would skip school to go to the shoot at eight thirty.

"At the loft? At the same place where the go-see was?"

No, of course it wasn't at the loft, it was at a studio in Chelsea.

Her next question didn't even make sense to Brooke. "Will Miro be there?"

"Who is Miro?"

"This BOY she likes," said Penny, her little sister.

"Shut up, Penny!" Cooper went off to her room and sat down, looking at Miro's designs.

The day of the shoot, Cooper sat in an aluminum-framed chair while a makeup artist went over her and then a stylist fitted her so she looked almost as cruel as she did in real life. She found herself impatiently waiting for the photographer and when he limped over to say hello, she blurted out, "Is Miro coming?"

The photographer seemed surprised. "Maybe later. He's at school right now."

Usually, Cooper thrived on being the center of attention. She loved having all eyes focused on her, the only sounds the clicking of the camera motor and quiet comments by the photographer asking his assistant for levels, strobe, and new backs. She loved the way the grown-ups worked so hard while she just stood there following simple directions: pout, more smile, less smile, turn, okay, try that, now really happy, now super-duper happy, more like that but with bigger eyes, really big eyes, biggest happiest eyes in the world, okay, now with mouth open—can we get a reflector in there, I'm getting some glare on the teeth—okay, now that big smile, with super big eyes, and—

But this shoot wasn't as much fun. Even if Miro did show up, she wouldn't be the center of attention, and he would never see how amazing and beautiful she was and anyway this supermodel Sophie was the superstar and Cooper was just this prop.

By the time Brooke showed up to pick up Sadie and Cooper, Cooper was already so disappointed she didn't even answer when Brooke asked how it had gone, and had to have Sadie tell her that the photographer seemed very happy with what he had gotten, and then the photographer limped over and kissed Brooke on both cheeks and said that they had met before and that he occasionally had coffee with her husband in the morning, after drop-off.

———

THAT EVENING, PENNY found Miro's designs when she was looking through Cooper's book. She removed them to trace because she, too, admired them. Cooper, panicked at losing Miro's drawings, stomped through the loft until she found them on Penny's desk and began shouting at her, "These are mine, mine, mine."

Penny began crying. "You don't have to scream at me. They're just some stupid designs."

Cooper grabbed them back. "They aren't just some stupid designs," she said, but she couldn't explain why.

———

AND FINALLY CAME the kind of humiliation that anyone who had observed Cooper—and that would mean every kid in the fourth grade and the entire faculty—found so unlikely that most weren't sure what they were witnessing when it happened. It was one of those moments that would be discussed with the kind of fervor that adults use when they talk about a particularly salacious celebrity scandal. In the middle of yard, with the entire fourth and fifth grades playing during a sunny spring afternoon, Cooper broke away, without a word, from her clique of girls. She walked all the way across the yard, past the boys playing tag and the girls in line for jump rope, past the yard monitor Lamont with a whistle on a cord around his neck, between the islands of backpacks and lunchboxes and jackets discarded in piles around the concrete playground. She weaved through all this to where she saw, backlit by the sun, the thin and slouching and so boyish silhouette of Miro, wearing headphones in flagrant contravention of school rules, leaning against the wrought-iron gate.

And she said, "Hey."

What happened next would become exaggerated through each telling. Miro had turned his back, stuck out his tongue, wagged his hand with thumb on nose, spit, flicked a booger, made moose ears. Actually, Miro had simply nodded without removing his headphones. It wasn't a snubbing so much as simple, pure indifference. Cooper backed away and walked through the yard to where her friends had stood. Already, her status was infinitesimally diminished. For the fourth-grade girls, this was the moment the fever broke, when the pain became bearable, when the soul was on the mend. Once Cooper had been exposed as having an unrequited crush, her powers dwindled. Her bravery at being bold enough to take a public risk was unremarked and unnoticed. Cooper herself hadn't felt brave. She hadn't felt anything at all as she walked toward Miro; it had been a compulsion, one that she had never felt before yet would act upon again.

The children didn't do a dance or sing a song to celebrate the end of tyranny. They continued their hopscotch and jump rope until the bell rang and they filed inside, aware dimly that something was different.

79 WORTH

We were told, several times, that the man who designed the Wally yachts also designed this yacht. As if that mattered to me. I don't know yachts. I don't pretend to. They are boats. And no matter how big they are, after a time, they seem too small. We had been invited by Francisco, a fund manager who managed the pension money of the entire Italian civil service, if I understand correctly. I am not in finance, but I know enough to know that is a very large sum, a sum from which it must be possible to slice enough many-zeroed crumbs and sprinkles to pay for yachts such as this.

Francisco had become friendly with Giancarlo at the restaurant, the two of them bonding while watching the World Cup in the bar. Soon, he was inviting Giancarlo to come to his house for dinner, which actually meant he was inviting Giancarlo to come and cook for him. Francisco represented for me the latest type moving into Tribeca. He was very wealthy; he sent his son to a private school uptown, and he chose to live here because very rich single fathers like him did not live on the Upper East Side anymore. He bought a vast loft in the building of Jay-Z and drove around in a ridiculous-looking yellow Ferrari. He had parties where a few dozen older European men would be joined by a hundred younger European and American women and they would do something like take ayahuasca and smoke a lot of marijuana.

I never understood why my husband would cook for very rich people for free but charge civilians $35 for a chicken breast. I've been watching these kinds of male friendships my whole life. Every one of my father's relationships in Tours had been built around some sort of commercial interest. The men he drank demis with, or hunted boar with, or played golf with, they were all somehow financially connected to him. For these men, their only personal relationship that wasn't based on family or money was with their mistresses.

Giancarlo and Francisco had become friendly enough that when they discussed summer plans, Francisco suggested he collect us in Ibiza and we would sail across to Sardinia. I told Giancarlo that I wasn't sure this was a favor. How were we to get from Sardinia back to Ibiza?

He waved me off.

We would carry our luggage, all that we needed for the twins and us, and then move on from Sardinia. To where? We will be like the Eurotrash version of the family Joad.

Okay, fine, I am flexible, I am easygoing, that is what we are like now, in America. Even with children. With restaurants. With a husband who is gone at dawn to the fish market and *carnicerie* and baker's. And who returns not after the kitchen closes and the slips are counted but after he closes Edward's, where they lock the door and smoke at the bar. Fuck Bloomberg, every European man thinks as he smokes in a bar.

So we give up the house at Can Furnet on the Friday, because that is when Francisco says he will be arriving. When? Which marina? Nothing is clear.

We have our bags packed and in the rented Fiat, the twins sweating in the backseat. It is hot already at ten a.m., and still we haven't heard from Francisco.

"Where is this fucking boat?" I ask Giancarlo.

I'm French, he is Italian, our daughters are American. We speak crap English.

He is smoking and studying his phone. I know there is nothing on his phone but he looks at it so he doesn't have to talk to me.

I know what Giancarlo is planning. He wants Francisco to partner with him on a new place. How many restaurants does he want? He is one cook. How can he be in six kitchens?

Giancarlo always has a reason for his friendships. He is like my father. He won't drink a coffee with you without knowing your bank balance.

We are sitting in the hot Fiat on the macadam outside the house we have been renting for two weeks. It is no longer our house. We have returned the keys to the Filipino caretaker, and now she walks by with her purse to her own car, looking at us curiously, wondering why we are still here. We have nowhere to go.

"How long are we going to sit here?" asks Amelie. Amelie and Anouk are not identical. Amelie has glasses. And it is awful for a mother to say this, but Anouk is much prettier and cleverer. She always has 4s on her report card while Amelie has 2s (and if I am honest, many 1s). And Amelie, her teachers tell me, has difficulty staying seated during class. She is wandering, distracting the other children. Yet they are twins, Anouk born six seconds after her sister and, apparently, the consumer of more of my womb's resources. I feel like I am always protecting Amelie, making sure she gets her share of resources outside the womb.

"It's so hot," Anouk adds.

"Aren't we going on a boat?" Amelie says.

"We can't stay here," I say. "It's too hot."

Then I make the switch to French, my husband's and my fighting language.

"Where the fuck is he? You told me you had a fucking plan."

Giancarlo exhales and starts the car. He slides on his Ray-Bans and as he goes, his famous hair, those golden brown Giancarlo locks that every magazine profile and television hostess mentions, sway in the breeze.

Ibiza is an island, I think. A boat can drop an anchor anywhere. Are we going to drive around the circumference of the island?

He lights a cigarette. He knows I don't like him to smoke around the twins and he only does it when he is angry.

We drive up the hill to the main road into Jesus, and then he swings out quickly to get ahead of a slow-moving truck.

His cell phone rings. He answers. So now he is driving with the cell phone in one hand, a cigarette in his mouth, and one hand on the wheel. This car is not an automatic. We are going down the hill in second gear, holding up the truck behind us.

"Allo? Allo? Hey! Where are you? Ahhhhh."

This yacht, this great Wally-like yacht, has encountered bad weather coming from Sardinia and is delayed.

How delayed?

They don't know. They will call us from Minorca.

―――――

WE ARE HERE to revive our marriage. Spending a few weeks of the summer on the Mediterranean to see if we can still be together. We have been living apart, seeing other people, but we have always shared a carnivorous sexual appetite for each other that never flags, despite the fact that we can't stand each other. It is still easy to see what attracted me to him years ago, when I was working the front of the house and he was the chef at Marais. We were already sleeping together when he convinced me to join him at his new place. We were formidable. I was the hostess, I ran the reservation book, I kept an eye on the bar, I negotiated with the Russian liquor wholesalers. And his cooking was amazing. Not because of his sous vide halibut or caramelized duck or truffled lardon, but because of what he can do in any kitchen, in

your kitchen, with *your* ingredients, in twenty minutes. That's how
he raised the money for the first place. We would be in someone's
house, and we would be drunk or stoned and everyone would
be hungry and Giancarlo would open the Frigidaire, peer into
the cupboards, and in a flurry of chopping, mixing, sizzling, sipping, tasting, pounding, and baking, deliver a two-course meal
that was better than what they were paying $40 an entrée for at
Chanterelle. He was magical then, and never so charming as when
he was working in the kitchen, a flurry of jokes and sad or happy
expressions depending on how his sauces tasted. I fell in love with
him in a kitchen, not at Marais but in the tiny kitchen of a bar on
Broadway after he returned from a bodega and in twenty minutes
had cooked a lamb, mushroom, and white-wine stew, goose-fat
potatoes, and frisée salad.

He had always been full of himself, but before the rest of the
world validated his haughtiness it was bearable, charming even.
The pluck of a confident little boy instead of, as it too quickly
became when he was featured on the *Today* show and in *New York*
magazine—when chefs became like pop stars—instead of the arrogance of an overpraised and vain man.

One restaurant became not two, or three, or four, but six.
There was the place uptown, the sushi place, the German place,
the bakery, the casual place, and now the restaurant in the casino
in Las Vegas and, soon, if Giancarlo finds more partners, restaurants in London, Paris, Hong Kong. I know Giancarlo. He is a
chef. But he also wants a yacht designed by the Wally people.

———

WE HAVE NOWHERE to go, so we drive into Ibiza *ciudad* and
Giancarlo steers through the city to kill time. It is hot and there is
traffic. The streets are narrow and so jammed with cars that we can
barely move. Old Spanish women with baskets full of today's shopping are walking along the sidewalk faster than we are driving.

"Can we park somewhere?"

Giancarlo tells me he is looking for a space.

There is nothing.

Finally, he lets us out in the Vara de Rey and we walk around the corner, rolling our bags over the cobblestones. Giancarlo says he will return the rental car and when the yacht comes, we will take a taxi. The girls want to have a burger from Burger King and normally I would not give them this but I feel that we have not planned our holiday so well and now have nothing to do today and nowhere to go so why not let them have something they like?

The girls order Whopper minis, Pepsi Max, *frites*, and when Giancarlo arrives, sweating from carrying our heaviest bag, which lacks wheels, he sits down at the table with a quiet, long exhalation. The great and glamorous Giancarlo, with hair like a romance novel cover model, is in Burger King. He says he hates to eat in restaurants like this, but I know he will pick at the girls' *frites* and even finish their Whopper minis if they do not.

How much time can we pass in a Burger King? We take our bags to the Hotel Montesol and leave them in a pile next to the short tables while we order coffee. I leave Giancarlo there reading *Le Figaro* and the girls and I go shopping at The End and The Pacha shop but soon it is too hot and every shop is closing for siesta so we must retreat to the Montesol where there is air-conditioning.

We give the girls Euro coins so that they can play pinball in the *glacerie* down the street and as I watch them go, Anouk walking in her even, almost adult-seeming gait while Amelie still walks like a child—she walked on her toes until last year—I worry again about the years to come, about middle school and how they will no longer be classmates next year. Anouk will get into one of the good public schools or I will make Giancarlo pay for a private school. But where can Amelie go? I have visited a few schools for those children who don't thrive in the usual schools, and they seem filled with profoundly troubled little girls, girls with scabs up and down their arms or who rock uncontrollably or have to wear a helmet like an American football player every day.

Next year, Amelie will have to repeat fourth grade. Anouk will move on to fifth.

In the summer, when she is not forced into a classroom and ordered to memorize multiplication tables (which she simply cannot master no matter how many sets of flashcards I make or tutors we hire), she seems more like any other child her age. She learned to swim this summer—Anouk learned three years ago—and Giancarlo even taught them how to use a snorkel and mask. They swam in the rocky little bay below Cap de Falco, though Amelie would sometimes panic and start screaming if her mask fogged up.

Outside of school, Amelie can pass for an average child. I want to keep her out of school forever. I want this summer to last forever; I would have preferred that we kept the house in Can Furnet and allowed the girls to continue pretending, probably for the last time, that they are equals.

They return, begging for change for an ice cream. I give it to them.

It is late afternoon and I am now thinking about where we might sleep if the boat doesn't come.

Giancarlo has been on the phone with New York, with his book agent—he is making a cookbook—and with his business manager. They could use a few more million, dollars or euros.

He looks around the restaurant, down the long oak bar, as if searching for investors. That is why we are going on the boat, of course, why we had to end our daughters' summer vacation, move on to Sardinia, and then fly back to Paris and New York. Giancarlo is insatiable. He wants everything. Such gigantism. His empire has already engulfed Tribeca, and now he wants the world.

"We need to think about where we are sleeping," I say.

Giancarlo nods and walks down the bar to the front desk. I watch him confer in Spanish with the girl there and then come back. There is nothing.

That is to be expected. We are in Ibiza in the middle of high season.

Giancarlo says he will walk down along the marina and then into the old city to see if there are any rooms.

I tell the girls to go play in the plaza behind the Vara de Rey. They say it is too hot. But really they are shy, I know, afraid to play football with the Spanish and Gypsy children.

———

WE HAVE DINNER in the French place next to the walls of the Old Fort, where Giancarlo knows the chef, who finds us a room on the second floor of a house on a noisy cobblestone street that leads up to the old city. There is one full-size mattress on the floor and another single the girls share. It is terribly hot and there are no mosquito nets and until nearly dawn we can hear the homosexuals walking by outside our window, becoming more and more bois-terous until finally they go to the nightclubs and it becomes quiet and there is an instant that feels almost un-hot. Just as I am finally falling asleep, the phone rings.

"Allo? Allo?"

It is Francisco with the boat. They are here. At Portinatx, a harbor in the North. We must go and meet them at once.

"It is early," I say.

"Get up. Get up," Giancarlo says. "We can rest on the boat."

The girls don't stir. The mosquitoes have been more aggressive with Amelie than Anouk and I can see the welts on her cheek and forehead. The girls moan; they want more sleep.

Giancarlo is up and has pulled on his trousers, sandals, and his faded blue shirt. His chest is deeply tanned, his face a shining brown like varnished wood. He is wrinkle-less and florid with health. I know that compared to him I look old, my lined face, my creased forehead, my freckles and spots darker from the sun. I look my age and I know it. Giancarlo is becoming ageless, frozen in time the way that the famous can become. His hair of course is his defining feature, the dirty-blond locks now luminescent and yellowing from the sun. He will have this hair forever; it's what the morning-show female hosts ooh and aah over when he shows them how to make truffled eggs or quail-egg frittata. They want to run their hands through it.

"Can we at least have a coffee?" I ask when we are finally standing in the cobblestoned street beneath the whitewashed buildings with their green shutters. The street is empty. Ibiza sleeps late. A few doors down, a dog pants in the narrow recess of a doorway, the thin strip of shade.

The girls are both squinting, unspeaking. They are exhausted.

"I'm thirsty," Amelie says.

"We'll buy water," Giancarlo says. "And Francisco says to bring fruit."

This is a pedestrians-only street. The closest traffic intersection is two blocks away and I must goad the girls the entire way, struggling with their bags over the cobblestones.

At the crossing, they sit down on their bags while Giancarlo looks for a taxi.

———

WE HAVE BOUGHT melons, peaches, nectarines, figs, and plums, kilos of bruised fruit piled into a leather-handled basket made from palm strips that sits on the stone jetty next to me. It is easy to guess which boat is Francisco's: the long, sleek, modern-looking craft with the silhouette of a shark that is moored farther out than the rest. A tender has put out and is coming toward the shore, two figures jutting from it as it bobs over the swell.

As the gray Zodiac comes up against the jetty, Francisco takes a long step and holds the tender to the jetty by standing with one bare foot on each. Sitting in the tender is a woman, very pretty, with long curly red hair. She wears a blouse through which her nipples are visible, and a bikini bottom.

"Come, come," Francisco says, scooping up my daughters. He places them on a bench in the middle of the tender. Francisco has a delicately chiseled face. His eyes are set under ridges of brow; his hair is brown and fine, held back from his face by sunglasses. A patina of silver-brown beard covers his jaws and chin.

Giancarlo starts swinging our bags in and Francisco piles them in the middle around the girls. Finally, Giancarlo steps onto the tender and I am left standing on the jetty, with the heavy basket of fruit beside me.

"Hand it over," the woman says. She is American.

I do.

Francisco holds out his hand and I take it and leap aboard.

"This is Shannon," says Francisco.

Shannon nods and then goes for the fruit. She takes a plum and bites into it, aggressively. She finishes it quickly, in just three bites, and then has another, spitting the pit into the sea.

After she swallows, she wipes her mouth with the sleeve of her blouse. "Oh my god, it's so good to have fruit. We haven't had fresh fruit since Sardinia."

Francisco pushes off from the jetty and sits beside the engine.

We motor out and disembark. The crew welcomes us aboard; they are Italian but speak to us in French. Francisco's son, Nicolas, is on deck, along with a filmmaker named Zen with a long, slender face; a plump, beautiful Greek woman named Micki who lives in Paris; and an older American man who we are told is a healer.

He sits by himself at the bow of the boat, deep in meditation.

The sailboat is vast and made from black carbon fiber, steel, and maple with teak trim all around. We follow Francisco through a spacious cockpit and down into the generous saloon. Our cabins are just off the saloon, each with a double bed and connected by a bathroom in between. There are two smaller cabins to the front of the saloon and ahead of them is the vast master cabin. The crew's bunks are somewhere below us, I presume.

Francisco urges us to get comfortable, unpack, but the girls cannot wait and change into their swimsuits and are back on deck. We are already putting out, motoring through the channel, rocking a little as we go. Francisco tells us the sail is something called a wing, a huge black cloth fin on a carbon fiber mast. He charters this boat every summer, he says.

The galley kitchen, fitted in below the master suite, is as well-equipped as most lofts: stainless-steel everything and easy access to a large cooler room. Giancarlo is carefully going through the inventory; the woman who usually does the cooking is looking on, displeased at this intrusion but afraid to object. This morning, one of the crewmen caught a fifteen-kilogram tuna that Giancarlo inspects and says he will prepare. He can make a carpaccio from it as well as crusted fresh tuna steaks with some tapenade. He digs through the kitchen and seems unhappy with what he finds and then asks one of the crew if they can lend him a blowtorch.

On deck, we are seated on the soft cushions that cover the wooden banquettes of the cockpit, bottles of cold Prosecco open. The Greek woman Micki rolling joints.

I can see now that Shannon is older than I had at first guessed. She was once very beautiful. She has green eyes that push out from beneath her bushy red lashes and eyebrows, a small, pleasingly turned nose, and fine skin. But there is something hard about her features. A scar runs from her ear along her chin line almost to the tip of her mandible. I later learn this was from a car accident, many years ago.

When I tell her we live in Tribeca, she says her brother lives there. She mentions the name of a photographer I have heard of.

"How did you meet Francisco?" I ask.

Francisco joins us, sliding in behind Shannon and taking the spliff from Micki.

Shannon says they met at a retreat in Topanga Canyon a year ago. Francisco has a house in Venice; he is often in California. She has children, but they are with their fathers.

Micki keeps rolling spliffs. She is like a little machine, so industrious, crunching up the hashish, breaking open cigarettes, making filters, rolling. She doesn't speak very much. If I understand correctly, the filmmaker is making a film financed by Francisco, or has made a film, I am not sure, and he is married to an actress who is not here. The healer makes his way back to the cockpit and sits down, taking a plum in his mouth, chewing quickly, and spitting the pit overboard. ·

He puts his hands together and bows. "Namaste."

He is very thin, with a pronounced indent at his clavicle that you could eat soup out of, his graying chest hair stringy and bone-white against his tanned chest.

"What do you heal?"

He takes a deep breath and opens his arms wide. "The universe."

I don't know what to say to that, or to any of these people. Giancarlo is of course gone, losing himself in the kitchen, leaving the socializing to me. I am not naturally talented at this. I am quiet and sometimes can't find the easy, flattering words that are the fuel for these conversations. My marriage with Giancarlo has meant that I have had to forge through the iciness of thousands of these little conclaves, a task for which I am unsuited.

I am still angry at having lost a day and then a night in the squalor of the mosquito-ridden rented room. No one has apologized for making us wait; no one has even asked what we did with our lost day.

I know that I have to let this go. That and the other troubles of my marriage, even the heartache of ending my relationship with another father at the school, of whom I was terribly fond. Brick was dependable where Giancarlo is capricious. He was loyal where Giancarlo is indifferent. Even the way Brick cared for his children and fought for them was special. I know that Giancarlo loves our daughters, but his first love is himself, his cooking, his food, his restaurants.

Nine-year-old Nicolas and Anouk were already excluding Amelie, Nicolas showing Anouk something at the bow, boasting that he could jump from here into the water, showing where he had cast when he caught a fish. I try to make Amelie feel comfortable on the boat while Nicolas is showing Anouk his little stateroom off the master cabin. Who will have to find a way to ensure that Amelie is included? It will be me, never Giancarlo. He won't even see the problem. I suspect that he loves Anouk more. No, that's not correct, he dotes on her more because she is beautiful and every man will dote more on a beautiful girl than a plain one, even when those girls are his daughters.

But I have to let this go as well. Here we are, motoring alongside the beautiful white and beige cliffs of northern Ibiza, the vertical faces fifty meters high. There is no other boat in the water and no house visible on the shore. The sea is almost green in places and I am startled when I stand up and look over the side. The draught of this hull must be at least ten meters, yet the water is so clear I imagine I can see the bottom. I can see fish swimming in the shallow water, blue darters shaped like teardrops that pop from the water for an instant and become almost yellow in the light.

Giancarlo has slaughtered the melon, sprayed lime over it, blended some of it with sugar, lemon, beet juice, carrot juice, and crushed ice into a gazpacho that he hands out in small shot glasses.

He has removed his shirt and his hairless chest is brown and smooth in the sun. He takes a seat between Micki and the healer and takes the joint when it is passed to him and inhales and exhales as if he is sighing.

Everyone gasps with pleasure as they drink the gazpacho. I stand up and walk to the front of the boat, putting Amelie's glasses on the table and urging her to come with me. She is reluctant and made nervous by having to keep her balance as we pass around the pilot's station on the narrow walkway next to the handrail.

The captain is pulling into a cove with sheer cliff on three sides. There are abandoned fishermen's adobe casitas on a tiny rocky spit, but I can't see how anyone could ever have climbed down to these little boathouses.

Nicolas is already wearing a mask and snorkel; he is looking back at the captain, who is steering us in. The motor has slowed so that we feel each putt-putt. Another crewmember scampers to the front and leans over the bow, watching the sea floor. "*Sí, sí, sí,*" he says.

The captain is nodding and also looking at a sonar gauge in front of him.

Amelie is standing well back from the bow.

"Amelie," I say, "come. Isn't this beautiful?"

She shakes her head. Nicolas looks like he will jump at any minute. Anouk seems suddenly ashamed of her sister as she now adjusts her own mask and snorkel.

"*Arrête,*" the crewman shouts, and the captain shuts down the screw and then reverses for an instant. The anchor drops with a satisfying cranking noise and sinks immediately, holding fast to the bottom.

Instantly, Nicolas and Anouk are over the side of the boat. I am surprised at Anouk's courage; it must be four meters from the bow to the surface.

Soon everyone is in the water, swimming for the shore. Only Amelie is reluctant. I assure her it is fine. The sea looks like velvet from here, warm, gentle, undulating. I see Giancarlo swimming up ahead with Micki. Francisco is making a powerful and overenthusiastic-looking butterfly stroke that propels him at great speed while displacing vast amounts of water. The filmmaker is in the water, with some sort of waterproof camera with which he films Nicolas and Anouk.

I don't see the healer anywhere.

I go down to my cabin to change into my swimsuit and come back up to find Amelie sitting alone in the cockpit.

"Let's go," I say.

She shakes her head. I won't let her give in to this, to feeling sorry for herself.

"We'll swim together."

On the shore, near the cliffs, Francisco and Giancarlo are already out of the water, standing in the sun atop white and tan boulders that look like the broken bits of pills at the bottom of prescription bottles.

I coax Amelie into a mask and snorkel and then into the water, urging her down the wooden ladder from the rear landing step by step.

We start to swim, Amelie putting her face down into the water to look around before she goes.

"Medusa?" she asks when she lifts her head back up.

We are treading water near the platform.

I shake my head. I don't think there are any jellyfish, but how would I know?

She finally begins to swim, slow breaststrokes, blowing out some seawater through the tube. I swim with my head above the water, watching her. She stops and puts her head above the water.

"The fish!" Then she is swimming again.

I am always so pleased when Amelie does things that every child can do, that Nicolas and Anouk do without anyone even thinking about it: they swim, they fight, they see fish. For Amelie each normal thing is cause for celebration. Or, I wonder, am I making too much of this? In the water I realize why I was so apprehensive about coming on the boat: Anouk would have a playmate in Nicolas and would be able to do everything at his level instead of slowing down for Amelie. It is not Anouk's fault, of course; she is just a child, and very patient, usually, with Amelie. But I know that in the years to come she will soon more frequently leave her sister behind; she will have no choice but to join the aggressive mainstream of life.

I swim alongside my daughter. The shore appears more distant than it looked from the boat. We are still many meters away, perhaps half a football pitch, and Amelie is not a strong swimmer. She is too busy looking at fish to realize how much farther she has to swim, but I am now gently urging her to quicken her pace.

After a few more meters, Amelie tires and I tell her to be strong, to keep swimming.

She puts her head down and makes a few more strokes but then she says she is too tired to swim.

I knew this was coming. I swim in front of her and urge her onto my back. She puts her arms over my shoulders and I swim for both of us, no longer keeping my head above water.

Everyone else is already climbing over the fishermen casitas, or up the rocky cliffs, or looking through the tide pools at the crabs and the fish. They don't see us. When I come up for air, I look for Giancarlo. He is seated atop one of the adobe casitas, facing away from us, next to Shannon.

I want to call his name.

"Amelie," I say. "Call for your father. I am tired."

She shouts, Papa, papa! but he doesn't hear.

I am not a young woman, and the final thirty meters give me wrenching cramps in my right arm and my feet. I urge Amelie off of me again, telling her I can't carry her anymore, but she won't let go. Please, I beg her, please let go.

"No, mama!" She sounds frightened, as if she can sense my weakening, my slowing down, imperiling us both.

I have no choice but to keep swimming. The sea that looked so inviting from the boat now seems thick and gooey, as if I am pushing my way through olive oil. Finally, I can feel the bottom, the round, algae-covered stones slippery beneath my feet. I try to stand up but lose my footing; Amelie falls from my shoulders and into the water. She comes up screaming, surprised at suddenly finding herself underwater.

"Come on, Amelie, it's not that bad." I am gasping, finally gaining purchase on the slippery stones and making my way to the shore.

Amelie is still screaming, trying to pick her way along the stones, but furious at me for dropping her.

"You pushed me in!" she shouts.

"Stop it!" I can barely speak.

And now, of course, everyone is looking at us, having heard Amelie's cries.

Giancarlo scrambles down from his perch to help Amelie the last few meters to shore. I sit down on the edge of one of the little channels hewn from the stone where fishermen at one point must have pulled in their boats.

"What did you do?" Giancarlo asks as he comforts Amelie.

I turn to him, furious. "I had to carry her. We were calling for you."

His eyes are red. Behind him I can see Shannon, her hair tied up. She is watching us, smiling.

"Come," Giancarlo says as he takes Amelie in his arms, carries her over the channel, and up the side of the casita to the perch on the yellow stone cliff where they are all sitting.

I want to shout that I am not the villain here. That Giancarlo should have swum out, should have cared enough about his daughter to wonder how we were doing, but I know that I have to let this go.

I am too exhausted to join the rest of them as they explore the side of the cliff.

GIANCARLO SERVES THE dinner and it is a wonder, the fish prepared two ways, the carpaccio and seared steaks, the tapenade, a frisée salad to go with a pan-roasted squid caught by the crew, potatoes seared in some truffle oil he somehow either found or brought on board. I'm sure this meal shines for Francisco and the rest of them even brighter because they have been on board for at least a week, and the charter chef, no matter how good, must have been running out of fresh ingredients. And anyway, how could she compare to the great Giancarlo? My husband, he is at his most charming, regaling everyone with stories: when he cooked privately for Muammar Gaddafi, who would only eat canned food that he saw opened in front of him. The culinary preferences of Silvio Berlusconi, Madonna. Their particular bad behaviors. I have heard these stories before, of course, and so have our daughters, who fall quickly asleep on the cockpit benches.

We are still anchored in the same cove. We rock gently as the color of the cliffs changes from yellow to green, the quartz sparkling in the last of the day as the sun pulls its light west. The cliff is blue and finally black, no sparkle in the moonlight. I try to imagine how we must look if there were someone up on those cliffs watching us, an intimate yellow rectangle of light as we dine, a few portholes in the cabins illuminated, the lights on the bow and the stern and the mast, the glows of embers as spliffs and cigarettes are smoked.

Anouk has found her bed on her own, tired from the swimming and the short sleep the night before; Amelie has her head in my lap, her glasses askew, her mosquito bites already diminished to brown bumps on her tan skin. I gather her in my arms and take her down to her cabin, lay her beside her sister, and remove her glasses. I slide the shorts from Anouk and then do the same with Amelie, and then pull the duvet over them. My girls, my girls, they are beautiful in the soft light, on the blue sheet, their skin dark from the sun, their brown hair streaked blond. I have that feeling that every mother has, the selfish wish to freeze time, to keep them forever small and away from the hurt and hate of real life.

––––––––––

WHEN I CLIMB back up on deck, I can see Giancarlo and Shannon seated next to each other on the stern, their legs dangling over the edge. Micki is, as usual, seated at one of the cockpit tables, rolling joints. The filmmaker has picked up a guitar, strumming something flamenco-ish from the bow, chords drifting back to us over the creaks of the hull, the soft clanging of pulleys against mast.

Francisco is smiling at me from across the table, the glasses of wine and mineral water on the table before him, reflecting the mast light and candles, the flicker of lighter against the end of a joint. He is very handsome, though too roosterish for me, with his big yacht and yellow sports car and overenthusiastic swimming.

"The girls are asleep?"

I nod. "It has been a long day."

He nods, takes a few puffs from the spliff, and then stands up and walks across the cockpit to hand it to me.

"No," I say, pushing it back toward him.

He sits down beside me.

"It's really lovely here," I say, just to make noise.

He nods. He is used to mooring in a Mediterranean cove, surrounded by beautiful cliffs and beautiful people.

He says, "Do you believe in one man and one woman?"

"What?"

"In the idea that you should stay faithful to one person," he says, flicking ash from the joint into an empty coffee cup, "stay faithful your whole life?"

"You mean monogamy?"

"Yes."

I know where this is going, but I don't want to offend Francisco if I can help it.

"I believe in love," I say.

He smiles. "Of course, we all do."

Micki has been sitting in the shadows. She now stands and comes around the table to sit next to me.

"What I mean is, can't we have more than one partner?"

I shrug. "Sure."

"Good, good." He nods, then takes a deep breath. "It seems Shannon is very fond of Giancarlo."

He points to the stern, where they are sitting shoulder to shoulder.

"And I find you very pretty, very attractive. Perhaps we can, all of us, just for tonight, have more than one partner?"

Does he mean have an orgy? I don't say anything. I look at his clear, smooth skin beneath the soft, bronze-and-gray bristles of his beard. He smiles and his teeth are unnaturally white; he has bleached them so harshly that they look like the fat on a raw steak.

The healer reappears in the soft light, crystals and turquoise charms hanging from silver chains and dangling amid his chest hair. He is mumbling, some kind of mantra in Spanish. He walks past us, then past my husband and Shannon, and then slips off his sarong and dives into the water.

"We can play with each other. Giancarlo with Shannon. Me with you and Micki."

I look at Giancarlo's back. Does he know what Francisco is proposing? Is he party to this? Is this his idea?

I don't want to fuck Francisco. I don't want to be anywhere near Micki and her joints. I'm not going to engage in group sex on the deck of a $125,000-a-week chartered yacht with my daughters sleeping downstairs.

I decide I will hide behind the language barriers. "Oh, I think that we should stay on the boat. I don't like to swim at night."

Francisco shakes his head. "No, I meant—"

"I'm going to check on the girls." I am across the cockpit and downstairs before he can say anything.

I take my toothbrush, a button-up white shirt, and underwear into the bathroom, where I brush and then go into the girls' cabin, pushing Amelie aside so I can squeeze in with them.

They are slender enough that we can all fit on this narrow mattress, which is cut to conform to the curve of the hull toward the bow. I listen for Giancarlo to come downstairs, and I listen, and I listen.

———

WE ARE UNDER way again before I am awake. I am vaguely aware of an engine starting up, and then the precise shouts of the crew as a sail is unfurled and we are soon tacking through deeper water, the sound from here as if there is a washing machine nearby. The girls are already up and gone, and for a moment I worry about Amelie and then immediately feel guilty for not worrying as much about Anouk. Gradually, I can make out more sounds from the galley, where Giancarlo must be baking them fresh brioche or something equally complicated for breakfast.

It is awfully hot in the cabin, the air still and smelling of my daughters' breath. I sit up on the side of the bed. I tell myself I don't want to know who fucked whom. I shouldn't care. But I know my husband, and this is a situation perfectly designed to spur his infidelity—fucking a beautiful woman to raise money for his venture. Unless part of the deal was that I also had to sleep with Francisco.

I hear the children run past and up the stairs to the deck, and I walk out to find Giancarlo in the kitchen, a white towel tucked into and folded over the front of his swimming trunks.

He is sipping an espresso.

He gets to work preparing eggs Benedict with spinach and

some smoked salmon he has found in the refrigerator, all of it to be laid over the fresh brioche.

He stops whipping his sauce and says, "I did nothing."

I shrug. "I don't care."

"I just wanted you to know."

"But you knew he would ask," I whisper. "Can I have coffee?"

He pours from the press.

He doesn't say any more. I look at him. Yes. He knew.

———

WE DROP ANCHOR off Calle Jondal, amid two dozen other moored yachts, and for a while the children swim in the sea, Shannon and my husband playing with them. I worry when I see Nicolas and Anouk competing to swim beneath the boat; I have to force myself not to intervene. I watch from the deck as Nicolas and Anouk hold their breath and dive, and Amelie pretends to be busy with her mask, looking at something a few meters from the boat.

I am seated on one of the cockpit banquettes when Francisco comes on deck. I watch him for any sign that he is disappointed or angry but he seems to have completely forgotten the whole episode. He and the healer begin speaking rapidly in Spanish, and I see the healer hand over to Francisco a small leather pouch.

Francisco winks at me, then goes back down below.

Somewhere, the filmmaker is playing his guitar.

Micki rolls spliffs.

Shannon climbs back on board dripping wet in a brown bikini bottom with no top. Her breasts are voluminous and her nipples vast. Her scar makes her look dangerous, somehow diminishing her beauty but adding to her allure. Giancarlo scrambles up the ladder after her. They take turns rinsing off using the handheld shower on the rear landing.

"Don't you miss your children?" I ask after she has climbed onto the deck. I know it is a mean thing to say. I say it because I am jealous of her.

She smiles, considers how to respond to this, but then walks past me down toward the cabins.

Giancarlo follows, hitting the side of his head with the palm of his hand to dislodge water from his ear.

When they come back on deck, dry, changed, fresh, the energy has shifted. They are all smiling, Francisco, Shannon, Micki, my husband, as if they have just shared a great story or joke. I ignore them. My daughters have come back on deck and I towel them off and tell them to put on shirts.

We are taking the tender to Xarco for lunch, for fish and *fidua*. We go in two groups. I ride with my husband, my daughters, Shannon, Nicolas, and Francisco. The others come in the next boat with the crew.

There are so many little tenders and Zodiacs tied up to the tiny wharf that we must step from ours onto the other little boats to reach the wooden planks. The beach is rocky and if I look to the west, it seems quite forbidding, with a brown-and-tan cliff slapped into the sea like a lion's paw and a hard current from the south crashing against the rocks.

"Can we swim?" the girls ask.

I tell them to stay in this area, where there are a few sunbathers on straw mats on a narrow spit of sand. "Don't go to the cliffs."

The rest of us climb the three flights of stone stairs carved into the hillside. A short, fat Spaniard in black trousers and buttoned-up white shirt greets Francisco with a warm handshake and shows us to our tables beneath a wooden lattice overlaid with palm fronds for shade, and solemnly promises that he will take care of everything. I look around. At each table I can see seated in the places of honor the patriarchs, the wealthy men who own the yachts on which the rest of us are merely guests. They are oily, tanned men, most of them fat, frequently bald, with cigarettes or small cigars in their mouths. Some of them sit with vast families, idiot sons and their pretty, vacuous wives and chubby grandchildren who demand ice cream. Or they are with similarly aged men and younger Eastern European women who look bored and cruel. They are eating vast plates of *dorado* and *salmonettas* and squid and sea urchin, mussels and oysters, *jamon iberico* and *fidua* and *paella* and *pimentos de padrone* and olives and garlic and big round loaves of bread. They are a Brueghel painting of rich bankers and their Russian whores, their fattened, dumb children, their old mothers, all of them mouths agape, glasses upturned, bottles emptied, fish deboned, lemons squeezed, pans scraped, stomachs stuffed.

Francisco is showing off for my husband, I realize. Trying to feed my husband as well as my husband has fed him.

There is something smug about the smiles and grins of Giancarlo, Francisco, and the others. The healer is the only one of them who is not giggling, or lying back in his straw chair with his mouth hung open. My husband is wearing sunglasses and I can see that his giggling is nervous laughter.

"What is going on?" I say.

"You didn't tell her?" Francisco says.

"What?"

"Honey, I, we, took a trip."

"Ecstasy?"

"LSD," the healer says quietly.

I look around the table. Shannon in her mirrored sunglasses is smiling. Micki is holding out a spliff. My husband is having a hard time keeping from giggling.

The waiter arrives with water, bread, and aioli. There is quiet for a moment as Francisco orders three bottles of Tavel.

"All of you?" I ask. "Acid?"

They nod.

I don't know what is making me angrier—the fact that they did not ask me, or that if they had I would have refused. My husband knows me too well. Who would look after our daughters?

I turn to Giancarlo. "You are so fucking selfish."

I stand up and walk to the wooden railing at the side of the restaurant. From here I can see the whole beach to the west, up to the lion's paw–shaped promontory. I watch the girls and Nicolas in the shallow water, playing with two very dark-skinned Spanish boys. They are taking turns jumping from a small rock into the shallow sea. Again, I have to remind myself to let Amelie be. When it is her turn to climb onto the little rock and jump, I feel a brief surge of panic and then joy when she makes the leap, splashing into the water like any other child. I want to shout out praise.

Behind me I can hear the setting down of ice buckets, the uncorking, a quick *salud*. A platter of *jamon iberico* is presented. They all become silent as they chew the sweet-and-salty ham.

I walk back to the table. They are all tripping idiots, operating their tongues, their mouths, their facial muscles, with exaggerated care and attention. "Think about this," I say to them, holding up a piece of bread with a fatty and pink slab of the *jamon* on it. "This is flesh. Animal flesh. A great delicacy. This female pig, she was kept in a pit so small she couldn't even turn around, and she was fed nothing but a mush of sweet acorns through a tube they shoved down her throat. She lived her life without moving and even if she wasn't hungry, she was force-fed these acorns. She never knew her mother, she never knew another of her kind, she never tasted any other food but acorns, she was kept from the sunlight, standing always in her own feces and urine. The only time she left her pit was to have her throat slit and to be bled out as she hung from a meat hook."

They all stop eating. Shannon moans.

Micki sets down her piece of ham and wipes her fingers on her napkin before picking up a joint from the ashtray.

Francisco starts laughing, slapping his knees. "Wonderful, wonderful."

My husband rips off another hunk of the *jamon*. "I know, I know, it is delicious."

I look at them chewing their *jamon* with gusto. I have lost my appetite.

The restroom is upstairs, behind the kitchen, next to a narrow road that descends in a zigzag. There is all around us the smell of fish stock and heated olive oil, of *paella* and *fidua* boiling on pans. That Spanish restaurant smell that I can't stand but that is inescapable in the Mediterranean in the summer. It reminds me of stomachaches and being thirsty and mosquitoes and oppressive heat. I don't know how they can all stand it; how it doesn't bother them to be spending thousands of euros for a lunch amid this rank stench. I sit down on the toilet, pee, wipe, and then I sit there in the stall for a long time. I don't know what to do. There are so many layers to my anger at Giancarlo. Of course there is the anger that he probably fucked Shannon last night. Then there is the anger that he took LSD this morning. Then there is my anger that he has put me in a position where to even express my anger about either of these issues makes me look a horrible shrew.

When I come back down the stairs to the table, where mussels, clams, and oysters have arrived, and more rosé, I see that Anouk and Nicolas have returned and are devouring the *jamon* with gusto. The swimming and diving must have stirred their appetites.

"Where is Amelie?" I say.

Nobody answers. Giancarlo looks around. "She is not here?"

I go to the railing overlooking the sea. I can't see her. I turn to Anouk.

"Your sister?"

She has her mouth full of pink flesh. She shakes her head.

I take the stairs two at a time and rush along the sand to where they were playing, the small rock in the shallow water now abandoned. I look for the boys they were playing with and can't find them.

I look out to sea, at the yachts, the tenders bobbing next to the dock. Could she have swum out to the yacht? That doesn't make sense. She knew we were in the restaurant.

I am cursing her, cursing my husband, cursing all of them as I slip off my sandals.

I turn to the headland, the lion's paw–shaped cliff. Running along the sand, I skip between the sunbathers on their mats, occasionally kicking sand onto them and listening to their curses in a wide variety of languages.

Nothing could have happened to Amelie, I tell myself. How long was I gone? Ten minutes? Fifteen? That is nothing. She couldn't have gone far. My anger shoots in different directions, toward my husband, toward Anouk, toward Nicolas, toward Francisco, and, finally, toward Amelie. Why does she always demand so much attention?

Oh my god, what if something has happened to her? She doesn't have her glasses. They are in my shirt pocket.

I am, of course, most angry with myself.

I come to the cliff where there is a trail next to a cork-shaped yellow quartz boulder. I climb the path, my bare feet becoming sore at the tendon where stones push into me, but I keep running until I am at a sort of hump over the promontory, the top of the lion's paw. Where is she?

For a moment, all my feelings converge, and I imagine she is gone, lost, carried out to sea, smashed against a boulder, drowned, and I feel some sick delight at being able to blame Giancarlo, at saying, "See, you take LSD and are a shitty father and husband and so now our daughter is dead!" I scramble down the steep hill. Did Amelie fall here? Is she sure-footed enough to have negotiated this path?

At the bottom are soft, mushy stands of dried kelp, as large as automobiles and slightly rotten-smelling, but comfortable to stand on barefooted. The sea shoots in around them and sends up small geysers of water. I leap from stand to stand, pieces of kelp sticking to my feet, and finally, near a massive block of rock, over the hiss and crash of ocean, I can hear the shouts of children.

I climb over the rock, using the many handholds of smaller stones embedded into the cliff-face, and then I see them. Amelie in the water, the boys on a flat stone spit that descends into the water.

The boys are laughing. Amelie is trying to climb out of the water, up onto the same flat stone where the boys are standing. They push her back.

"Swim around," they are taunting and laughing.

Her face is wet. She is crying.

I shout, "Amelie!"

She can't hear me. The boys, however, turn.

"What are you doing?" I shout in English.

They don't understand but they both become suddenly quiet.

My daughter stumbles ashore. She collapses on the flat stone for a moment to catch her breath, then looks up. "Mama!"

I scurry down to her. The boys stand by, shamed.

"Cerdos," I call them in Spanish. Pigs.

I help Amelie over the square boulder, up the trail, and then down. I can see Giancarlo coming down the beach. He is waiting at the bottom when we descend the trail but I ignore him, walking with Amelie not back to the restaurant but over the little jetty to the tender, which I untie and manage to start up myself by roughly pulling the starter. The boat is easy to navigate, just a handle jutting from the engine with a throttle on it, which I can turn to direct the screw. We are back on the yacht in just a few minutes, and while Amelie waits on the rear landing, I go to our cabin and collect our bags, mine and Amelie's and Anouk's, in a rush, and carry them on deck, where a crew member helps me to bring them down to the tender to stow. The crewman also insists on helming the tender back to shore.

"What are we doing, Mommy?" Amelie says.

I hug her. "We are going."

I expect her to fight, to beg to stay, but she is silent.

"Here." I hand her her glasses, which she slides on, and then looks over the side at the fish.

————

WHILE WE ARE waiting for the taxi, Giancarlo says good-bye to the girls. To be on LSD and to be losing your family can't be a good trip, I am sure, but Giancarlo is not like other men, and I can imagine him walking away from us and going back to the table and laughing with the rest of them as they suck the flesh off the fish bones and order more wine and smoke more spliffs until finally Francisco invests with Giancarlo. I already know that they will open restaurants in London and Paris and perhaps even here, in Ibiza.

When the taxi finally arrives and the driver has arranged our luggage in the boot, I climb into the backseat while Amelie and Anouk hug their father. He is still wearing his sunglasses. Behind him I can see Shannon walking up the hill to us, Nicolas running ahead of her.

Giancarlo turns to Shannon and smiles and raises his eyebrows in a gesture as if to say, "See what I am dealing with?"

But Shannon walks past Giancarlo and holds Nicholas by the shoulder while he says good-bye to Anouk. When he is finished, Shannon bends and kisses her on both cheeks. Then she does the same to Amelie, giving her a long hug. "I know," she says, "I know how hard it is when you are so different from your sister."

The girls climb in. I help them with their seat belts.

Go, I tell the driver, go.

87 LAIGHT

S o erratic was Levi-Levy's parenting, fidelity, and wakefulness that his abandoning his loft following an argument with his pretty (if always exhausted-looking) wife, Charmaine, elicited neither comment nor even notice in the neighborhood. When he had been living with spouse and five children—all boys, each spawned in two-year intervals, coinciding, Levi-Levy had once noticed, with the new staggered interregnum between Winter and Summer Olympics—his comings and goings from his North Tribeca loft had no correlation to school starting times, office hours, market openings, or retail schedules. His peregrinations stemmed from one obvious source: his pathological sleeplessness that rather than medicating with any of the newly derived sleep aids, he would occasionally drink and eat into submission with martinis and steaks so that he might pass out, say, from three p.m. till six p.m. and then stay awake for the next seventy-two hours.

His stumble down Laight Street at five a.m. on a Monday morning, wearing a New York Mets cap, women's orange-frame sunglasses, and oversize black-leather police jacket, was exactly as statistically probable as his stumble down West Broadway at five p.m. on a Sunday night. In other words, Levi-Levy was perfectly unpredictable. So when Charmaine threw him out after opening one of his credit card statements and learning that in one month he had spent $10,523.67 on steak, liquor, Holocaust literature, and comic books (oh, and he had bought a cello!)—during which he had furiously denounced her "Cheney-like, Ashcroft-like, Yoo-like, Gonzalez-like" invasion of his privacy ("What's next, you prying NSA bitch, wire-tapping?")—not even the children had noticed that their father was no longer living under the same roof.

Charmaine had been angry with him for so long that she had gone beyond forgiving him, passing straight through to resignation: Levi-Levy was an unrepentant recidivist. The catalyzing incident had been the sight of their ten-year-old, Ely, behind the wheel of the family Town & Country, as the boy, his face frozen in attentiveness, his eyes parallel to the top of the steering wheel, drove their minivan up Vestry. Alone. Charmaine was standing in front of their building with their youngest in a Snap-n-Go seat. And Levi-Levy, who had said he was going to get the car, was nowhere in sight. He had apparently given the keys to Ely and told him to go pick up Mommy. Charmaine recalled the lessons Levi-Levy had given Ely in the driveway up at the country house, as Ely, his lips pursed in concentration, signaled left and came to a stop within two feet of the curb.

And where was Levi-Levy? Charmaine asked after she had angrily yanked her son from the car.

"What?" Ely said. "What did I do?"

His father, he explained, had recalled an urgent errand, handed Ely the keys, and hailed a taxi going uptown.

At that moment she realized that Levi-Levy's impulsiveness might kill them all.

———

SURPRISINGLY, TAKING UP residence in his office—a studio apartment in the East Village where he kept his comic books and various antique martini mixing sets, and where, at some point in the Nineties, he had shifted his entire VHS porn collection— meant he was more assiduous about being on hand in the morning to walk his children to their various day-care centers, preschools, kindergartens, and elementary schools, and in the afternoon to various sports leagues and lessons. He also now made it a point to catch *SportsCenter* on ESPN during his sleepless nights, so that he could discuss with his sons the various baseball results and could dissuade his middle boys, Elan and Ezra, from lying to him about the exploits of ballplayers. (He had once gone half a day believing that Bobby Parnell had pitched a perfect game.)

It was infuriating to Charmaine that all the boys remained besotted with their spendthrift and capricious father, and each and every one of his ridiculous habits—from his prodigious red-meat consumption to his profligate comic-book buying to his seemingly ceaseless assembling of plastic model battleships. Their loyalty sprang in part from their childish wonder that Levi-Levy could actually, physically, simultaneously lift all five of them. He was forklift-strong, almost hunchbacked, but like an insect able to lift more than his own body weight. As if all those steaks were actually being turned into muscle.

The boys would giggle and holler as they rode him, balanced on his arms and astride his neck, precariously perched on his shoulders or standing with their toes curled around the top of his belt. They were like some six-headed monster as they made their way down Greenwich in this manner. "Here come the Levi-Levys!" the older boy, Ely, would shout—an entire basketball team, with coach!

———

LEVI-LEVY'S INDIFFERENCE TO other people's schedules, to his wife's financial worries, to his own deadlines, stemmed partially from his insomnia, but more fully from his believing what had years ago been occasionally said and written about him: that Levi-Levy was a genius.

He had been a precocious success, writer of a funny and poignant one-man show performed by an actor who would go on to great acclaim. Levi-Levy hadn't intended for the show to be a comedy, yet that was how it played, in part because the actor's performance perfectly mimicked Levi-Levy's manic behavior. A smash Broadway run was followed by award nominations and offers to work on new plays, television scripts, book contracts—all of which Levi-Levy accepted and then promptly failed to deliver.

Levi-Levy had never really been the toast of the town, but enough glasses had been raised in his name that he could still convince himself and a few others that whatever had made that now-long-ago hit show a success would happen again. In person, if you weren't married to him and he showed up close to the agreed-upon time, and you fed him steak, he could be funny and personable. His erratic nature and frequent sexual innuendo and surprising shtick of self-aggrandizement still could net small writing gigs from those seeking to produce or direct something funny.

But, again, as Charmaine would occasionally remind him to his reliable ire, that show had been a long, long time ago. Several administrations ago. Several economic expansions and contractions ago. Before cell phones or hybrid cars. Before, in fact, the Internet. Before the kids, before they had even moved down to Tribeca, where Charmaine had shrewdly borrowed a half-million for three thousand square feet on Laight. She had called the mortgage brokers, secured the loan using her good credit—at some point, she had warned her husband, his age and his credit score would intersect—and signed over a check to herself from Levi-Levy's agent to make the down payment. Levi-Levy, naturally, had fought her every step of the way. Now, it was this loft, second- and third-mortgaged, that was keeping the kids dressed and Levi-Levy knee-deep in T-bones and Beefeater.

WITH LEVI-LEVY NO longer expected to show up at home with any regularity, Charmaine was sleeping soundly; she could, for the first time in years, count on Levi-Levy to actually deliver at least 40 percent of the children to their schools, and she could make it to the agency before ten a.m. She did occasionally miss his big, boozy, hairy body, but the truth was she had been missing that for years anyway, since early in their courtship, when she discovered that Levi-Levy would actually get dressed after they had made love and go out to the kitchen, order Chinese food or a pizza, and then fall asleep on the sofa in his clothes.

But she had found him powerfully attractive. Blue-eyed, fair, curly hair, muscular, broad-shouldered, thickly chested in the manner she had associated with those Israeli commandos who had raided Entebbe. (In fact, she realized watching an old rerun one night, he *had* resembled Stephen Macht, the actor who played Lieutenant Colonel "Yonni" Netanyahu in the made-for-TV *Raid on Entebbe.*)

She had compromised for years. Their marriage was based on some theoretical value of Levi-Levy's genius and striking looks leveraged against her stalwart ability to earn a living as a literary agent. There were periods—brief, fleeting, noisy, early in their marriage—when Levi-Levy had been flush: first payments for screenplays, first halves of book advances, the gate from a touring version of his show with a lesser actor. Levi-Levy would run through it with shocking profligacy. It had been funny the first ten times he did it, but a few years into their marriage, when Charmaine accepted that she was virtually on her own—Levi-Levy had even failed to accumulate enough points to continue his Writers Guild health insurance—she found it less charming and more selfish.

"What would you rather have?" Levi-Levy would ask when she confronted him about his spending. "A boring schmuck with a pension and a 401(k)? Or a sexy genius with a big cock?"

And he said this over dinner, in front of the boys.

Now, with his credit cards cut off from hers, his checking account no longer linked to hers, even his cell phone number sliced off from her account, she could at least be assured that he was no longer doing *more* damage; she had contained it, cauterized it. And she did take some smug pleasure in imagining Levi-Levy, in his stupid women's sunglasses and Mets cap, finishing his martinis and steaks and bottle of '95 Leoville and then finding that his credit card had been denied.

Which was happening with more frequency, Levi-Levy noticed. So thank god that Tribeca during the boom had been as fertile for steak houses as for luxury condominiums. When they had moved in, there was only City Hall. Now, there was a Palm; there was Wolfgang's, Dylan Prime, and Landmark. The staff at each of them knew Levi-Levy well (he and the five boys were actually caricatured on the Palm wall near the bar). So whenever his card was declined, he could rub it, spit on it, do a little incantation and faux-rabbinical mumble-prayer before finally telling the maître d' he would be back shortly with some cash.

He had aged well, Charmaine admitted; yet she hated to concede she was so superficial that that was partly why she had put up with his shit for so long. And he would periodically turn on the same charm he had displayed when they met: the unintended self-deprecation, the self-aware (or was it?) grandiosity, the liberating disregard for social convention that could make her feel like she was in college again. But after pushing out five kids, Charmaine was savoring the prospect of being single, and when one of her clients asked her out for a drink—no, no, not a writer, she wouldn't do that again—a chef, Giancarlo, whose cookbook and memoir she had sold for good sums, she shrugged and said fine. She had always been skinny, and after each birth she was a regular and frequent sight up and down Greenwich trotting in black tights and Prada parka behind a jogger stroller. She had just now worked back to her old 125 pounds, two years after Etan was born. And she didn't mind saying it, she felt hot again.

————

IF YOU WERE raised in a certain privileged part of New York City, and stayed, you assume that somehow, by the time your children are school-age, or at least middle-school-age, you will have accumulated wealth sufficient to send them to a good private school. After all, your parents did it, somehow, so why not you? But those children grow up fast, so you settle. You decide, well, public primary is fine, the schools have improved, the test scores are rising, and you've moved into a great neighborhood with a famously sought-after K through 5. Surely, by the time middle school rolls around the funds will be there to send the kids to Brearley or Dalton or Collegiate. Middle school looms quickly, however, and still, after those years of stretching for the loft, for the summer place, for the car (and insurance) to take you from loft to summer place, it turns out that $40,000 a year per kid (after taxes) hasn't really materialized. (And, come to think of it, how the fuck did your parents manage it? Maybe, just maybe, it's because your dad was an accountant instead of a fucking playwright?) And now, suddenly, you are too entrenched. The city, Tribeca even, has become so much a part of your identity that you can't move out to the suburbs, you can't uproot the kids, the wife's business, your network of friends, and so you stay and confront what you swore would never happen to your kids: public middle school.

The schism of parental haves and have-nots, of kids with rich grandparents and kids without, becomes clear when parents begin touring the various public middle school options. For one thing, some parents barely pay attention to the test scores other parents fret over, because the test they are interested in—the HSPT—is completely different. A few of the more privileged might go through the motions of touring Nest or Lab or ISE or the other good public middle schools, but many won't even bother, smug as they are that little Gabe or Nat or Julie or Sammy will be going elsewhere. Other parents, almost frantically, show up at every middle school night, exchange dozens of e-mails with middle school coordinators, and convene in worried klatches with other parents, fretting about the 3.97 scored on State Assessment English when a 4.0 was required.

With five boys, Charmaine knew she didn't have a choice. Levi-Levy, having lost track of the years, still assumed middle school was seasons away when, for the oldest boy, Ely, it was next year. When Charmaine handed to Levi-Levy (who had shown up in the loft to collect a milk crate full of books about the Holocaust, which he intended to reread) a letter from the school informing them that Ely had been tardy twenty-six times, he shrugged and said, "That's my boy!"

Yes, you arrogant fuck, that is your boy, she had told him, and he will not be getting into Lab or Salk or any of the other prized public middle schools with twenty-six lates.

"That counts," she told him. "They won't take him."

There was, however, a solution. She handed to Levi-Levy a flyer that had accompanied this Dear Parent letter, saying that perfect parental attendance—four Tuesdays in a row from eight forty a.m. to ten a.m.—at the Independence School's Punctuality Improvement Program ("A District 4 Best Practices Honorable Mentionee and *Downtown Tribune* Way to Go Award Winner") would scrub the offending tardies from the child's academic record.

Levi-Levy was outraged. "This is classic—blame the parents."

"And they are fucking right in this case."

The rest of the fathers were surprised when Levi-Levy, with little Ezra on his shoulders and a Holocaust historical atlas under his arm, waved off coffee with the guys and explained he had to attend the Punctuality Improvement Program. The sound editor looked at him, shook his head, and asked Ezra, "What have you done with Levi-Levy?"

CORRINE, THE WOMAN who had conceived the Punctuality Improvement Program, had once suffered from chronic tardiness, before finally hitting bottom and deciding she had to change her life. She told this to the eight mothers and one father uncomfortably seated around the short-legged library tables in the middle of the second-floor school library. It surprised Levi-Levy that some of the mothers here, each of them bearing their Dear Parent letter, were attempting to convince Corrine that their sons or daughters hadn't actually been late the reported number of times, or that they were late but it was the fault of the bus system, the subway system, the weather, the kitchen, the father, the sibling. But Corrine, with hair dyed a reddish-brown and deep worry lines across her face, simply urged these mothers to admit they were powerless over their tardiness.

Each attendee this morning was encouraged to identify the specific causes of their lateness—they could just look at their excuses for a convenient list—and then figure out a solution to each of those problems. If the subway was the reason they were late, then they had to allow an extra half-hour for the ride. If getting the kids dressed was the issue, then perhaps they needed to prepare outfits the night before. But those strategies would come later. This week, Corrine explained as she passed out a worksheet, they were to go through their morning routine and note how much time was allotted for each activity—getting dressed, eating breakfast, brushing teeth, etc.—and then figure out how much time each actually took. (Unnoticed by Corrine was the irony that Levi-Levy's presence here with his second-youngest son meant that Ezra would be an hour late for his drop-off at the Washington Market toddler program.)

Levi-Levy was pleased to see the late mothers were an attractive bunch. He recognized a few of them from the yard during drop-off: the mulatto with the French accent, the tall Canadian, and even the sound engineer's broad-shouldered wife. What's her name? Brooke? Good-looking shiksa brunette, seated next to him, studiously bent over her worksheet, filling it out.

Levi-Levy looked at his worksheet. He had no idea how long it took for his son to brush his teeth, get dressed, eat his waffles. Though he suddenly had an inspiration.

"What if my son sleeps in his clothes and skips brushing his teeth?" Levi-Levy asked Corrine. "That's what I do."

Frisky Brooke surprised Levi-Levy by laughing and gently slapping him on the thigh, as if she were in on the joke too.

But he hadn't been joking.

"I was thinking of limiting my daughter to just one cigarette in the morning, you know, with her coffee," Brooke added.

Everyone laughed at Levi-Levy's next suggestion: that his son could simply drive himself to school.

Brooke handed Levi-Levy a note saying, "I'm so stoned I don't think I can handle this." She stood up and walked out, her black denim–clad ass making a circular motion as she went. Levi-Levy had been made excited by the presumed intimacy of Brooke's note. He quickly gathered up Ezra, who had been flipping uncomprehendingly through Levi-Levy's historical atlas of the Holocaust, dribbling spittle onto Treblinka and Majdanek, and followed her.

"Remember, next week, bring your strategies!" he heard Corrine shouting after him.

———

RUNNING WITH EZRA in one hand and the Holocaust book in the other, he caught up with Brooke downstairs.

"Let's get some steak," he said.

And she was just stoned enough at 9:45 a.m. on a Tuesday to say yes. It is difficult to find quality steak in the morning, even in the new Tribeca, so after dropping off Ezra, Levi-Levy agreed to come back downtown to City Hall to meet her, though it was risky having breakfast with another mom at such a local spot.

Levi-Levy's infidelities had to this point been contained to formerly young actresses lured by Levi-Levy's promises of impending staged readings of his impending work at the theater company with which he remained loosely affiliated. Or he occasionally would bang a student taking classes at the company, though the manager had several times warned Levi-Levy about this—or, rather, reminded him that only teachers doing actual company work with students were supposed to be screwing them.

Yet he found initiating an affair with a fellow parent, a mother of his son's classmates, someone, in other words, who by her routines and circle of friends, by her own marriage to one of the guys Levi-Levy had coffee with occasional mornings, someone who knew him and his kind, and could understand his references and his jokes and nod knowingly when he mentioned Ornette solos or John Williams novels, even if she didn't really know what the fuck he was talking about, he found this presumed mutual understanding to be exciting and conducive to higher-quality screwing. She seemed to find his eccentricities and unconventionality charming. Levi-Levy knew Brooke's husband, the sound engineer, was a pretentious, boring type. A geek, really. A techie posing as an artist, not a real creative, certainly not a genius like Levi-Levy. In fact, as he now concluded, those coffee guys were generally a cut below: the ambitionless sculptor, the crappy memoirist, the producer, the gangster, all of them second-rate, sub-geniuses, certainly. It must have thrilled Brooke, Levi-Levy thought, to be lying with such a talent as him, after that sterile, overscrubbed little half-Asian she was used to.

Their late-morning meetings in his studio—a toxic-smelling cavern with opened tubes of dried-out epoxy lying around atop stacks of superhero comic books and the grainy black-and-whites of emaciated concentration camp victims in his Holocaust books—would become almost a narcotic for Levi-Levy. Brooke, in her yoga togs to maintain her cover, would beg him to open a window to clear out the fumes so she could smoke one of her half-marijuana, half-tobacco cigarettes. Afterward, he would fall, deliciously, into long, uninterrupted, rejuvenating sleep.

After rousing he would hail a taxi to one of his sons' schools, where he would collect Ezra or Elan or Ely or Elmer (the youngest, Etan, wasn't yet putting in a full day at preschool) and walk them home, resuming his usual jocularity with his sons for an hour or two at the loft until Charmaine came home; she then sent away the nanny, and the evening ritual of feeding and bathing would begin.

Separation is supposed to be hell on the kids, Charmaine knew, yet her boys were thriving, though the oldest was beginning to suspect that even by Levi-Levy's quirky standards he was home less frequently than before. But the younger boys, who were in bed by eight p.m., never noticed their father slipping out and away.

Imagine the injustice Charmaine felt, then, when she went out for a drink with the chef, returned home after the kids were in bed, and then the next morning received angry silence from her betrayed boys. Even Levi-Levy, it turned out, had made an appearance that night, barging in with Chinese food, steak sandwiches, and Justice League DVDs for the boys, who, after a certain hour, kept asking where Mommy was.

"Where were you?" Ely demanded of Charmaine as he sat sullenly stirring his bowl of cornflakes.

"Out with a client," she answered.

Something, Ely knew, wasn't right about his family, but what exactly was amiss? He had no ready answer, or even the tools to formulate a coherent question.

"We're going to tour ISE today," Charmaine reminded him. "So you don't need to bring a lunch."

"Where's Daddy?" Etan said.

The elevator doors slid open and Levi-Levy strode back into the loft, ready to deliver children.

Charmaine was forced to admit that their marital dissolution had made Levi-Levy into a model father. Present (almost ubiquitous), dependable, and patient. After his initial, strenuous protests, he had completed the PIP without further complaint. And, even more perplexing, for the first time since early in their relationship, he seemed centered, calm, and (she couldn't believe she was thinking this) relaxed. He cheerily passed along to her the strategies he had picked up at the PIP—get the boys only one color and type of sock so you don't waste time looking for a match, pack their lunches the night before, and Levi-Levy's reluctant concession: no more steak for breakfast.

It was when she was on her way to work that morning that she concluded his about-face, his improved demeanor, meant that Levi-Levy was probably having an affair.

Instead of anger or betrayal or frustration or jealousy she felt that perhaps it was for the best. She had noticed among her circle, among the fellow parents, an enhanced friskiness in the air: an upsurge in mufky-fufky that was leading to some divorces, separations, and broken homes. She wondered, how many other affairs simply were being quietly buried? Why shouldn't these husbands and wives have a fling now, during this last stage where they might reasonably pass as sexually attractive, or at least before the sight of their own naked bodies repulsed even themselves. They were going soft, losing hair on their heads, and sprouting new hair everywhere else. They worried that a missed period meant the beginning of menopause rather than an unwanted pregnancy. They lived in fear of the moment arriving when they could see, however distant, but certainly there, the end. Before we are all horribly gone to seed, why shouldn't we fuck our brains out one last time, Charmaine concluded.

That was also the self-justification of the cuckolding wife, of course, as she was sure she would be in a matter of days. She was initially surprised by the chef's interest in her. She was flattered, of course, for he was flagrantly handsome with his ridiculously expensive coiffed hair and Italianate features and his chest-thrust-forward strut. They had met to discuss an easy-to-package memoir project: a food magazine editor would ghost the proposal and the chef would meet with editors to pitch the book, his telegenic looks and almost comical accent ensuring he would be an easy talk-show booking. Before too long the offers rolled in at the high end of the six-figure range she had predicted, the mood of their meetings and conversations increasingly celebratory, the flirtation that she had at first correctly taken to be his default demeanor gradually increasing to an unmistakable intensity. And it even turned out that their children attended the same school.

———

FOR LEVI-LEVY, BROOKE's abrupt cessation of fornication—it happened mid-thrust, the stoned Brooke pushed him out, stood up, and got dressed, as if waking from a not entirely pleasant dream—meant a return to his sleeplessness. A few days later, chewing a New York strip at a Village steak house, he considered the facts: Brooke hadn't been to see him in a few days. His texts were unanswered. So this is what middle-aged dumping feels like, he thought, pouring more wine and flipping through a catalog of an upcoming comic-book auction. It felt similar to getting dumped as an adolescent, only without the public scorn. It had been so long since he had felt reflective about anything that as he considered his life without the prospect of morning sex with Brooke he felt an unfamiliar pang of nostalgia. He started thinking about the recent past: the good, fun sex; and then further back, to his life with Charmaine, his children, the chaotic years of so many kids and so many uncompleted projects. He hated to consider it but now felt compelled: what had he been doing all these years? Numerous failed plays that never made it out of readings. Unfinished film scripts. A third of a novel about time-traveling superheroes who journey back to stop the Holocaust. It was an output incommensurate with his genius.

What if his greatest achievement had been his family: his beautiful boys, all well-brought-up and fully vaccinated? Each praised
by their teachers as being clever, funny, and, though they never
said this because they weren't allowed, potential geniuses like their
father. So who was he to have decided that his great genius had to
be deployed in the service of scripted or written entertainment?
Perhaps his genius was as a father.

In the school gymnasium, he took up his position on the side-
line, having arrived in time to catch the second half of his second-
oldest son's basketball game. He was used to how unathletic all
these eight-year-old boys (and the few girls) looked in their basketball jerseys, shorts, and absurdly expensive sneakers. Among these
little boys, there lurked no prospect for athletic scholarships, to say
nothing of professional careers. But as the Hornets, Elmer's team,
built a small lead in the second half, something strange seemed to
be happening: Elmer was having the game of his life. Every time
he got the ball, he shot. And every time he shot, he scored. He
was in the zone, and feeling it to such an extent that he wasn't
even smiling or laughing or celebrating his baskets but merely
running down the floor to take up his defensive position. The
other fathers—Rankin the gangster, even Brick the sculptor—had
also noticed this, and a few had even begun shouting, "Pass it
to Elmer." The most ridiculous confirmation of Elmer's heat was
when he received the ball near the top of the key, pivoted, then
began dribbling up the lane, reversed course, and began dribbling
away from the basket and put the ball up over his left shoulder. He
wasn't even looking at the basket. By then, a few dads had come
over to Levi-Levy and were patting him on the back, as if Elmer's
performance were somehow related to Levi-Levy's parenting or
DNA or at least keeping the boy alive long enough so that this
fifteen minutes of basketball were possible.

After the game, after the *two-four-six-eight, who do we appreciate*
for the losing Celtics, when Levi-Levy and Elmer were walking

up Greenwich, Levi-Levy couldn't restrain himself from reaching over and tousling the boy's hair repeatedly. He was so proud of his son, he realized; he was happier than he would have been at his own achievements. The boys were his life. His family was his life. When he got home, he decided, he would give Charmaine the good news: he was moving back home. He was ready.

———

CHARMAINE LISTENED TO Levi-Levy, but found all his arguments for moving back in to be flawed. For one thing, he was a better father now that he was no longer living under the same roof with the kids. And she rejected categorically the prospect of remerging their finances, or, more accurately, remerging her finances with his debts. She had other reasons she didn't want to admit to Levi-Levy. She had met the chef three times this past week for surprisingly enjoyable sex, despite her initial perplexity at the chef's technique of using his penis as a sort of pestle he would swirl around, as if somewhere in her vagina were sesame seeds or cardamom that had to be ground into powder. Now she was looking forward to her next pestling, and found that prospect more exciting than any potential reconjugation with Levi-Levy. The simple facts were that Levi-Levy was a better husband and father when she wasn't screwing him; and the screwing was better with a man who wasn't her husband or the father of her children.

They talked after the children were asleep. But it was no, no, and no, and Levi-Levy, reduced to undignified begging, saw that he could not persuade her. Sooner or later, he convinced himself, she would relent. He gathered up another box of his books and took the elevator down to the street and went out into the cold night as if he wasn't terrified of the world.

47 LISPENARD

B efore she had heard of capitalists and proletarians, owners
and renters, haves and have-nots, Sadie was aware that
there were economic distinctions between families. Some clans
carried themselves with a quiet sense of entitlement, the fathers
visible but taciturn, the mothers in their fancy kitchens with stone
counters and European appliances, giving gentle directions to their
help and, sometimes, to babysitters like Sadie, before vanishing for
the evening. These homes were tidy, swept, and, when Sadie first
learned the word *bourgeois*, she immediately used these carefully
designed and sparse lofts as her frame of reference.

Sadie came to think of her own family as being like aborigines:
indigenous peoples cowering in their fifth-floor walk-up with its
soggy butcher-block kitchen counter, Dynavent open-flame heat-
ers, illegally mounted boiler, and bathroom floor through which
she could see the downstairs neighbors' bathroom if she opened
the cabinet beneath the sink and peered through the hole where
the plumbing snaked south. Her father had moved into the place
when nobody else had been interested in living here, and their
tenancy was guaranteed by a loft law whose continued jurisdiction
her father was constantly signing petitions to ensure. The space

was worth millions now, and the landlord was eager to push out Sadie's family, renovate this unit into one of those tidy, swept designer lofts, and sell it to a member of the bourgeoisie. Yet her father, protected by the legal system he had once professed to despise, was immovable.

Her father had once, in a serious moment, told Sadie that whatever she did, no matter what great odysseys she embarked upon, she must always return to this apartment to maintain her residency and therefore ensure her legal claim. This rent-controlled tenancy was, presumably, her inheritance.

In elementary school, there had been plenty of girls and boys like her. Progeny of artist parents, or at least parents who looked artistic, who had lucked into good deals and now were mingling with the wealthy. But the rich seemed to be arriving in ever-increasing numbers. She hadn't noticed the transformation at first: the change from battered Fords with hoods as long as ping-pong tables and Volvo station wagons with duct tape instead of rear windows to late-model Mercedes and Land Rovers, looking equally forlorn parked in the dull street light but each, in its shining "notice me" eagerness, a sign the neighborhood was gentrifying, one unvandalized vehicle at a time. Of course, a child doesn't explicitly posit concepts like gentrification. But Sadie began to understand it intuitively by the end of elementary school, when some of her peers were enrolled in private schools named for saints or rich men while others, like her, would be going to schools with numbers instead of names. She knew, without ever asking her parents, that those fancy-sounding schools were out of the question, just as she knew, without ever asking her friends, that those schools promised entrée into a network of people with fancy kitchens, a world of rich kids.

Those kids, the ones who had gone on to private schools, had indeed become part of a wider social network of young adults. Though they still lived in the neighborhood, and she would run into them from time to time, their friends came from all over the city: from the Upper East Side, from Sutton Place, Brooklyn Heights, Central Park West. They were involved in school activities that took them to Europe, social events for which you bought drinks by the bottle at nightclubs, and in the summer they were inevitably away at their Summer Houses. Sadie remained close to the neighborhood girls and boys who had attended the local junior high school and high school, the public schools. She had a few friends, the pretty girls who, though their families lacked the means to send them to the private schools, had, by virtue of their looks and charms, been included in certain of those tribal rites of the wealthier. Being beautiful, Sadie concluded, was almost like being rich.

There was nothing wrong with Sadie's looks, but one would be hard-pressed to remark on them. Black hair, brown eyes, a thick arc of black eyebrow, good nose, freckles, thin lips. Pretty enough, analyzed feature by feature, but then, step back and Sadie was just a few crucial inches too short to pass for normal. And she wasn't thin. The effect of her, then, was like being in the presence of a beautiful block. But what is wonderful about a perfect square?

She had concluded early on that she would have to work hard. And living in close proximity to these successful families afforded her plenty of opportunities to study them, all while making a little money caring for their children after school and in the evenings.

———————

HER FATHER HAD moved to New York to become an artist, and they lived now surrounded by vestiges of that putative vocation. In their railroad loft, along the brick wall that ran east to west, was evidence that he had dabbled in painting and worked for years as a puppeteer. The vinyl cases arranged spine-out in bookshelves made from planks and old phone books were proof that he had also produced some sort of unwatchable video art about those puppets. Sadie had the only proper room in the house—a windowless cavern that served as her bedroom. Her father slept at the rear of the loft, beneath the air-shaft windows. There was one bathroom that he had years ago jerry-rigged with cheap panels, and, for some reason, a Jacuzzi-style bathtub whose jets had never, in Sadie's recollection, functioned, and were now calcified to a kind of lime-green. His skill, it turned out, was as a tinkerer. Whenever one of the families Sadie looked after would need to dispose of some out-of-favor appliance or component part, Sadie would lug it home or tell her father about it and he would show up with a hand truck and roll the dishwasher or television or karaoke machine back home. He would pull apart the devices, spread the parts across the living-room floor, rendering this space uninhabitable for days, as he patiently studied the array before him, before deducing which was the flawed belt or shaft or cowling or housing, and then he would head down to the last remaining hardware store in the neighborhood to seek a replacement. He had rebuilt dozens of machines, and that was the reason the family had a wide-screen television (in its heyday, a shockingly expensive model) that displaced as many cubic feet of prime Manhattan real estate as a parked car. (The screens of the sleeker families were all flat.) They had a double-door fridge and, stacked in the living room disrupting the viewing of the monstrous television set, was a washer and dryer that Sadie's father also had resurrected.

Her father lamented the closing of each mediocre neighborhood restaurant though they rarely dined in them, every crappy discount store that you only went to when you were too lazy to walk to Staples or J&R, even the Dominican-run pawnshop down on Chambers in which he had never set foot. He saw each closing as setting the stage for further gentrification. And Sadie knew that if there was one thing her father was not down with, it was an upgraded neighborhood.

Her mother, Caroline, worked at Harvest House, a nonprofit that coordinated the distribution of free meals to indigent families.

She was, more than anything else, gone: she had moved out of the loft when Sadie was twelve to a floor in a brownstone on the wrong side of a park in Brooklyn. Sadie's custody had been determined by her school district, the one in Tribeca generally considered better, i.e., whiter, than the one in Brooklyn.

Her parents had maintained cordiality, primarily because of Sadie—drop-offs, pickups, forgotten homework, parent-teacher conferences, and emergency babysitting. Now that Sadie was largely determining her own wheres and whens, she suspected her parents would soon go months without speaking, then years, and then eternity.

She was guiltily aware of her father's deep and unrelenting love for her. The way he watched her, the quick smile and up-turned eye-corners whenever she would roll back into the loft. He who was so indifferent to food, could live on rice crackers, peanut butter, and marijuana for months, would order takeout from Zen Palate or Takahachi if Sadie was home. He asked her about everything, told her about everything, and wished the world for her, but for a long time, Sadie wanted nothing to do with him. It had to do with the sense, steady as cicada buzz, that he had succumbed to life rather than seized it. She had studied the other dads, and they had this eager, unvanquished quality; Pop-pop, on the other hand, seemed to shy away from life. Still, she was coming to appreciate his steady current of adoration and feckless gestures of support. He would never be good for tuition, but if you needed the tube changed on your bike he would get that done lickety-split.

Fathers are mysterious to their daughters. For most of their youths, girls barely stop to wonder about the middle-aged male in their life. He's good for a shoulder ride, or to hang up a white board, or to teach you how to ride a bike or swim. But he is also distant, quiet, confused, bumbling, sleepy, indifferent, slow to anger but once riled unmerciful in handing out groundings and confiscating cell phones. But he was there, always there. And Sadie was just now beginning to see who he was, and that he was the only person who saw Sadie as the absolute center of the universe. And that would always count for something.

———

SADIE WALKED DOWN the five flights of creaky stairs to the grimy ground-floor landing. Here, the building's tenants haphazardly leaned their bicycles into one another so that pedals became enmeshed with spokes and handlebars caught brake-lines. Gradually, those bikes that were infrequently used would migrate to the back of the metallic jumble where tires would eventually deflate, chains rust, and seats become covered with dust. Sadie's big old Baker Continental, the discard of a publicist mother who had purchased the vintage bike on sight without ever riding it, was among the most used and therefore nearly always at the outside of the pack. The one-speed bike was heavy, creaky, and slow to pick up speed. Once in motion, though, the bike's weight and bulk seemed to give it a momentum of its own and only a minimum of effort was required to keep the Baker moving at a stately pace down Hudson and then across Duane.

She parked on the street, unfurling from around her chest the heavy chain and alarm clock–size lock she used to secure the bike to one of the bicycle docks that had started popping up around the neighborhood. She let herself into the building and rode up to the third floor, where she found the Asian-looking father standing by himself before the stone counter in the kitchen, looking at a photocopy of a flyer—a badly reproduced image of a man who looked like him.

He smiled as he greeted her but she suspected he was unsure of who, exactly, she was. Sadie knew that he worked in the music or entertainment business; that he did something technical with sound for television shows and films. He was often distracted, coming and going from the loft with no discernible schedule. He seemed similar, in many ways, to her father, only with much more money and far less resentment.

The girls were in their part of the apartment, and Sadie found her way across the loft to the vast area that the mother referred to as the nursery. Sadie was fond of the girls, and the youngest did not yet fully comprehend that Sadie was an employee and not a friend. So her arrival meant to them the presence of another playmate.

Her job, if she were asked to summarize it in one sentence, was: Keep the girls in their nursery and then, at some point, remove them from the loft. She deposited them in ballet studios, gymnastics classes, or music practice rooms. Sometimes she brought the girls to their friends' houses for playdates, where Sadie would sit in the living room, often accompanied by a fellow nanny of Caribbean or Asian descent, the two of them having nothing to say to each other and, seemingly, little in common save their similar relationships with wealthy people. And lately, she'd had to bring the elder one, Cooper, to various modeling go-sees and castings.

It was while walking to and from these various appointments that Sadie and the girls engaged in long and often surprising conversations. They were still young enough to be clueless as to the ages of adults. The younger, Penny, guessed that her mother was eighteen years old and that Sadie was twelve. Sadie was, of course, close to eighteen now and the girls' mother was closer to forty. The girls asked Sadie if she liked various Disney shows she was vaguely aware of, and then what she wanted to do when she grew up. This last question Sadie always found to be a challenge as she walked, a little girl's hand in each of hers and her backpack filled with juice boxes and other kid detritus—Missus Possum plush toys, notebooks, pencils, sunglasses, hats, towels, jewelry, and, of course, iPods and/or iPhones—she had stuffed in before leaving the loft. (When did American children begin to emulate mountaineers in their view of how much gear was appropriate when leaving their homes? Sadie recalled leaving her house with what she could stuff in her pockets. These kids needed a Sherpa.) What did Sadie want to be?

She had applied to a half-dozen colleges, liberal arts institutions spread throughout the Northeast and Midwest, with little idea of what she might actually study when she was there. She suffered from the misconception endemic to a certain kind of New York childhood: she had been raised to believe that each human endeavor, from science to art to finance to animal husbandry to music, was equally valid and necessary. Rich kids, those she had grown up amidst, had that idea drilled into them by their winner parents. You can be anything you fancy. As if the world had an unlimited appetite for artists and designers and actresses. The neighborhood lent credence to this mistaken belief. Weren't there such creative types all around them, living effortlessly in lovely places? Yet Sadie had seen the flops too and, rather late in high school, had concluded that perhaps all professions weren't created equal. Her father, she had long ago realized, was not going to miraculously emerge from his rent-controlled cocoon to become a great, well-paid, creative butterfly. Yet by now, with her leaky arithmetic and indifference to algebra, it was too late for Sadie to change course and indicate to prospective universities a great interest in accounting or finance.

So she was destined, she suspected, for the English department of whichever college would pony up the biggest saddlebag of financial aid. Her transcript had been fine, her test scores on the lower end of good, and she had deduced that the same meek, respectful, good nature that allowed her to win favor, and $15 an hour, from these families might also win over admissions officers. She had preferences: she'd prefer a private liberal arts school to a large public institution. The girls from the New York City private schools, she guessed, would go on to private liberal arts colleges, at least those who weren't admitted to an Ivy League school.

Her father had been a non-resource during that period of

filling out applications and gathering recommendations. Having never attended college himself, and never one to expertly fill out a form—save those that guaranteed his continued occupancy—he had encouraged Sadie with platitudes about expressing herself and then gone back to studying the inner workings of a food processor.

Her mother had been more helpful, sliding on reading glasses to study Sadie's essays, and she proved to be of particular use in completing the financial aid forms in a manner intended to elicit not pity but sympathy.

Unstated during this whole process, by her mother, by her college and career counselor, had been that if massive financial aid were not forthcoming, then Sadie wasn't going anywhere. Or, there was always the junior college on the West Side or Hunter uptown, but she wouldn't be joining and catching up, finally, a little, with those girls who had headed off to private school all those years ago.

Now, as Penny and Cooper asked her this simple question—*What did she want to be?*—Sadie couldn't help but run through these calculations in her head, and had to resist answering that if the money doesn't come through, she wouldn't be anything.

———

SHE WAS STILL in touch with a few of the girls she had known in elementary school, when they had all been tucked into the cute little classrooms behind the wrought-iron gate; when their world extended only to the cut-out letters on the wall, their names and birthdays written on the white board, and whatever art projects the teacher had festooned throughout the classroom. (Oh, and the innumerable Indian projects they worked on. By now, there must have been as many elementary school projects devoted to Native Americans as there had actually been pre-apocalypse Native Americans.) At what age was she aware that some girls were different, that their parents had the means to live in a certain mode while Sadie's folks were outmoded? They were done with that little school at the end of fifth grade, but she must have noticed the differences earlier. Fourth? End of third? The girls with summer houses, with mothers who drove around Lower Manhattan in SUVs, the girls who were collected in the yard after school by nannies instead of a curious-looking father in crooked sunglasses and paint-smeared Chuck Taylors. Those girls had begun to pair off, to arrange themselves in quivers of better clothing, fancier shoes, suntans after Christmas and winter break. And these days, as she often found herself back in that yard to pick up Penny and Cooper after school, she could see the girls segregating themselves in the same manner. Cooper seemed particularly adept at befriending those similarly stationed and Sadie saw a hierarchy emerging; the more powerful females rejecting the weaker, the prettier and more desirable already segregating themselves. It broke her heart, a little, to see the suddenly bewildered and less powerful females tossed from the pod, left to wander at the fringes of the cliques as the classes made their way out the double-doors into the yard. Broke her heart, yes, but also filled her with a kind of hatred for Cooper and girls like her, who were already castigating, ostracizing, selecting in or out.

Sadie occasionally saw a few of her old friends. They texted periodically, inviting her over on slow nights when they had nothing better going on. Often, Sadie would end up watching television while her better-connected acquaintances iChatted on their laptops or texted other friends, engaging in a long and winding loop of gossip about boys and parties, a vast and glittery-seeming world whose primary attribute, from where Sadie sat watching muted DVR episodes of shows that before this evening she had barely been aware of, was that Sadie had no part in it.

Yet it was Sadie's gift that she could sit by while her friends made their more glamorous plans and never make them feel even a flicker of pity. She was used to being the one who got a little less, who wasn't cut into the good deals or added to guest lists or there for opening night. And these girls liked having an audience. They enjoyed safe, nonjudgmental Sadie, easy-to-impress Sadie, Sadie from around the way who they had known forever and ever and who they could call whenever and she would roll up—on a bicycle!—and it didn't matter if they didn't have cool people over or chronic or Krug, she would show up and hang, impressed that they had a Wii for fuck's sake. It was a little embarrassing that she worked as—for real!—a nanny. But Sadie was good people. Even the badass girls, the connected sirens who fancied themselves as manipulative as nighttime teen soap biddies, needed a low-maintenance friend.

Here, in the center of so many cultural and financial circles, amid families connected to the power and wielding the power, why was it so hard to envision a future anywhere but in nightclubs? Kids around the country, around the world, didn't they dream bigger? Didn't they have grand notions of the law or medicine, of directing blockbusters or dreaming up a killer app? But these girls, nominally her peers, they seemed to have become mired in the quicksand of their parents' success. Because wasn't one of the reasons those kids in flyover states dreamed of making it big was to make it here? To be on the list at The Box on Friday? And for Sadie, who took so many of her cues as to what she should be, how she should act, what she should think, from the families of the children she cared for and, to an even greater extent, the better, fancier-heeled girls from just around the block, it some-times seemed like nobody was casting a glance much past, say, Friday night. She hadn't yet encountered the word *provincialism*, and though she had been suspended and choked in the web of stultifying thought thrown off by that blindered sensibility, she was now, for the first time, catching gusts of fresher, less cloyingly perfumed, cleaner air. You look through those college handbooks, an unlikely source yet still, for Sadie, the aspirational antipode of fashion magazines or *The Hills*. You study those photos of kids walking on diagonal paths across broad lawns, backpacks slung over their shoulders, or the trio of students—one white, one black, one Asian—engaged in an earnest conversation around a microscope. They didn't care about being on the list. They had reached some nirvana, where, Sadie had come to believe, the means of your family was irrelevant. Maybe college was an El Dorado for the moderately attractive financially challenged. Strangely, the girls she knew in her hood, like this crew this evening, were called privileged by the media. They were from Saint Anne's and Dalton, sitting around the—what was this room, this little elbow segregated from but somehow linked to the den? Did it even have a name? This extra little spit of living space, like an afterthought larded with a flat screen and a Wii and sectional leathers?

Sadie slid onto the floor, her butt against some sort of carpet that felt old and thick and hairy, like the hide of a prehistoric mammal. They were talking about the girl who had been molested, just down the street. The guy totally followed her into her building, then into the elevator to the basement, where he, like, forced her to blow him and then shot it all over her face. Some of the girls knew her. She was a freshman at Claremont. Brunette, sort of cute but no sizzle. So, like, why did that freak pick her? There were so many hotter girls.

But, eeeewwww, it was so gross, that guy, that, you know, *black* guy, not that that mattered because they all knew brothers who were totally hot, but, just thinking of—

"I heard," said one girl, "that he totally butt-raped her."

Eeeeeewwwww.

"But he wasn't black?" Sadie ventured, recalling the poster she had seen around the neighborhood. "He was, like, Mexican."

Whatever. It's still gross.

WHY DID CERTAIN girls rule and others follow? Was it entirely a matter of wealth? Was it permissive parenting that forbade nothing? That took the view that every misbehavior, every cruelty perpetrated by one kid on another should be let slide in the name of letting kids be kids? (Let them be kids, really let them, and you will end up with a tribe of bulimic eugenicists with huge amounts of credit card debt.) No, Sadie had to admit, for in every bloom, there was the girl or two who wasn't rich, but she had something else. Looks helped, of course, but some girls just knew how to be mean in the right way. They knew how to be mean first, to gain the upper hand in every relationship by being cruel before anyone was cruel to them. Sadie had failed at that. In elementary school, when the ostracism had begun, she had been stunned when the pretty girls modeling for *Vogue Bambini* or Gap Kids shunned her when she approached them in the yard, with a quick, smirking, "You know, Sadie, you don't stay friends with the same people forever."

She backed away at a loss for words, hoping she didn't look too hurt. It was like finding out the devil was real.

She wondered what those girls had that she didn't. Was there a mean gene? Or could meanness be learned, and if so, should she learn it? Wasn't good-natured Sadie, helpful, decent Sadie useless? Wasn't she obsolete? Was it time to learn to be mean?

She had decided Sadie 2.0 would be unveiled in college. But how would she ever get to college, with her deadbeat dad and her mother barely subsisting? Sadie earned as much as she could nannying, picking up and making the rounds with Penny and Cooper, the long afternoons and Saturdays, the Wednesdays and alternate Friday nights. The hours-long stretches of Candyland, then Monopoly, and now, god help her, Cranium and Apples to Apples.

How much could she make? She often calculated this as she rode the Baker around Tribeca on her way to pick up the girls at school. At $15 an hour, sixteen hours a week, that wasn't even two honeys a week. And college cost, what, a zillion dollars a year? She didn't like to read that part of the brochures, the part where it broke down tuition, housing, meal plans, activity fees, and books. Sometimes Penny and Cooper's mom would talk to Sadie about college. She had attended Sarah Lawrence, and she either carefully avoided the subject of tuition or, more likely, Sadie believed, just couldn't imagine that it could ever be an issue. For these people, the money was always there, magically replenishing, like a child's conception of how an ATM worked. She recalled walking with Penny and Cooper through SoHo, past a store that Penny and Cooper insisted on stopping at, a fancy clothing store that Sadie had assumed wouldn't sell children's wear. But there, to one side, were little dresses and cute kids' jeans and tiny little wool coats with fur collars. The girls had begun picking through the racks, finding jackets and dresses they liked, oohing and aahing. Sadie had glanced at the price tags and was shocked by the numbers: many hundreds of dollars for little kids' clothes that would be outgrown in a matter of months. "This stuff is crazy," she said, more to herself, "nobody would buy this stuff."

Then later, back at home, as she was pulling off Penny's dress, she noticed a label from that very store.

So how could these people even imagine that you could get into a college, a good college, and then not be able to go?

She thought about the girls she had gone to elementary school with, girls not unlike Penny and Cooper, and wondered again about the mean gene, and realized that if she didn't have it, then she would have to learn it. She could be, what was it? What were those girls? Ruthless, that's it. The girls were like that, and their parents must have been too; that's how they got here.

THERE WERE SO many bright girls in New York, her College-and-Career Lady warned her. She sat behind a plain white table with chrome legs that ended in little black rubber cups, presumably to keep them from scraping the linoleum floor. Piled on her table and atop the filing cabinets in her office were hundreds of those brochures, the marketing paraphernalia of the education industry, trade schools touting Personalized Professional Training and liberal arts colleges promising Higher Learning with a Purpose. The ivy, the granite, the old buildings, the stadiums. It was like they were selling four-year package tours instead of school. Sadie had lacked the scratch to pay for the Kaplan Test Prep classes and Kumon math tutorials, but she had nonetheless tested respectably; her grades had been good but not great—the overall impression created by her transcript was of moderate intelligence and academic diligence. Would it be enough? In this city of bright Asian girls from Stuyvesant and the carefully curated extracurricular résumés of rich girls with fancy last names from Trinity? Of course not, Sadie decided. Not if she needed hundreds of thousands in financial aid. Wouldn't they give that money to a brilliant Gujarati with science chops or to a Korean violinist?

There were state schools, she was reminded, that provided a comparable education at a more reasonable price. How about SUNY Purchase?

No. She dreamed of finally leveling the playing field. This ambition caught even Sadie off guard, appearing one day as this vague desire to finally get a taste of what it felt like to be in instead of out. And the idea wouldn't let go, so that even after the applications had been sent, with her safety school, Rutgers, dutifully included, she refused to consider that possibility.

So when a trickle of acceptance letters started arriving— Wellesley, Kenyon, Vassar—and she showed them to the College-and-Career Lady, she was taken aback by the praise she received; it was given as if, see, you are every bit as smart as those other girls, now you won't feel so bad about what you are missing while you're at Purchase. But bullshit, she thought. No. Just because they weren't offering much scholarship money, and just because even with PELL grants and Staffords she wouldn't be able to close the gap, never mind eat or sleep in a bed while she was there, she refused to admit she wouldn't be attending one of these prestigious, fancy institutions of higher learning. She had conceded so many times and in so many ways. Enough.

————

ONE AFTERNOON, AS she was emptying the girls' mac 'n' cheese plates into the compactor, she decided she would just ask. What could it hurt? They were rich, right? They might even enjoy such an act of philanthropy.

After the girls' bath, when she had gathered up her backpack to go, she knocked on the door to the guest bedroom, Brooke's office space.

"Hi there." Brooke turned from the computer where she was reading about the memoirist who had made everything up. He lived just a few blocks from here, Sadie knew, and Brooke had known his wife, or they had worked together or something like that.

"What's up?"

Sadie set down her backpack and then took a seat on the fold-out sofa. "Um, you remember when we were talking about college?"

Brooke smiled.

"Um, so I think I want to go to Wellesley."

"That's awesome."

Sadie almost didn't ask but then just blurted it out. "Can you guys help me?"

"Help?"

"With the budget issues."

Brooke inhaled. She furrowed a brow. Sadie assumed she was thinking about the question when what she was really thinking about was how to say no.

"Sadie, we love you. You are an incredible girl," Brooke said.

"But we're not your parents. And we have two daughters of our own we are going to have to get through college. Not to mention private school for six years before that."

Sadie nodded. Suddenly, she felt ashamed she had asked.

————

SO WHAT WAS Dad thinking anyway? She was sitting on the sofa, eating a bowl of Kashi and soy milk, watching a cartoon. Sadie blurted it out: This was her big dream, and, well, what did he ever dream about?

"What was yours? What is yours?"

Her father, who still had a swirl of white spackle in his hair from some work he had been doing to the rear of the loft, turned to her. His beard was growing in gray and erratic, the follicles going everywhere like the whirly antennae of lobsters you see in Chinatown tanks, his facial pores seemed to be widening as he aged, black holes in flesh, tunnels into his head. But Pop-pop, no matter how he aged, he just kept looking more and more like himself. He was so totally and completely himself that he could almost pass for invisible as he walked down Tribeca streets nowadays. The other grown-up dads wore Steven Alan or Rogan, and looked like overgrown little kids; her dad walked around in denim overalls from the fucking Gold Rush and old work boots.

"I, I . . ." He was about to say, his dream, his big idea, but then he paused.

Her dad looked at her for a while as if trying to think of what to say, and then went to one of the cinder-block-and-plank bookcases piled high with waterlogged paperbacks and old art magazines and came back with a videotape. He still had a VCR wired into the big-tube TV, and he popped in his video and grainy black-and-white footage soon tracked into focus. A robot, assembled from tin cans, with a rolled-back sardine-can top as a quiff, marched onto the screen and did an elaborate and primitive dance. It moved,

Sadie imagined, sort of like cavemen would move, or Indians dancing around a campfire in front of their wigwams. The robot's dance was appropriately jerky, a Frankensteinian clunkiness that was just how a robot like this would dance. It was a puppet, Sadie knew; there was a hand at the back of the robot, and strings controlling the condensed milk–can legs. The puppet's movement was so perfect, so robotic, that Sadie for the first time—she had seen this footage before, she must have—understood what her father had been doing with these strange videos.

The video then cut to an anthropomorphic monkey wrench with iron-filing hair, the oddly feminine-looking tool bouncing up and down in a state of childlike distress. The rusty monkey wrench was agitated about something, was frightened, its fear communicated by her father's manipulation and careful movement of—of a monkey wrench! He was making a monkey wrench seem frightened, seem like a little person. By simply moving it a certain way, holding it at an angle, bouncing it up and down once or twice, he was imbuing this monkey wrench with humanity.

And then the robot bounded into the frame and, okay, this was weird, sort of raped the little monkey wrench. But it was also somehow funny—totally insane, no doubt—but still, really fucking funny.

She began laughing. She had seen these old videos her father had made decades ago, had watched them as a child when she was too young to appreciate them, and they had always just seemed dark and dreary and just weird, the total opposite of the bright, airy happiness of the Tribeca she knew and worked in. But now she was old enough: she got it. They were dark and dreary, and they did make you uncomfortable, but that was because they were supposed to make you feel that way.

She watched the whole series of them, eight little short films, seeing the full scope and range of the human spirit reduced to metallic puppets bashing into each other, fucking each other, giving birth to each other, and betraying each other. It was amazing, she began to think, but it was so unlike any other *regular* achievements that it was no wonder they had been forgotten, or, actually, never really discovered. It was a uniquely weird thing he had done, and beautiful, in a crazy way.

She was proud of him.

"Why did you stop?" she said.

"I don't know," Pop-pop said. "I let things get in the way. I let people get in the way. I didn't—"

He rubbed his beard. "I wasn't, I wasn't, I was, I—" He picked up Sadie's empty cereal bowl and stood up to take it to the kitchen.

"Ruthless. I wasn't ruthless. That's what you have to be. That's what everyone who makes it is. Everyone around here. And you have to be that, because there's no penalty for ruthless. Only upside."

———————

SUCH WAS HER state of mind as she dolled up that night to meet a few of her old friends for drinks at a local tavern. It was one of those cash-only joints over on the other side of West Broadway, where the bars were lax about policing IDs, so there were enough cute girls to offset the suits pouring in from Citi a few blocks away. The mood of this gaggle of girls was celebratory. Most had been accepted into a college, if not the college of their choice. Most of the institutions were in or near New York—Sarah Lawrence, NYU—with one or two of the girls being bold enough to venture as far as Bennington or New Haven.

Sadie didn't find the bar comfortable. It was a little paneled room with doors that looked like hatches on a submarine and straight-backed booths with mirrors over them on which were crayoned specials. The staff was a hirsute, mustachioed bunch of dudes wearing string ties and white shirts, the desired affect being Roaring Twenties, Sadie guessed. But then why was the waitress turned out like a Spanish peasant, thick-soled, clunky heels, black dress with floral top, and a red flower in her carefully tied-up bun? It was tiring to try to understand where this was all coming from, or going, and after two of the meticulously measured, blended, and poured cocktails—Sadie was drinking old-fashioneds, each running her nine carefully hoarded dollars—she decided that she wasn't fond of bars, and never understood why among her girl-friends it was considered a coup when they got all glammed up and tricked a local into selling them drinks.

Sadie saw him as he walked in. At first, he didn't recognize her, his eyes adjusting to the light. Penny and Cooper's dad, after an instant, saw the friend he was meeting at the bar and joined him, the two of them taking stools and turning their backs on the rest of the room. Sadie became suddenly self-conscious, wonder-ing if her being at this bar would disqualify her from caring for his daughters. Suddenly wary, she gulped her drink, the sickly sweet bourbon making her queasy for a moment as she forced it down.

Her friends, noticing Sadie gone more taciturn than usual, asked her what was going on.

It was embarrassing to explain the awkwardness, but she saw no alternative. The dad she worked for, she explained, the father, was over there.

They craned. They saw.

One commented that he was kind of cute.

"Eeeeew," another one said. "He must be like forty!"

Sadie shrugged. She was thinking of slipping away when the father walked past, on his way out the door to smoke a cigarette. He stopped when he saw Sadie. Smiled. And continued on his way out.

They kept their discreet distance, Sadie downing another cock-tail, the father over by the bar, drinking, turning once in a while to see if Sadie was still there. At one point, they both ended up outside the bar smoking and So, hey, how are you doing?

They didn't talk about Penny or Cooper. Instead, the father began asking Sadie about what she was planning to do with her life, where she would be going to college. She mentioned her desires, her choices, Wellesley, Kenyon, or Vassar. He nodded. He told her he had gone to a state school in California. He wasn't the student type, he said. He'd been more into playing in bands, the music scene, and he was probably lucky that he wasn't as successful as some of his friends, because he had found his way into the whole sound-editing business and had sort of grown that into, like, this whole *business*. It never would have happened, he said, if he had been in a more successful band. You never know how it all adds up, or doesn't. Something seems like a bad break and ends up lucky. You are pissed off at what goes wrong and then, a few years later, you realize it was a stroke of good fortune.

Her father occasionally spun such long-run nonsense, but coming from this dad, from the head of a successful family, it had a certain credibility. It almost sounded like wisdom.

He wasn't a bad-looking guy, she now realized. With his long black hair, prominent nose, he reminded Sadie of the cartoons of American Indians they had studied when she was in grade school.

They continued talking at the bar, the father even buying all the girls drinks, which lent Sadie a little more status than usual, seen as she was to be jocking this older guy. She ordered another old-fashioned, her dizzying fourth, then another.

———

SHE REMEMBERED WALKING with him, down the darkened street, leaning into him, both joking that he had to protect her from the molester who was supposedly still at large.

———

THERE ARE IDEAS that arrive fully formed, complete with words and images, and even our ideas *about* those ideas are in place as

soon as the thoughts manifest, so that the concept as edifice can be
studied, walked around, so to speak, and then more axons fire into
more dendrites so that an even denser supporting structure for the
idea is built.

Sadie would later marvel at this process, at the sudden appearance of her big idea. It seemed to have arrived simultaneously with
the seduction, but already it was *so* there: of course that's what she
already had been thinking.

And Sadie had to smile, for she was already becoming more
calculating than she had ever thought herself capable of being. Like
those other girls, those richer, prettier girls.

Ruthless.

————

THEY WERE AT his sound-effects studio, in a darkened little
room with a box of gloves and little children's shoes and what must
have been a hundred belts. There was a shoebox full of zippers and
another of different kinds of light switches and remote controls
and various domestic objects that clicked. Where did he get all this
stuff? she drunkenly wondered, as he worked on unbuttoning her
blouse. When they were finished, the act still unfamiliar to Sadie,
though she was not completely inexperienced, the simplicity of the
solution was before her. She would ask him to pay for her education, or at least that part of it which wouldn't be underwritten by
scholarships and grants and loans, and of course he would pay for
it. Or she would tell Brooke, the pretty brunette wife, what had
happened here, would explain that he had bought her drinks and
then had his way.

What choice would he have?

104 WEST BROADWAY

B y now you have heard of the scandal.

My first book, that one about Japan, had been a critical success. It allowed me to secure a staff writer's position at a prestigious monthly American magazine and then to move on to an even more august periodical. My next book, nearly a decade later, the memoir about growing up in Nevada, about my high school drug addiction, subsequent stays in rehab, arrest for breaking and entering a physician's office to steal narcotics, and my eventual incarceration in a state hospital, has become a bestseller. The scene in which I break the nose of one of my counselors at the rehab center and then piss on his desk has become almost as notorious as my boarding a plane with a broken jaw and Transportation Security agents following the trail of blood down the aisle to my seat. In the book, I fight off three of them before they finally subdue me with a Taser in full view of my fellow passengers.

I finally beat my nasty drug problem with a combination of martial arts discipline—picked up during my years in Japan—and a tough, go-it-alone ethos that I summarize in the book as Seven Times Down, Eight Times Up. It's an old Yakuza saying indicating the relentlessness of the *ronin* (wandering warrior), who will always rise no matter how many times you knock him down. I abbreviate this in the book to the acronym 7TD8TU and repeat it as a mantra. Unbuttoning my shirt to reveal the 7TD8TU tattoo in Gothic lettering on my chest has become a regular feature at my readings and television appearances.

The book was becoming a phenomenon—a bestseller, of course, but somehow more than that, an inspiring tale that teenagers, young adults, and those down on their luck were reading over and over again and buying to give to their friends.

I had come a very long way since Tokyo.

I hadn't heard from any of my old Tokyo colleagues in years. Trey, a fellow writer and editor at the Tokyo magazine where we had worked, had stayed behind, continuing on at the magazine for a year before moving back to America. We met in New York when he came through a couple of years later, quite a few pounds heavier and tired-looking. He had finally managed to place a story in a good magazine and secure a book deal of his own for a very modest advance. He wrote his book, it was published to general disinterest, and then he surprised me by moving back to Tokyo, where he began working at yet another new English-language magazine, this one a weekly spin-off of our old rag. He periodically sent me story ideas to show my boss at my magazine. I never passed them along.

Maxine had been the founder of the magazine and she had sold her share of the company and went on to edit another magazine, this one in Japanese, which eventually folded. I heard she had gotten a nose job, remarried a Japanese man, and was looking for work.

Yoshimi had married a salaryman and had settled in Saitama, a suburban prefecture, where she had two children of her own.

They all had their reasons for resenting me. I had left them all behind. We had been close, working together, until my resentment of Maxine—I felt I was doing all the work and she was

getting all the credit—finally caused a series of arguments culmi-
nating in some very nasty exchanges. It had been Maxine, in fact,
who had encouraged us to take liberties in the writing and editing
of stories. We began making up some facts. The magazine needed
the copy and she hadn't cared how we produced it.

I didn't think about any of them very much at all, busy as I
was with my life and the impending paperback publication of my
book. The publisher wanted me to visit twenty cities on my tour;
my agent was trying to get them to agree to just a dozen. I had sold
the dramatic rights, for a six-part mini-series, to HBO, and my
co–executive producer was Sumner, a neighborhood guy who the
development head at HBO had wanted detached from the project
but who I insisted should stay on. They wanted a producer with a
better track record as a show runner but I explained that Sumner
had believed in the project from the beginning, from when he first
read a galley of the book. I couldn't dump him now.

They agreed and we made a deal that I would write the first
two episodes myself.

———

THE DEAL FOR my next two books would be a blockbuster, a
huge sum divided into four payments, the first of which would be
nearly seven figures.

This, then, was the life I—we—had been dreaming of back in
Tokyo. I was thirty-seven years old and married to a former editor
I had met at the magazine. Marni was self-confident and pretty,
sure enough of her looks to have actually written an article for
New York magazine about what life was like for a pretty woman
in New York City. She had been prominently social before we
met, though never quite as wealthy as her society coverage would
have suggested. This was a city on a bender similar to what Tokyo
had experienced when I was living there: presumptuous, flush,
drunk with certainty about its station and wealth. Real estate was

a cloying and far-too-frequent topic of conversation—we had just purchased a spacious loft in Tribeca, and we were shopping for a house on the North Fork of Long Island—just as it had been back in Tokyo. Only now I was partaking in the prosperity, swimming in it, rather than feeling excluded.

I could never have imagined that I would appreciate literary and financial success primarily because they ensured better treatment for my autistic son, but that was turning out to be the great benefit.

Marni remained a powerful social force, though she no longer flew the flag of convenience of any of the glossy titles. She still inspired jealousy and a hint of fear in her peers, even among women you would assume were too pretty and too smart to give a shit. For the first months of our relationship I had wondered what she saw in me. Marni, who at one point could have married any of a dozen bankers or lawyers or trustafarians, had shacked up with a writer—and at that point, not even a successful one. Never mind that I had subsequently thrived so that my success now seemed commensurate with her status. She had chosen me when I was nobody. She must have loved me.

———

WHEN I STARTED at the magazine I was a contract writer in a borrowed cubicle—not as low-status a position as it sounds, but still, an enlisted man while Marni was clearly in the officer corps. I had always had a certain bluster about myself when it came to women; I wasn't shy and being a writer had made rejection more familiar than feared. Yet my first glimpse of Marni, at the distant end of the table in a story meeting I made the mistake of attending because I happened to be in the office—writers *never* attended these meetings, I found out later—was electrifying. She exuded presumption. Her brown hair was curled down to her shoulders and her long head sat on a neck as graceful and flawless as a swan's.

Her eyeballs were heavy and protruding; she saw everything. Her cheeks were pink and shiny and her mouth thick-lipped and sensual. I remember she was wearing a white jacket, blue blouse, black pants. She seemed simultaneously bored and ahead of everyone else.

Stories were suggested, discussed, dismissed. It was only later that I found out that very few articles emerged from these meetings. Those came from smaller, more discreet conclaves. But Marni did suggest something fashion-related and it was immediately approved.

Later, when I was back at my cubicle, Marni came over and introduced herself. "Marni Saltzwell."

I took her hand.

"You've been writing those Japan articles," she said.

"That's me."

"They're unbelievably good."

She walked away, back to her distant office.

We went out for drinks a few days later, ostensibly between editor and writer though I would never write a story for her. We had martinis at the Oyster Bar and she said I should join her for a gallery opening. We went to the opening and ended up in a little galley kitchen at the back of the gallery, where we were crowded in with Damien Hirst, Anthony Haden-Guest, Patti Smith, and Arne Glimcher. Then we joined the artist in his limousine to go to a nightclub where the entire second floor was roped off in his honor and we sat at his booth. Nobody seemed surprised that I was there once I explained I was with Marni, but actually, what *was* I doing there?

That was the question I asked myself many times during the first few weeks of our romance, half-expecting strangers on the street to congratulate me because I was fucking Marni Saltzwell. My being with her was almost that ridiculous, as if I were suddenly dating Madonna. For the first time, my picture was showing up in

Patrick McMullan layouts as "and friend" before he bothered to figure out who I was.

I didn't dare mention my enthusiasm or excitement at being with Marni to Marni, but I looked forward to our assignations as if each was a long-sought-after first date. It never occurred to me that she might be feeling the same excitement. I assumed she would soon be moving on to her next guy.

She was still living up in SoHo then, in a corner loft on Grand Street with huge casement windows that faced south and east. I loved being in that apartment with her, reveling in the couples-y things we did, the Sunday *Times* reading (although she had already read most of the paper by Friday), the brunch-cooking, the dope-smoking. I was intoxicated by her glamour and pulchritude, of course, but there was also an easy connection, a steady and untroubled rapport. Marni was so fast and bright, possessed of vast computational power and analytical skills. She hadn't become Marni Saltzwell only by birth and beauty; she had also been, I was now discovering, at the top of every class she'd been in, from Spence through Brown. She still remembered with mawkish regret that in third grade Willow Roebling had mastered long division before she had.

At the time, there was much discussion about the president launching air strikes against targets in the Sudan and if that was an appropriate use of U.S. power. How quaint it now seems that the loss of nineteen U.S. soldiers in a rescue operation in Somalia a few years earlier had generated the widespread belief that Americans would not tolerate any more combat casualties. It was Marni who first pointed out to me that as long as there was no conscription, then Americans would soon be willing to go to war again. She was always surprising me with that kind of analysis. I know it sounds awful and sexist, but I found it thrilling to hear such well-formulated ideas pouring out from such a pretty face.

We never spoke about what exactly this thing was but I knew it was serious when she called me up sobbing at four a.m., confessing that she had just slept with Mark McGrath, of all people, and felt horrible about it.

"Can I please come see you?" she said.

I said fine. I wasn't sure who Mark McGrath was, but liked how this was playing out.

She came over and we sat on the sofa in my Eleventh Street apartment and she told me she had discovered something about herself, and about me.

"I need you," she said. "I need you because you're the one real thing in my life."

IN THE MORNINGS, I would bring my son, Alexander, to his preschool over on the East Side. We had tried to mainstream him at the pre-K at the local public elementary school—it had embarrassed Marni to have a child in public school—but I liked the other dads, with whom I had coffee many mornings. Alex had been diagnosed as autistic—a wide-ranging disability, I was discovering—at around twenty months, but he was showing signs of perhaps being on the higher-functioning side of the spectrum. He walked at eighteen months and climbed steps soon after. Motor development, I read in the numerous books on autism that were now piled in our loft, was a key early indicator of IQ, which meant that Alex, beneath all the messed-up wiring and synaptic misdirection that experts now say is a cause, or perhaps effect, of autism, might have a relatively healthy mind. Marni and I, like all parents of the developmentally disabled, desperately hoped that was the case, and believed we saw in Alex small signs that he was improving. At age three, he was responding to his name, smiling more often, and when he sat with us at the table, he would allow his milk to be served in a receptacle other than his orange sippy cup. Because of the success of my book—and, of course, Marni's money—we could afford the recommended phalanx of speech therapists and behavior-modification professionals, and these childhood-development experts were becoming a regular part of our lives, as constant a presence in our loft as Marni and I were. They seemed a little bit thrilled to be working with the son of a literary celebrity.

At first, it worried me when Alex seemed occasionally indifferent to my presence. That was, of course, a putative symptom of autism, and pediatric neurologists had warned us that it could make for a trying parenthood. I was reluctant to talk about it with the coffee guys. And even they were careful not to joke about Alex—virtually nothing else was off limits, so I was grateful for this forbearance. I thought of my tattoo, 7TD8TU, and was vaguely embarrassed as it now seemed that such warrior braggadocio was meaningless when I was confronted by the simple fact of Alex's autism.

When we switched him to the special school on the East Side, I continued to have coffee with the guys as if my son was still among their children's classmates. But while Alex didn't show affection, he took great pleasure in my company as we took walks around the neighborhood, visiting the little park over by Greenwich Street or stopping in to the deli where I buy newspapers and a gluten-free peanut butter bar for Alex. (We hadn't determined if Alex was gluten-intolerant, as are allegedly so many of the autistic, but thought it best to take as few chances as possible.) The Korean lady used to give Alex a straw, which he liked to chew on as she told him he was a handsome boy. Like so many autistic children, Alex possessed an otherworldly beauty. Or perhaps he had just inherited his mother's good looks.

———

I DIDN'T GO into my office at the prestigious monthly very often, but I knew it was important that I maintain my position there. The magazine gave me the kind of credibility I could never have dreamed of back in Tokyo. But I believed the magazine now needed me almost as much as I needed it; the success of my memoir had made this a mutually beneficial relationship. I was also making friends with other writers in New York, the novelists from Brooklyn, the blue-blooded fellow writers at my magazine, the literary-lion types I met at *Paris Review* parties and PEN benefits.

On one of my infrequent sallies into the office, the editor in chief popped into my little windowless space and said, "You have a stalker." He was a handsome man with wire-frame glasses and shiny black hair that he combed straight back. It was he who had first published my stories about Japan, a long time ago. Among our other topics of conversation were our autistic sons. His own boy, Roman, had Asperger's syndrome and was already twelve years old. When Alex was first diagnosed, the editor in chief had been a great resource for advice, giving me the names of first-rate specialists and helping me to place Alex in the special day-care program on the East Side, for which I paid $36,000 a year.

"What?" I smiled, imagining that yet another deranged reader of my second book was trying to get in touch with me. Success has curious side effects.

He was holding in his hand a manuscript that he now passed to me. "Read this and let's talk. Now don't freak out about it."

It was ostensibly an article submitted to my boss for the magazine's consideration. In reality it was an unsigned, systematic, footnoted, fifty-nine-page takedown, beginning with my first book about Japan, which it went through almost page by page to demonstrate that I was not only mistaken in my reporting but that I was willfully misleading. It then went through my career at the old magazine back in Tokyo, citing articles there to prove I had always faked it. And then, most damaging, it went through my earlier stories for this magazine, those that had been about Japan and for which I had gained my first small measure of literary and journalistic success. It pulled those pieces apart and splayed them, as if dissecting cadavers, pointing out the myriad places, characters, and instances that could only be pure fabrication on the part of the writer.

I could only bear to read it in short bursts, pausing after every paragraph to consider the detail and precision of the attack. It was an etiological document, exhaustive, thorough, and linear. I didn't even remember writing most of the passages quoted and then ripped apart. As I read, I felt my heart racing and very quickly realized this might be the second worst thing to ever happen to me; the gradual, creeping realization that something was wrong with Alex had been the worst.

The author had two lines of assault: there was the basic, simple idea that I made countless spelling and factual errors—the names of villages, the population of prisons, the view out a coffee-shop window. All wrong. But I knew that those were inconsequential errors of the type other journalists and writers had made and which I knew were excusable, particularly in work that was a decade old.

The other line of arguing was more sophisticated and ultimately more troubling: too many of the characters, in particular in those early stories for this magazine, simply did not exist. There was the Japanese motorcycle gang boss, the political fixer, the porno actress, all of whom had been the central figures in my early stories for this magazine—which back then had never run photographs— and who, the author of this document concluded (who *was* the author of this document?), could not have ever existed based on his extensive reporting. This person had gone back and spoken to experts quoted in my pieces, to other characters in my stories, and visited the addresses and buildings mentioned to prove that these characters and settings were fictitious yet had been presented in this magazine as fact.

Now, my magazine is famous for its fact-checking, though staff members know that the fact-checking is really only as good as the writers' notes. And I had known going into my first assignment that they had no fact-checkers who could speak Japanese, and so were entirely dependent on my version of events.

The author of this document was making a reasoned argument that for a decade I had exhibited a pattern of fabrication and dissembling. What was making my back tingle was that this was a well-argued and systematic prosecution, persuasive in tone and well articulated; it was a condemnation of me as much as my work. After you read it, you were ready to convict me of almost any crime.

I IMMEDIATELY WONDERED who—besides my editor in chief—had seen this.

I asked him.

"I showed it to Tyler," he said, referring to the editorial director of the company, nominally his boss. "Nobody else needs to see it."

He said he didn't care about the stuff in Tokyo and what was in my first book. What he felt we needed to do—just in case, he said—was prepare a defense about the stories of mine he had published in this magazine. It was heartening to hear that he was proceeding from the point of view that I was in the right; that my stories were solid, and all I had to do was rebut the allegations.

Then he said something chilling. "I've already gotten a call about this." He mentioned a Web site that intensely covered New York media. "So it's out there."

I tried to laugh dismissively, but it came out so loud that I sounded a little bit like I was barking.

"Do you know who this is?" he asked.

I shook my head. "I have a few ideas but no, I'm not sure."

I walked back to my office and sat for a while, staring at my terminal and trying to think of who this could be. Maxine? Trey? It could be any of a dozen hacks who had been in Tokyo while I was there and who were jealous that I had not only gotten out but had succeeded. But Maxine had been the angriest, the most resentful, and in many ways I had been most dismissive of her, reminding her in subtle ways—and sometimes not-so-subtle ways, for I was in my early twenties and possessed the arrogance of youth—that I was more talented than she, more brilliant, and was only passing through Tokyo. My future, I assured her, was in New York, in the media capital of the world, the seat of literary culture. She was, I implied, a bush leaguer, destined to remain in this provincial backwater—at least when it came to publishing in English.

I went back through the document, now looking closely at the allegations about stories I had written for this magazine. I felt like I could almost hear Maxine's Texas drawl in them. Did my boss really expect me to produce notes and backup for articles written nearly ten years ago? And anyway, I felt it was a better strategy to ignore completely these accusations. To respond, I decided, would be to take them seriously, and how could we take seriously an anonymous accusation?

I e-mailed these thoughts to my editor and found it ominous that he didn't immediately reply.

I had to go pick up Alex from day care and take him home for his speech therapy appointment. He was smiling when he saw me, but as I walked toward him I realized he had been fixated on something else, behind me, in the distance.

———

LATER THAT AFTERNOON, I got an e-mail from my boss saying that he, Tyler, and one of the magazine's attorneys wanted to meet with me the next morning. Nothing serious, my boss added, just an informational meeting.

When Marni got home, I showed the document to her and she withdrew into our bedroom to read it while I busied myself in the kitchen.

She was nodding when she came back out. "So?"

"What?"

"Is it true?"

I was shocked. Was the document so persuasive that my own wife would have her doubts about me?

Marni just that day had her brown hair blown out and had that fresh-from-the-salon glow. She was tall and had broad shoulders, which she insisted had resulted in great financial benefits for our family since she could seldom find expensive outfits that fit her frame, and so was now recycling outfits she had been given by designers. She had a small waist and when she wore jeans, as she did now, the narrowness of her legs made her upper body seem almost disproportionate; in build and carriage she seemed a little like a miniature wide-receiver in pads.

Still, she had known me for eight years, and we had been living together for the last six. She didn't wait for me to answer.

"This is going to come out somewhere," she said. "This will end up online."

"But it's unattributed," I said.

"Doesn't matter, you're famous now. Sort of. You're important. This will titillate people. But, but is it true?"

Ah, that was the question. What had so bothered me about the allegations, about the attack, was that it was an almost entirely truthful recitation of my inaccuracies and fabrications. Marni and I had never discussed what she knew or didn't know about the veracity of my work. If she hadn't known when we met, I believed, then she had to have been alerted when she read my second book, which plainly dissembled several stretches of my life that she knew—she must have known!—diverged widely from my actual history.

But success, I had discovered, can blind people to the facts. And I had even come to believe the "facts" of my books and to consider those versions as reliable and accurate as any other. Certainly the proceeds from those books had been real. Look at this condominium. This speech therapist working right now with my son in his room. That diamond on Marni's finger.

I could see, however, that she did not like to admit that all this—or most of it anyway—was based on my prevarications. She was happier when it had all been unstated. And now I handed her this, a document stating that it was all built on lies, and she couldn't help but be reminded of her own doubts.

"What is truth?" I said.

Those big brown eyes betrayed a sudden sadness. Those sensual lips pursed.

"You have to fight this," she said. "You cannot give an inch." She asked what my boss had said.

I told her about the impending meeting.

"Get your own lawyer," she said.

Still, even as Marni gave me this sound advice, she seemed a little bit distant. She was too sophisticated to show any disappointment and too worldly to believe that I was the first journalist who may have fudged it. What she was silently reprimanding me for was putting all of this, our lifestyle, at risk, even if that risk had been laid in long ago.

I suggested to her that this wasn't a big deal. That these stories, my first book, those old articles, it was all old news, literally. "Who cares about stories from the Nineties?"

She didn't respond, but I knew what she was thinking. None of my work could stand up to this kind of scrutiny.

———

BUT WHO WAS making these accusations? Trey? Maxine? Ah, what about Yoshimi? She had once been a studious young journalist. Could this be her life's work? I thought back to my departure from Japan. I had completed my first book and was moving to

New York, where several magazine editors had implied I could expect enough work to make a living.

Yoshimi had been my interpreter for much of that first book, and she had also been a great source of information, of reporting, of wisdom about Japan. She had, in more ways than I care to admit, made the book possible. And I had been generous in my acknowledgments; hers had been the first name I mentioned.

And through the reporting and writing of that book, we had grown close, developing one of those rare relationships where the sexual intensity actually seemed to increase after the initial romance, in part because she had been physically nearby during the writing of the book. During any lulls in the work I would wander into the next room to where she was watching television, slip out of my tracksuit pants, and she would be waiting for me. (I have to admit, I never would feel the same level of easy sexuality with Marni.)

When it was time to leave Japan, it never occurred to me to ask Yoshimi to join me. I didn't need her in New York. She would be a burden, I figured. Assimilating her into Manhattan would be an extra task I did not need at that propitious moment.

With Yoshimi, it was possible to achieve our parting by never talking about it. I knew she was unlikely to bring it up and when I began my preparations, she simply sat on the bar stool next to my kitchen, smoking her ultrathin cigarettes until the day the taxi came to take me to the train station.

I saw her a few times after that, on trips back to Japan, but we never resumed our relationship. Or talked about it.

Had she been quietly seething at having been abandoned by me? It was hard for me to even picture her face now; I could see her body, in the black stirrup pants she always wore back then, behind a cloud of cigarette smoke. She'd always been so loyal. I couldn't imagine her turning on me now.

No, it had to be Maxine.

My agent suggested a good libel attorney but before we could meet to discuss this issue, a Web site about Japan had picked up the document and was running excerpts from it. A link appeared on Gawker almost immediately, along with a terrible photograph of me in a kimono that had appeared on the contributors' page of a travel magazine a few years earlier. This was a perfect schadenfreude item: successful author turns out to be a fraud, sort of, a long time ago, allegedly. They were having fun with it. But anyone who bothered to click on the link to the Web site about Japan would see the damning evidence for themselves.

I had badly underestimated my own fame. And Marni's residual fame. Page Six picked up the item and in the wake of all the other journalism scandals at the *New York Times* and the *New Republic*, this seemed even more titillating, since I was, after all, a best-selling author, and august institutions like the *Columbia Journalism Review* were now on the case as well, calling my boss at the magazine to ask for a comment.

Sumner called me to say that HBO had called him to ask about the controversy. "They didn't know the book was nonfiction," Sumner said. "So I cleared that up. I told them this will all blow over. I reminded them of *The Hitler Diaries*."

"But those were fake," I said.

"Yeah, but didn't the Germans make a movie out of them anyway?"

"Anyway, this is about my first book, not the book they bought."

"Good point."

I had already hung up before I realized how strange it was that HBO was now calling Sumner instead of me.

My attorney had asked the magazine to delay any meeting on the subject until he could go over all the material. He claimed that since I was being libeled by an anonymous source, in Japan no less, this was an exceedingly complicated case that required him to consult with attorneys in Japan before we could respond.

My boss, meanwhile, had asked his research department to dig up whatever documentation existed on those stories. These files, he had been told, were somewhere in Pennsylvania.

The worst thing that could happen to me, Marni and I concluded, was that I would have to resign from the magazine. I talked to my agent about this and he agreed that while it would damage my literary credibility, it would not affect the large advance for my next book. We had an agreement with the publisher, but had not yet gone to contract.

As long as this stayed in the distant past, and was about Japan, how many people would actually care?

A legitimate question could be raised about my work, and that was, did any of it actually seem like nonfiction? The tone, the scenes, the interior dialogue, the entire style of the writing was fictional. Fiction, nonfiction, I never worried about labels and I had learned early on in Tokyo that it didn't seem to make much difference to readers. I had ended up writing nonfiction instead of fiction because of the realities of modern publishing. Magazines wanted journalism; book publishers wanted nonfiction. Who was I not to oblige?

Of course I couldn't tell anyone this, or defend myself by claiming, as I knew very well, that tons of writers were fudging it, faking it, creating composite characters, making up scenes, taking broad license depending on what they felt they could get away with. Nobody ever talked about it, but I couldn't be the only writer who had given in to this temptation. There simply were no rules. A book is published. If it is received as literature, then nobody wonders at the veracity of every detail, and reviewers use phrases like "richly imagined" instead of saying that it is "full of lies." Readers knew, I was sure, that my first book had been "richly imagined," and reviewers had both praised and condemned this attribute. Still, it had stayed steadily in print for more than a decade—twenty paperback printings—and the success of my second book had ensured that it would stay in print forever. (The publisher hadn't yet responded to any of the allegations, but they were requesting a meeting with me to talk about the situation.) But where did a writer go to answer this question, of how much fakery was kosher? In a court of law, none. But in the real world of writers, where was the line?

Nobody knew. This was a game that changed as you played. And who gets caught? The unlucky. Seven times down.

I couldn't tell my boss that. We were meeting in the magazine's conference room, my lawyer seated beside me. My boss, Tyler, and the corporate attorneys—two of them!—across the table from us.

"Don't say too much," my lawyer had advised me.

It was obvious from the venue, the attendees, the body language, that my boss's only concern here was covering his own ass. He did not want to get dragged down like the executive editor of the *New York Times* had because of the malfeasance of an underling. An investigation cost him nothing and provided maximum defense against accusations the magazine hadn't acted quickly enough.

I was maintaining a pose of indignation, both at the accusations and at the fact that the magazine seemed to be taking them seriously. This was an anonymous document; why should that have catalyzed this convening of high-priced legal and editorial talent?

The magazine's position was that it had to take seriously any complaints about the accuracy of its stories. In this climate of intense scrutiny of journalistic ethics, it had no other choice. Tyler tossed out bromides like "The reputation of our brands is built entirely on integrity."

"Thank you for that," I said.

In the past, as my boss and I had discussed one of my stories or our sons, I had seen in his expression, in the cast of his features, the eager widening of his eyes as we spoke, great energy and enthusiasm. Now there was a dullness behind his wire-frame glasses. He had in front of him my notes from those stories, years ago, or at least what could be found at the warehouse in Pennsylvania.

What was apparent was that the stories were entirely sourced to my notes, and, as far as the notes went, the stories were accurate. My attorney argued that was the end of it. His position, and it was a clever counteroffensive, was that all of us, the magazine and I, should be working to find out who was disseminating this material and sue them for libel.

But the notes, I well knew, had been as fabricated as the stories. I had written them *after* I had written the articles—faked interview transcripts, phony description—all of it submitted ex post facto to the research department that was incapable, because of language barriers, of checking for itself.

My boss was still suspicious.

"To completely exonerate you," he said, "we are going to go back and check all of your stories again. To prove beyond a doubt that you are in the right."

My attorney was a tall, skinny gentleman going a little bit bald on top. Still, when he sat back, as he did now, he almost appeared to have a full head of hair from the front. He was smart enough to see that too vigorous an argument against this tack would appear self-incriminating. Why would a reputable journalist argue against a thorough checking of his work? He should, in theory, welcome it.

How many pieces had I written for the magazine? At least twenty; only the first few had been about Japan. The rest had been wide-ranging, but mostly situated in countries where there was a serious language barrier to reporting. A few of them, mostly profiles of famous businessmen, politicians, or athletes, had been more or less accurate. The rest were as full of fancy as my books.

I shrugged. What else could I do?

WHEN I TOLD Marni about the magazine's plan, she shook her head. "How long is this going to take?"

"I don't know."

"If they fire you, we lose our health insurance."

With Alex's disability, his frequent interactions with medical professionals, that would be a costly blow, but considering my vast income, the impending payment for my next books, the TV money—and wouldn't I soon be in the Writers Guild and its excellent health insurance program anyway?—we would survive.

I was no criminal; nothing I had done could be considered a violation of any law. There was still, however, an anxiety I felt at not being able to speak with anyone about the reality of my situation. I had prevaricated, fabricated, whatever you wanted to call it; the document, in many ways, was accurate, and I would become strangely excited as I reread it, which I did frequently, almost gasping as the writer—Maxine?—concluded each carefully constructed argument with a veritable *j'accuse*. In tone and style, I realized, this was a kind of denouncement, similar to what might have been submitted by a neighborhood committee about a class enemy to the Communist Party in Mao's China. But also, in its careful litany of evil deeds, journalistic heresies, it had a little bit of the measured hysteria that might convict a witch in seventeenth-century Germany. All that was left was throwing me into the well to see if I would float.

Why then did I feel a slow-burning desire to walk into my boss's office and level with him, to bare my soul and admit that I had faked it, piped it, cooked it—that I was a fraud? This is why criminals confess: because they are too lazy to work hard on fabricating their innocence and they are too bored to wait out their eventual conviction. It is a little like quitting a game of chess that you know you are almost certainly going to lose anyway. Just get the embarrassment of defeat over.

But Marni, thankfully, was more clearheaded. She would ask what my lawyer said. She would weigh the pros and cons of various approaches. She would advise me on dealing with the media, hiring a publicist. But through all this, I could detect a certain distance, as if she were among those disappointed by me. She had told me she wanted me to be her one true thing.

My conversations with my attorney were clipped, concerned as I was about his fees. He had required a $5,000 retainer, and I was afraid to ask how much he charged per hour, per phone call. But he had come so highly recommended and was so frequently in the newspaper, associated with high-profile cases, that I knew this was going to cost me new-car kind of money, at least.

Still, my wife pointed out, repeatedly, that this would blow over. These were still, ultimately, old accusations. And so what if the magazine dug up some obscure factual discrepancies or incomplete verification of old stories? That was still trivia as far as the general public, the book-buying public, was concerned. This was still all in the realm of inside media, the kind of hair-splitting that New York journalists and editors did while the rest of the country happily went on reading books like my second one. They cared about the story, she reminded me, about my ability to put you right there, with me, as I struggled with my demons.

———

PERHAPS ONE OF the saddest aspects of fathering an autistic boy is that you wonder how much of his experience he is filing away. Is he building up a well of happy memories? We want our children to have these joyous recollections, a sense of well-being about their childhoods. Why? So that in life's inevitable dark moments, they can call on this as evidence they were once happy and thus will be happy again. But with Alex, even as we took a walk on a beautiful spring morning to the playground, and then to the river where the light and the warming but still brisk air were so gorgeous you knew that through the course of your whole life you get maybe ten days like this, as I pushed him on the swing and he did his liturgy of mumbled consonants, "De-de-de-de-de-de-de," and he twiddled his fingers together and rocked his head—I knew I was supposed to curtail his self-stimming whenever it happened, but he seemed so content at that instant that I was reluctant to intervene—I found myself lost in that question: if Alex is so existential that he can't recall happiness, does that make him less cumulatively happy?

He was so pretty, sitting there in his swing, his blond hair bouncing in the breeze. He had my wife's sharp nose and almost feline eyes—he was lucky in that—but he had my mouth.

It seemed so unfair that anything this bad should happen to me while I had just suffered the misfortune of having a developmentally disabled son. Where was the justice in that? I decided that was why this would blow over; I just had to hold steady. This was the bad part, and even if I had to resign from the magazine, I would still be fine. Eight times up, right?

———

WHEN ALEX WAS diagnosed, Marni had thrown herself into the autism world, joining the board of Autism Speaks, socializing with the celebrities who were now flocking to the cause. Having been born too late to witness the March of Dimes and the campaign to eradicate polio, I had never seen a disability marketed and packaged so successfully. When I began noticing the television commercials of lovely actresses sternly facing the camera and spouting statistics—1 in 250, then 1 in 170, then 1 in 70—I realized they had rebranded autism, a lifelong, chronic condition, as a childhood disability, as the March of Dimes had done with polio when they renamed it Infantile Paralysis. But as I considered Alex's future prospects, I knew that all the autistic boys and girls will grow up, and while the funding and research were now being intensely focused on ever earlier intervention and treatment, the reality was that there would be millions of grown-up autistic men and women. What about them?

It had been Marni who came up with selling the kids. That is, she had chaired the Autism Speaks committee that had worked with the agency to conceive the strategy. The kids were adorable, after all, far more beautiful than the grotesque and often unkempt adult autistics. Who wants to give money to a self-destructive middle-aged man who can't talk? But the children, like Alex, were cute. Millions were now pouring into the foundations funding research, all because, I wanted to tell Marni, of a little lie.

―――――――――

AT NIGHT, I would lie awake trying to figure out who hated me so. We flatter ourselves to think that all those we have known spend much of the rest of their lives thinking about us. But here, in this document, written with such barely restrained animus, was evidence that someone indeed had spent a great portion of his or her life thinking about me.

But who, and when would they stop? I had gone online and noticed that Trey's new magazine was giving a great deal of space to the controversy on its Web site; a reporter from the magazine had e-mailed me asking for an interview and I had passed the query along to my attorney. The story was rousing interest over there because my first book had joined the canon of books by foreigners about Japan. Perhaps Trey had been jealous. I had detected a certain distance the last time we met, years ago, in New York. Did I too easily reveal my dismissiveness? Perhaps I had shown that I considered him beneath me, but should I have pretended otherwise? Yes, I now thought, perhaps it wasn't Maxine. It must have been Trey.

In the U.S., however, the furor over my little scandal was showing signs of petering out. The magazine continued its investigation, and I took a leave of absence. According to my attorney, as long as I never pushed for reinstatement, it was very possible that the matter would just be dropped, as long as the media interest in the subject continued to wane. No one else, apparently, had the energy, ability, or inclination to investigate a bunch of decade-old stories. My attorney, when he had been reached for comment by one of the media Web sites, had been masterful at downplaying the significance of the accusations and overstating the Byzantine complexity—"We don't think the correct transliteration of the name of a thirteenth-century Shinto priest should be a matter of much hand-wringing." He assured me this would just become one of those curious little footnotes to an otherwise fine career.

I WOKE UP that morning with several concurrent thoughts. There was the practical matter: at some point I had to get over to our garage to pick up the Range Rover—and while I was thinking about the garage, had I mailed in their monthly payment? (Our choice of automobile had lately become a source of concern for Marni, now that she had become a resolute environmentalist.) Then there was the issue of children, as in should we have more of them? Since this small scandal had begun, Marni and I had postponed the conversation about whether Alex should have siblings. It was complicated by the fact that we both believed it would be too much of a burden for any child to only have Alex as a sibling. But if we had two—or twins, as Tribeca couples now seemed prone to spawning—then that would make it somehow easier for all of them. Marni had worried that two more children would mean at least five more years before she could seriously get back to work.

She, too, had books she wanted to write, magazine articles she had turned down, board positions she could have accepted. The sacrifice, she correctly argued, was hers. There was no financial reason for her to go back to work, we both agreed, but the human ego is a fragile thing and Marni, as pretty as she was, had always been a little bit concerned about not being taken seriously because of her looks.

Marni had done the research, checked into our genealogy, and while there was a slight chance of a second autistic child, it seemed worth the risk and, I really believed this, it would be better for Alex in the long run. Marni and I were not going to live forever.

We couldn't wait that long to make a decision, however. The many women's magazines that came to the loft were constantly reminding us that every year past thirty-five a woman loses some alarming percentage likelihood of becoming pregnant. Perhaps we just had to charge ahead and see how far we got.

I was also, for the first time, feeling like this little brouhaha was finally blowing over. At coffee a few mornings ago, the guys never even mentioned my pseudo-scandal. I no longer went into the magazine and, to tell the truth, I didn't miss it at all. I had my HBO script, which I needed to begin working on. Perhaps I would resettle out on the North Fork for a while, work on my script and my next book, and enjoy the leisure I had earned. But: Alex. We didn't have a program for him out there and so I would have to head back into the city frequently anyway. Maybe we should just move one of the behavior-modification specialists out there with us, install her in a guest bedroom. Thank god for the money I was making. Right?

———

I WAS ALMOST out the door, hoping to get a quick cup of coffee with the drop-off guys, when I checked my e-mail and felt a sinking sensation in my shoulders. In my inbox were two dozen

requests for interviews and comments from various news organi-
zations and magazines. There were twenty-seven new messages in
my voice mailbox.

It took one Web search under my name to turn up a new document, clearly prepared by the same person, posted on that same
Web site in Japan, but now about my second book. Someone had
searched through arrest records in Nevada and discovered the only
court document that included my name related to an appearance
in traffic court. No mention of an arrest for breaking and entering,
no mention of a brawl with TSA officers. The article made very
clear that the incidents described in my book, on pages 97–111 and
134–156, could not have happened. They were fabrications, which
threw the rest of the narrative very much into doubt. In other
words, this best-selling book, with 260,000 copies in print and a
few hundred thousand more paperbacks now making their way to
bookstores across the country, was a fraud. This new accusation,
which built convincingly on the old document, was immediately
reverberating in the media echo-chamber—CNN and Huffington
Post already had it high up on their home pages.

I was momentarily dazed as I rode the elevator downstairs and
walked to the garage to pick up my car. Marni had dropped Alex
off at his day-care program and was presumably on her way home.
I thought of calling her but instead called my attorney, whose assistant had been giving out no comments on my behalf all morning.

"What is this shit?" he asked me.

Another caller was trying to break into my line. I checked my
phone and saw it was my agent.

"I don't know. It's bullshit. What do I do?"

"This isn't a legal matter anymore," he said. "No one is taking
any action against you. The magazine is no longer the center of
attention. This is for your publicist or your agent."

I called my agent. "How bad is this for me?"

"I don't know," she said. Then her tone changed slightly, almost to pleading. "Are they wrong, are they completely wrong?"

I paused a moment too long. I had to say they were wrong, but when the truth leaked out, as it would, I might then lose her as an ally. Still, right now, what choice did I have? "Of course they're wrong."

She had noticed how long it took me to respond. "Don't say anything to anyone. Not yet."

I asked if I should talk to my book publicist.

My agent pointed out the publicist worked for my publisher, not for me. I was surprised to hear that our interests were not necessarily aligned anymore.

One of the guys I had coffee with, the playwright Levi-Levy, texted me, "Whos a full o'shit bastard?"

Then another: "Steak&martinis on me!"

Then Marni's number showed up on my caller ID. "Everyone's calling," she said. "It's disgusting. Their tone, they are almost gleeful that you've been taken down."

I was in my car now driving down Greenwich. Where was I going?

Several times I turned toward the West Side Highway and the Battery Tunnel, planning to head out to Long Island, each time turning back around. Part of me felt I should just go ahead, look at a few houses, fuck it all, but then I would feel another wave of panic. It reminded me, actually, of swimming in the Caribbean off an otherwise pristine stretch of beach and then suddenly seeing a Portuguese man-o'-war hovering in the water just a few feet away, that sudden jab of panic, a primal waking up of my flight instinct. I could only imagine the fun all the media Web sites were having with this, perhaps the biggest takedown yet, a blockbuster writer exposed as a fraud.

I frequently had to pee.

I would pull the car over, on Chambers or Warren or West Broadway—I was spending my morning driving all through Tribeca—and just freeze for a while, mumbling, "Oh fuck." My career might be over. I would leave my car with emergency lights on in a red zone and trot into Giorgio's or Giancarlo's Bakery or Bubby's and use the toilet—the staff all knew me and didn't think twice about seeing me running through the restaurant.

Again, I wondered, who did this? This document, this admirably thorough work, combing legal databases for court documents, that was in keeping with Maxine's diligent character. She had always been relentless at pursuing her ideas: the founding of the magazine in Tokyo had been her pet project and she had stuck with it for years after I had left, despite having little aptitude for magazine editing. When I Googled her, I could see that her last job had been working in the English language division at a Japanese publisher, but the publisher shut down that vanity project a year ago. So she had time on her hands. And there was a relentlessness to this that also seemed in keeping with her character. She could work tirelessly.

My wife called to tell me the news was on CNN. "They have a dean from some journalism school talking about journalism as a public trust, and you, apparently, have violated that trust."

"But this wasn't, isn't, journalism."

"Nobody cares," she said. She actually seemed to be enjoying this, a little, the publicity, the notoriety, the unfolding scandal.

I told her I was freaking out, that I couldn't believe people were making such a big deal about this. And then I added, with hope, "As long as we're together."

"Of course," she said, and then told me she was going to pick up Alex.

As I was driving back to the garage, I thought of all the ways a writer's life could go wrong: never actually writing anything (somehow, that seemed the most pure failure), losing one's nerve, never having enough time to write, never getting published, never achieving recognition, never making a living, never fulfilling early promise, spending one's career doing the wrong sort of writing, having one's work censored, being imprisoned, always feeling un- derappreciated, becoming jealous, bitter, angry, resentful, dying undiscovered.

I seemed to have come up with a whole new way to fuck up as a writer.

———

OR HAD I? In all the stories written about my career, nobody pointed out the obvious, that writers have always fabricated their stories. Instead of comparing me to Jayson Blair, Stephen Glass, Janet Cooke, why not compare me to Daniel Defoe, Stephen Crane, or a host of other fine writers whose fiction was first published as nonfiction? Why not Bruce Chatwin or Ryszard Kapuscinski, whose fabrications were always celebrated as metaphorical mas- terpieces? Why wasn't I considered one of those writers who used invention not to falsify truth but to sharpen it, enhance it, make it more vivid? Anyway, what was the damage, really? Shouldn't the success of my book have at least elicited a comparison to a better writer than a daily newspaper hack who made up some quotes? They could at least have compared me to Clifford Irving or that lady who wrote as if she was a gay truck-stop hooker.

I did make the mistake of going on a television talk show, where I tried to explain that personal memoir had always been an impres- sionistic rather than factual genre. The white-haired newscaster—in person, he had a tiny head shaped like a pencil eraser—then brought up my work for the magazine, and I was reduced to pointing out that the allegations were all anonymous, and that no independent expert had proven that I'd made mistakes. Another major misstep. Nearly a half-dozen Web sites over the next three days came up with dozens of examples of errors and flaws in my work.

My editor at my publishing house was very disappointed by my performance and told me the publisher was considering suspending publication of the paperback, or at the very least putting in a disclaimer about the accuracy of the material.

The other parents at Alex's program started to shun me. They brushed by me after drop-off without saying anything, avoiding my glance, not that I particularly wanted their company. But come on, soon the autistic themselves would shun me, though avoiding such interaction was a symptom of the condition anyway, so how would I know I was being shunned?

The TV deal was off, my agent told me. I could keep the money I had already been paid for the option—less than a year of special education for Alex—but the larger, deferred payments would not be forthcoming.

I called Sumner. If HBO was no longer interested, how about Showtime? Or FX? Or perhaps it could be a feature? Sumner was quiet and then told me that based on what he had been reading online, he didn't feel he could in good conscience work with me anymore.

IT WAS AMAZING to me how quickly my circumstances had changed. Marni would look at me accusingly, and I could read in her expression an implied question: what are we going to do now? There was still her money—does it always come down to money?—and more coming in from the paperback publication. The disclaimer—practically a stamped FRAUD! on the cover—had been negotiated by my agent and publisher and didn't initially put off readers; BookScan numbers over the first few weeks were good enough to keep my book on bestseller lists everywhere. But what was the trendy phrase everyone was using now? My book didn't have a long tail. Those early sales, it seemed, were fueled by curiosity about this book being in the news.

Marni told me at one point: "I do not want to sell the loft."

I actually thought it would be better to sell it and move some-place remote where nobody knew me. Ibiza. Bali. Philadelphia. But Marni wouldn't have it. She had never been as wealthy or connected as the gossip columns suggested, but still, this was her world, and she had no intention of sacrificing it so that I could rehabilitate myself.

And what would we do with Alex? He had his programs, his professional support. We couldn't just move him to a new country and restart his learning.

This wasn't the time to mention that despite all the expensive programs, therapies, operant-conditioning sessions, Alex didn't exactly seem on the road to wellness. He was still profoundly distant and, I had to admit, pretty damn weird. I doubted he would ever be a regular kid in a normal school; I didn't think he would ever understand that it wasn't acceptable to pick his nose and eat his snot in public. But oh how I loved him. Plus, in the midst of this whole scandal, Alex, of course, had been com-pletely oblivious.

I was watching Marni with Alex one morning, spoon-feeding him gluten-free breakfast cereal, and I suddenly realized that the main reason Marni was staying with me was him. Our son, our autistic boy, was simply too much for her to handle on her own. Otherwise, I suspected, Marni would have a few months ago taken Alex and left me to my sad little fate.

————

I DIDN'T WANT to go out, to meet old friends, to join other writ-ers and editors. Book parties would have been horrible, and dis-tracting for the author whom we were ostensibly celebrating. The community that had once thrown its doors open to me, asking if I could host a table to raise money for this cause or appear on behalf of this literary journal, was now offering me only silence. Not surprisingly, nobody asked me to write for them. I was in a kind of internal exile.

Marni, on the other hand, was getting more assignments than she could handle, more board requests, more invitations. Her byline became, in a matter of months, the most sought-after in town, a symbol of a certain connectedness. The editors who gave her those assignments always asked after me, sent me their regards, but always stopped there. It was the kind of best wishes sent to the family of a convicted murderer: you pitied them for their hardship while knowing full well that the guy was a guilty bastard.

DEFEATED MEN, IN the best of times, are only interesting when they still have some power. Pompey, Marc Antony, Hannibal. True defeat leaves a man alone and therefore of much less interest to historians, I suppose, and to women. Compare Napoleon at Elba versus Napoleon at St. Helena. In the first instance, he still has his court and all the intrigue and possibility that entails; in the second, he is reduced to begging for a larger sugar ration from the English captain who commands the rock on which he is exiled.

In my defeat, I had become similarly uninteresting. Nobody called, nothing new happened in my life, and I soon found myself wondering if perhaps I should take up the study of a new language, learn Spanish and read Cervantes.

I had spent plenty of time mulling over who had taken me down and concluded that on my own, I might never discover who it was. It was better not to know, I decided. Revenge isn't sweet unless you can show yourself to the victim. So for now, I took some small pleasure in not being sure who it had been. Trey? Maxine? I didn't know and told myself I didn't care.

I took long walks with Alex. I delivered him to school in the morning, and picked him up in the afternoon. Marni was busy with her writing and charity careers and I couldn't think of anything else I would rather be doing. These were Alex's first five words: Corn, Book, Dog, Ball, and Dad.

I knew that annoyed Marni.

It was only a coincidence that Alex said "Dad" the day she served me with divorce papers. That wasn't a terrible surprise—is it ever, really? She had discussed it with me several times, but I had always assumed this was one possible scenario and that there were others that we hadn't discussed.

She looked happy, like she was thriving. I was the one who wasn't happy. We were sitting at our round table, in the portion of the loft that served as our dining area.

Are these conversations always so cliché-ridden? Working? Not working? I thought of one of those contraptions where you drop a marble into a tube and it rolls through all sorts of tunnels and turns and then bumps into a domino that sets a whole row of dominos falling until one drops onto a scale that tips so that water pours from a bowl into a pipe and so forth so that in the end, after a dozen other little connections are made, a lightbulb turns on. I guess a marriage is sort of like that—this ultimately trivial-seeming set of connections that has to be in place so that in the end, there is either light or darkness.

Marni looked at me and I recalled my first glimpse of her across that editorial meeting. Electrifying.

"I don't believe you anymore," she said.

I couldn't really make any argument against our divorce. Marni had always been smarter than me and, truth be known, probably a better writer.

———

WHEN MARNI'S BOOK about our marriage and my scandal was published a year later, it was greeted warmly, sold respectably, and was optioned to become a film. She was attached as the screenwriter. Her income and her family's money now kept her and Alex comfortable and the stream of specialists steadily paid.

When I read her book about our lives, I wasn't surprised to discover she had made the whole thing up, cooked it as thoroughly as I had my own book. But then that made sense, didn't it? It was published as a novel.

I told you she is smarter than me.

––––––––––

I MOVED FOR a time to Jersey City, working for a semester as a substitute teacher and tutor for children for whom English was a second language. If I had the money, I might have gone back to school to get a teaching certificate. As it was, I needed to pay for my car and the insurance so I could drive into the city every weekend and several times a week to see Alex. He lived with his mother, in our old loft, and it was agreed as part of the divorce that I would have unlimited visitation and the option of joint custody. Marni and I were forced by Alex's condition to be far more amicable than most couples are in similar circumstances.

One Tuesday, we attended a conference with Alex's teachers: he was now sorting shapes and patterns—and even holding a pencil and drawing shapes—but had no interest in people, even in other children. He had also developed a disconcerting habit of immediately dropping old words when he picked up new ones, so that his vocabulary seemed to have frozen at about two hundred words. He was getting dressed by himself, could brush his teeth, and— Marni was particularly jubilant about this latest achievement—was almost completely toilet-trained. Marni and I knew all this about Alex, of course; parent-teacher conferences about the autistic are usually a formality. But he was beautiful, his teachers said, such a lovely child.

After I returned home to my apartment in Jersey City, I found a letter from my old magazine. At first, the sight of the magazine's venerable logo excited me. Even the coarse, heavy stock of the envelope quickened my blood for a moment. In an instant, however, I recalled my status, my permanent exile. I opened it to find a forwarded envelope on thinner stock, from Tokyo, Japan, sent months before.

I knew what this must be. Somehow, I'd been waiting for it.

I opened it to read the handwritten note from Yoshimi. She had researched and authored those attacks and now she wanted to be sure I knew it. I was surprised that she still seemed angry. It seemed that such effort should have at least freed her from hating me. Otherwise, what was the point? Near the conclusion, she gloated, "You could never cut it in MY game." She added that she had found one additional mistake in my book, a very basic one. The old Yakuza saying, in actuality, was "Seven Times UP, Eight Times DOWN."

She was wrong. That had not been a mistake.

In the end, I still believe, you don't always lose.

113 NORTH MOORE

T he last day of school, already warm, the mothers in summer dresses, pale arms not yet brown from sun, the fathers in T-shirts, shorts, sandals, the children making their noisy way through the gate one last time, their backpacks now worn out of habit rather than necessity, the year's class work already sent home. The oldest of the children, the fifth-graders, were making this turn for the last time. They had already visited next year's middle school but were too young to be apprehensive about that impending transition. For now, they looked forward to summer, to camps and beach houses and trips upstate or to Europe, to swimming, splashing, to ice cream and the sun-soaked hubbub of the hot months.

Here they were, the sculptor, the playwright, the memoirist, the producer, the sound engineer, the photographer—even the gangster made an appearance, did a fist bump with each of the men, wishing them a great summer before he climbed into his large black vehicle and drove north. His son was graduating this year, and though his daughter was only going into fifth grade, she too would be leaving for a new school in September.

They were not necessarily liked, these men, but they were known by the community, and could be seen as a core of sorts, the masculine center of power and wealth and prestige, or at least the appearance of such. The producer, Sumner, led them down Chambers, past the vacant retail spaces where there used to be a bakery the children liked, and another retail cavity where there used to be a bar, and so forth. All the men, occasionally, in the quiet early-morning hours when sleep eluded, worried at their diminishing wealth, at their cracking nest eggs. Rumors spread of short sales amid a loft market frozen in nuclear winter—no buyers, no sales at any price. If just a few months or a year ago the nominal value of their lofts and property had given each an expansiveness when it came to imagining their prospects, they were now seeing futures that seemed just a little more cramped; their three thousand square feet in Tribeca was worth 30 percent less than yesterday. So as they walked past the shuttered retail spaces, the signs proclaiming 2000SF RETAIL alongside a commercial realtor's name and phone number, they didn't comment, but to a man, it made them uneasy.

They reached their destination, their last remaining breakfast joint. The steak house they once loved no longer served breakfast; the market that had stood on the corner for decades, Bazzini's, was gone; Socrates on Hudson Street closed, the proprietor sending them off his last morning with an *"Adios amigos"*—so they now were stuck with a restaurant where on Sundays they sometimes had to brunch *en famille*; on weekday mornings, they could order overpriced eggs, bland toast, only one kind of bagel. There was the usual argument, to sit inside or out, alfresco in Manhattan meaning sharing the sidewalk with bike messengers, dogs on their morning constitutionals, the bleet trucks backing up, and the stench of exhaust. But they sat outside, and newspapers were spread open and coffee was ordered and there was nothing to mark this occasion, no ceremony to note that these men would never all be together at the same table again. There was just more of the usual banter and small talk, the self-aware wittiness verging on smugness that would put off anyone who wasn't them, the vulgarity and obscenity that men delight in when there are no women around, the quick disseminating of summer plans, the polite asking after children and wives.

What held these men together? Even now, looking around at each other they wondered. The sound engineer staring at Sumner with disgust, the playwright thinking the sculptor a dull-witted goy, the memoirist resenting all of them for not speaking up on his behalf during his public castigation, the photographer thinking, generally, why did he ever hang around with such a gang of unattractive mediocrities. They were pulled together by coincidence, having children roughly the same age in the same school. They felt some kinship because of who they weren't—they weren't attorneys or bankers or hedge fund runners as were so many of the new fathers just moving in to Tribeca. But from this idea of what they weren't, could a real bond be forged? Did they just not want to eat breakfast alone?

This is what fell over them each as they picked through their disappointing eggs and oatmeal, drank thin, watery coffee—Why were they here?

For each man saw in the others his own shortcomings. None of them was as successful as they once dreamed. Each might be wealthy by some global standard of accounting, but by the local measures of bankers and entertainment moguls they were middle-class. Levi-Levy asked himself, Why did the photographer live in relative splendor while a genius like me makes do merely with a very spacious loft? Why, Mark thought, is the sculptor allowed to carry on his affair with impunity while my drunken dalliance could end up destroying my life? Why, wondered Brick, is the photographer celebrated as a fine artist—a special issue of *V* devoted to his work, Lehmann Maupin curating his photographs of celebrities—while I still have to supplicate in hopes of a show at BravinLee? It could drive men apart, these small jealousies. The easygoing friendships of college and young manhood were as distant now as a collegiate summer romance. The relationships now all felt freighted; each felt like the others were the reason for his disappointments.

————

THE MOLESTER, MARK told them, he was never real—or so the indifferent law enforcers concluded. The girl was making up her story, the voice on her phone nothing more than a few minutes of Jerry Orbach from an old *Law & Order*. She tearfully admitted such to a female juvenile crimes officer. The whole story had been in the local free weekly. Her father still refused to believe it, couldn't bring himself to confront her, and accused the detectives of manufacturing this tale to hide their failure to bring the perpetrator to justice. This gossip hadn't been passed along with the same gusto as the initial news of the alleged crime.

"They are dropping the case; the girl's story has inconsistencies. The father knows something horrible happened to his daughter," Sumner reported. "But the police aren't interested in pursuing it."

That, Sumner proclaimed, was the real scandal. And then more innuendo, more confusions, rumors, the girl was bought off, the father was hiring private detectives, the local community rags weren't covering this story anymore because of the further hit to property values such an anecdote might cause.

So the anxiety was left to simmer, now unfocused and undirected. Who or what was now threatening the children? The fathers couldn't say, but there was still the notion that something sinister was at large.

Sumner, the producer, was always eager to mention the threats, the fears, the siege they were all under. It wasn't enough that a guard now patrolled Washington Market Park, that cameras were trained on the play structures, that you couldn't enter the school during school hours, that to sit down at Bubby's on a weekend unencumbered by infants and toddlers made you the recipient of suspicious glances. Sumner had inveigled for more. He suggested the erection of an electrified fence around Tribeca, as that would keep out the molesters. (Unless the molester lived among us!) The rest no longer gave him full credence, but his insistent drone of concern had its unsteadying effect. It was Sumner's voice they would hear when they considered perhaps letting their eleven-year-old walk the three blocks to the playground by himself. No, better not, for what if, what if?

There was no way to refute a rumor, no argument could be made against irrational panic. So that even Mark's measured, careful explanation that it had all turned out to be a false alarm, a bout of teen hysteria, the hoax of a confused girl, drifted into an eddy of cross-talk and conjecture.

"What child-molester?" the playwright Levi-Levy asked, having forgotten, or never really considered, the threat.

And so the whole matter was explained again by Sumner; between coffee sips and forkfuls of eggs, he again laid out the causes for alarm.

And Mark said again, "Shut the fuck up, Sumner, why are you doing this again?"

"What?"

"Talking nonsense."

But Sumner stared him down, and it seemed to Mark as if Sumner knew about his dalliance with the nanny—of legal age, but still, guilty, guilty, guilty. So Mark kept quiet.

———

BRICK THE SCULPTOR decided then and there, because of his fear, because of his worry, that he would stop joining for breakfast. Why spend twenty dollars on eggs and coffee, twenty dollars he might not be able to afford in the near future. Perhaps the right move was to start hoarding canned goods, he decided, head out to Peconic, start laying in staples, some fuel, maybe a hunting rifle.

He explained his idea to the gathered fathers, to become a survivalist, of sorts, to hoard against the day civilization breaks down.

"Have you lost your mind?" Mark said.

"When the masses rise up and we can't use our iPhones anymore and Wolfgang's runs out of steak, will you open for me a can of beans?" Levi-Levy said.

"You're on your own," Brick warned.

"Well," Sumner said, "I might as well tell you guys now. We're moving. We put our place on the market, rented it out. So, assuming our tenants pass the board this afternoon . . ."

Mark hadn't realized Sumner was trying to rent out his place. Or had he known and forgotten?

"To where?"

"Westport."

Mark knew Westport, Connecticut. Big houses, good schools, white people. (Basically just like Tribeca, only more so.)

"Oh, well, that's good," Mark said perfunctorily. "Probably safer for the kids."

"Definitely," Sumner nodded, "definitely. A lot of folks are moving out."

"I hadn't noticed that," Mark said, "but that doesn't mean it's not a trend: Escape from Tribeca."

"Yeah, while you still can," Sumner said.

———

MARK TURNED RIGHT upon leaving the restaurant, staying close to the buildings and out of the spray of a light rain. And just as he was making his way home, he saw Sadie, pedaling over cobblestones on her big, old bicycle. Shit, he didn't want to see her now—ever—and intentionally avoided Lispenard because that was her street, but this was Franklin and here she was.

She didn't look like a child. With her scarf, thick-frame glasses, and vintage romper, she looked more like, well, Amelia Earhart.

He couldn't fathom whatever lust had momentarily swelled for her. She had nothing of that nubile, prosthetic sexuality too familiar now from Internet porn and music videos—Sadie had the sexuality of a stenographer at work.

He had embarrassed himself not only with his act, but by his partner. But wait a second, he thought, who was he, late thirties, verging on middle age, heading into the third turn perhaps, to be judging?

Sadie saw him making his way down Franklin, past the atelier with an Asian name no one in the neighborhood had ever seen anyone enter or depart, and steered in his direction, immediately, without hesitation.

Over the past few months they had been often in each other's vicinity, she still had been caring for his children, yet they had had no more than ten minutes of conversation between them. Drop-offs, pickups, payment, hours, that was all arranged by Brooke. Mark spent more time arranging bank transfers from his studio account to her account, figuring how to hide them as equipment purchases and lease payments, than he had spent talking to Sadie. Which was fine with him.

"So," she said, putting her plimsolled feet down on the pavement, steadying the bike.

He nodded. "Hello, Sadie." He didn't know what tone to take. Angry? Sad? Defeated? Indifferent? He opted for a mechanical monotone.

"So, I'm going to Wellesley," she said, as if he had been awaiting her decision.

He didn't know what to say. "Did you consider a state school?" he said.

"You mean Purchase? Or Binghamton?"

He didn't know the names of state colleges. He shrugged.

"They're supposed to be good," she said, "but I decided to go to the best school I got into, because, you know, I'm not worried about the money."

"I guess not," he couldn't resist saying.

"So, I told Brooke my last day is July first. I'm going to be a counselor at this camp, and then, you know, college."

Mark felt a sudden surge of pride at Sadie's success. "Wellesley? Isn't that where Obama went to school? No, wait, Hillary Clinton? Right? Didn't she go there?"

Sadie nodded. "Well," she said, "Mark, I want you to know that I really love your kids. You have two great daughters, a really cool family."

Where did an eighteen-year-old get this kind of composure? he wondered. Oh yeah, in Tribeca.

Sadie continued, "And I don't want to ruin your family. So, well, after these funds I've gotten from you, that's it. I'm not one of those people who is going to keep coming back and back and asking for more. So, I wanted you to know that, because I feel guilty and weird."

You should, he almost said, you should feel guilty and weird. Then he thought, so that was the price? A hundred thousand dollars? And now he is free?

"Sadie," Mark said, "you're going to do very well."

"Thanks, Mark."

She mounted her bicycle and pedaled away down Franklin.

———————

HE MADE A decision at that moment to tell his wife everything. He was tired of this hiding. His initial calculation, that the marriage was worth the dishonesty, that the value of the unit was greater than the integrity of any of its constituent parts, was mistaken. Marriages must rest on sound foundation—he surprised himself by his embrace of this bourgeois notion, but then look at his life: he surrendered to the perquisites of that class long ago, so how could he now be questioning the values that came with it?

But how to inform his wife of his transgression, his only

transgression, albeit with the babysitter? Does it being a cliché make it less or more of a violation, easier or harder to excuse? Brooke would be furious. At the act, and then, he supposed, at this woman for staying and working in their loft these past several months. Sadie was to go off to college in the fall, that being the terms of their blackmail. And she was such an unassuming girl, to pull a stunt like this.

The rain now diminishing, sunlight popped through hazy clouds, and for a moment there was that disorienting sight of drizzle amid sunshine. Mark decided he wasn't quite ready to see Brooke, and would instead go to his studio and check the schedule. Work was slowing down, for sure. Marketing budgets had contracted, meaning advertising spends were down, so fewer commercials were being produced and so less studio time was required. Everyone was trying to get a deal, saying they would take off-peak, short-notice space if that meant a better hourly rate. He had no choice but to accommodate, which added up to a few thousand dollars less a month in income—he had long ago set aside and subtracted the tens of thousands for Sadie. But he had somehow known during the boom years, when his loft and his studio spaces were all appreciating and his income rising, that that was aberrational. Rich people were, well, different, mysterious in their sources of wealth—dynasties or trusts or vast timber or mining holdings, or at least they did something unfathomable and now discredited in finance. You were not supposed to become wealthy by, essentially, owning space and letting it by the hour, like the proprietor of some No-Tell Motel, yet that was exactly what Mark's income stemmed from, all those hours, which during the good years had been a great many hours indeed.

Of course, it helped that Brooke could tap vast family resources. His girls would never know a day of hunger, an hour of insecurity about shelter, clothes, warmth. He knew enough to know that he had no real financial problems.

Yes, he could end up living on scrambled eggs, or takeout Thai food and the bar menu at Odeon if Brooke decided enough was enough. Could she ever forgive him? Should she? Or would there follow the predictable moving out to a rental somewhere in the Financial District and uneasy joint custody, sales of the real estate, the business, dividing of assets? And he the cast-out man, the philanderer who destroyed a charmed home, the schmuck who tore apart his family lusting after a kid, barely eighteen. Wives were fickle, wives were unpredictable, you just never knew if they would stay or go. Look at Rick; his wife, Marni, scrammed at his scandal. But who knew what else Rick might have been doing? Perhaps in addition to fabricating memoirs he, too, had been screwing the help.

But still he felt that telling his wife would be, as politicians caught in a scandal always say, the right thing to do. This is the time, he thought, this is the moment when he can start all over, with or without beloved Brooke. The time has come, he tried to convince himself, to come clean.

He was walking down Church, past one of the terrible Italian places, when he came upon Sumner again, with his two daughters riding on Razor scooters. Ah yes, he remembered, last day of school is a half day. Brooke must be with the girls right now.

Sumner had not yet noticed him, and so he considered a hasty crossing of the street, but then there was Sumner's grin.

"Hey Mark."

Mark nodded in greeting. He didn't want to see Sumner, not now, not ever. But he was stuck.

"Well, it's official," Sumner said, folding his arms. He had sunglasses folded into the top of his V-neck T-shirt.

Official? Mark worried this was more molester-related news. Some new statistics perhaps, the latest white paper from Protect the Children?

"We're definitely moving. Our tenants passed the board."

"Hm," Mark said. "Escape from Tribeca before your children are sodomized."

Sumner didn't find that funny.

The daughters were becoming impatient, their silver scooters at rest on the slick sidewalk. Their helmets glistened from drizzle. Sumner turned to them. "Val, Chantal, stay out of the street."

"And Mark," he said, "let's get a drink, before we go. Or coffee."

Mark nodded. He was sure he would never have to see Sumner again.

———

MARK WANTED A drink. He walked over to the steak house and sat at the bar, where he ordered a martini, which he knew was a mistake, and then decided he may as well have lunch and ordered a rib eye and spinach and a baked potato and said he'd take lunch in the dining room. The floor-to-ceiling windows at the front of the restaurant looked out on Greenwich, at the investment bank across the street—whose employees filled this restaurant at night—and the line of town cars idling next to the curb. Across Hubert was another stalled condominium complex. He recalled reading online about the sponsor's financial problems, the buyers suing to get out of their contracts, yet as he studied the building now, the graceful arches, the vast windows, the elaborate masonry, it looked like the structural embodiment of prosperity. Only now, instead of a rich man living on the third floor, a yoga studio had rented the space. Perhaps if his receipts kept on declining, he, too, would have to sublet to a yoga entrepreneur. The yoga industry seemed recession-proof.

In walked Levi-Levy, wearing heart-shaped sunglasses, a Hulk T-shirt, and pants with rainbows on them.

He was genuinely pleased to see Levi-Levy, though he detected, for a moment, an uneasiness in him.

"Aren't those rainbows the symbol for gayness?" Mark said, attempting to make a joke. "Are you wearing pants that are sending coded messages to other guys that you are available?"

Levi-Levy smiled at this, and whatever initial reservations he'd had when spotting Mark now seemed to have evaporated.

"I hope so," Levi-Levy said, and took a seat at the table.

He ordered a martini as well, and steak. They talked for a while about Sumner and his moving to the suburbs, about other families who were fleeing Tribeca.

"Pussies," Levi-Levy said.

Mark regarded Levi-Levy as capricious, flaky, unreliable, a bad husband, failed artist, and lazy drunkard: the perfect person with whom to discuss his newfound desire for clarity and truth in his marriage.

Levi-Levy was quiet as he listened to Mark describe this potential scandal—so much more interesting than anything they had ever discussed during their innumerable morning coffees together. And Levi-Levy even forgot during the tale that he had, for a brief and wonderful while, been cuckolding this man himself. Only a genius like him, he reasoned, could separate his emotions and own interests from those of his lunch-mate and fellow steak-eater.

To accompany steak, wine followed martinis, and Levi-Levy recoiled in horror at Mark's declaration that he was going to tell his wife the whole truth.

"Who does that?" Levi-Levy said. "Are you new here or something? Though I have to admire the chutzpah of this babysitter of yours. And I had no idea you were so wealthy."

"I'm not. But don't you want there to be no secrets between you and your wife? To know everything about each other?"

Levi-Levy chewed his steak and didn't know where to begin. "Wow, you can have breakfast with someone for years," he said, "almost every morning, and still have no idea who they are."

Levi-Levy urged restraint. "How about you start by telling

the truth from now going forward? Future-facing? Who wants to spend all that time sorting through the messy past?"

Mark shook his head. "But the past is precisely the issue."

"What are you talking about?" Levi-Levy asked. "Guilt? You've gotten away with it! You're *getting* away with it. There is no guilt."

"I would want to know if Brooke had screwed around."

No you don't, Levi-Levy thought, or, no I don't want you to know.

"Take it from me," Levi-Levy said, "you don't want to shine the harsh light of probity upon your marriage. A marriage is like a very sensitive virus that thrives in darkness, in the damp, airtight dungeon of secrecy. It will die upon exposure to the light."

"And this coming from someone who is no longer living with his wife," Mark said.

"That doesn't mean I'm not right. Besides, my marriage has actually improved a great deal since I moved out and stopped speaking to my wife."

———

IT WAS THREE p.m. by the time they finished lunch, the rain and overcast now blown over so that they emerged into hot afternoon light. They squinted, weaved, the gin, vermouth, and wine now making them feel too warm, slightly queasy in the sun. Levi-Levy checked his phone, said he had to go pick up two of his boys from a last-day-of-school picnic.

"Your summer plans?" Mark said before they parted.

Levi-Levy seemed surprised by this question. "I'm going to wear lighter clothing," he finally said.

———

THIS IS THE day, Mark was telling himself, of big changes. Associates were leaving, renting their lofts even—he had thought you couldn't do that in this market—the older kids were moving on to middle school. And he too could now affect great transformation. Perhaps what he wanted was an end to his marriage, perhaps that's what he was really trying to achieve. To tell Brooke what happened in the hopes that she would call it off, would tell him to go so he could return to being himself? Is that the dilemma of the husband in marriage, that he felt he was an impostor, that all this, the home, the wife, the children, it was a long detour keeping him from the path he was supposed to be on, the women he should be screwing, the drugs he should be taking, the grand, decadent life he was sacrificing to be a dad?

But who was he kidding? Who did he think he was? Bob Evans? He would be another forlorn, single guy in his late thirties, the oldest guy in any nightclub he happened to wander into. He had gone out for dinner and drinks with his divorced friends before—they always had plenty of time—and despite their freedom they seemed even sadder than the shackled husbands. And what about the kids?

He walked up Greenwich, stopped at 'witchcraft for a cup of coffee, and while waiting for his Americano, he saw through the window a black Escalade like the one Rankin drove, waiting at the light for the left turn onto Laight and then, presumably, the West Side Highway, the FDR, the Midtown Tunnel, the BQE, and so forth until the Hamptons.

Why did a guy like Rankin stay married? Mark wondered. What was in it for him? Or consider it this way, if a guy like that could stay married, then why couldn't he?

Coffee in hand, Mark walked east again, bloated, unsteady, unsure of his destination. The mistake of midday drinking, wiping out thought and decisions. And decision making was not his strength. He was at his best with technical calculations, with analyzing digital files, manipulating sound waves, with hearing, not speaking. Even getting married had not seemed like his decision; he had simply stayed with the prettiest girl who would have him, he now realized. Of course, he loved the perks, but it was never a matter of Mark saying yes, rather it was Brooke never saying no. So this wasn't about that stupid affair, the blackmail, the mistake of infidelity, no, this was about the marriage, the act of will of staying together. Mark now concluded that what he was thinking about was not the affair, not telling the truth, not honesty or love, it was whether or not he wanted to be married to Brooke.

That old question, again.

He went home.

———

BROOKE AND THE kids were out, presumably at some last-day-of-school picnic festivities. Mark lay down on the sofa. He needed a nap. But he kept seeing the faces of the families they knew, the other fathers, the mothers—he tried to keep his focus on the attractive mothers—the other children; he wasn't very fond of other people's children, actually, just his own. But he had to admit, these men and families, this crowd and this place, as flawed and embarrassing as it was, this was his life now.

———

THAT EVENING, OVER dinner, as he watched his children pick through their Thai food, he looked around the loft and appraised the art. If they were splitting up, he would like to have a general sense of what they were splitting up—there was the Daniel Richter abstract, the old totem-pole sculpture by Marisol, those would each have to be worth close to six figures. Maybe even the modest-size George Rouault over the piano was worth something now, and when was the last time he'd even noticed that dreary little smudged clown?

Later, after the girls were in bed and he was trying to reset the television, which one of the girls had managed to deprogram into static, Brooke mentioned that the mother of one of Cooper's classmates (the gangster's wife, he dimly realized as he half-listened) had confronted her today.

"She said her daughter was still upset that Cooper and Amber could never get along—"

He nodded. Which was the input again? HDMI 1, 2, 3, 4, or 5? And why are there five anyway? What can you input? Say, the cable system, a Blu-Ray player, a computer, a game console. And then what else? Maybe a camcorder? Do people still use those or is it all iPhones now?

"—she said that Cooper had still been excluding Amber from jump rope or whatever. Amber was very upset—"

There it is. HDMI 5. Still nothing. Unplug the cable box and wait for a reboot.

"—Cooper told her, apparently, 'We don't have to stay friends forever—'"

Ah, there it is. Back on NY1, the official you-have-successfully-rebooted-your-cable-box channel.

"I talked to Cooper about it and she said that she and the girl just didn't get along and why should she be friends with a girl she doesn't like. If Cooper doesn't like Amber, then why should she be forced to like her? *Can* we force her to like Amber? I can't even get Cooper to eat a piece of broccoli. I mean, the school year is over, why bring this stuff up? She should just tell her daughter that sometimes people change, friends change, relationships evolve, you know?"

He agreed.

Relationships evolved. People changed. Perhaps all this extra-marital activity was simply part of that evolution. Why should he impose his morals and standards upon his marriage? It was an organism larger and more varied than he could comprehend. He needed to let it flow, to let the marriage have space and oxygen rather than examine it for flaws and imperfections. In time, he was sure, this was the kind of personal trial that makes a marriage stronger rather than weaker. Fucking the babysitter, in other words, was good for his marriage! It sounded ridiculous, but how else could a man know whom or what he really loved or needed? You learn from the deed, not from the theory.

Another drink in him, and he felt the rekindling of his afternoon buzz, the soothing, vague assuredness that his life was, somehow, in its own rather predictable way, working out. The art on his walls, the children, the wife, it was all flawed, perhaps, but it was all good enough.

BROOKE WAS IN the guest room/office, and she reappeared now, a serious expression on her face.

"Can I tell you something?" she said.

"Anything."

"Okay." She took a deep breath. "I think I should tell you this because I want to be honest and I think it's better if we just get this stuff out in the open so that . . . so that it doesn't grow and become something worse."

"Sure," he said, not liking where this was going. Hating, in fact, where it might be going.

"I've kind of realized that I have a problem with, with smoking too much marijuana. I need to stop, I think, and I've been seeing a therapist about it, someone my friend Anna suggested, and he told me that it might be helpful for me to go to NA meetings or MA or one of those, and so I went to one, on Broadway down near Wall Street, and I don't know about those meetings. I mean, I hate meetings, and joining stuff. That's not really me. But anyway, I do know that I need to quit, because my behavior when I've been smoking—and this was an everyday thing for me—hasn't been very positive, very, um, yeah, not positive."

Behavior not positive? He did not ask in what way. He had not been a shining exemplar of positive behavior himself.

———

THERE WERE NO revelations and recriminations that summer but instead a growing tension and discomfort in each other's presence, a short-temperedness with each other that reached the point where Mark took to sleeping in the guest room/office of their loft, where, if the truth be told, he slept quite soundly.

What was awful about this situation was how every past malfeasance, misbehavior, or fuckup was now trotted out again: Mark's early-in-the-marriage drug problems; Brooke's dope-smoking. And then, of course, Ed.

Brooke had always maintained that Mark had never understood her heartbreak and anguish at losing her brother. Or, even more troubling, at never finding him. The lack of a corpse had caused in Brooke an anxiety that Mark did not understand. "Ed is gone," Mark had once barked in a fit of impatience. "Let him go!"

But all these points and counterpoints were just circumlocution to cover the starker truth, that whatever mutual lies and complicities had been told or untold to keep the edifice of their marriage going were suddenly crumbling. What kept two people together for year after long year? A recalled sexual spark? An *entente cordial* of forgiving each other's annoying habits? An ability to ignore each other for extended stretches? The kids?

Even the best of marriages are based, to some extent, on being willing to overlook how much you can hate your spouse. And when something stirs the coiled snakes of convenience, fatigue, resignation, and disinterest, and you glimpse through the writhing bodies the thing itself, then you see how much you hate her. And the feeling is mutual, all concealed by the elaborate staging of a modern, affluent lifestyle.

———

LATER THAT SUMMER Brooke took a trip up to Maine to spend a few days with her tattooed and now fifteen-years-sober mother, who lived in a Bar Harbor barn with a woman Mark assumed to be a girlfriend but that Brooke never conceded as such. The purpose of the trip, according to Brooke, was to think things over, take stock, and make a decision about the viability of the marriage, because she knew in her gut things weren't quite right—as if such things could be decided. Mark had always felt a distant warmth for Virginia, a mother-in-law whose unobtrusiveness—the best trait of the truly self-involved—limited her interactions to odd Christmas presents for the kids—patchouli-scented candles, vintage *Sweet Valley High* novels, and, one year, a set of costume mustaches—and an annual visit on her way to an Earth Day dance somewhere in Pennsylvania. She had been a handsome woman, now grown wide in the hips but with a still-formidable carriage over-scrawled by too many tattoos. Her own marriage hadn't fallen apart so much as had become irrelevant. One Labor Day, when her husband had packed the car to drive back to Connecticut, she had simply decided to stay on. Brooke and Ed were already flown. Brooke's father had shrugged, climbed into the Saab, sparked up a roach, and headed south.

Brooke packed a bag, hailed a cab to the airport, and was off, the first leg, Mark knew, of the multi-leg journey from New York to Bar Harbor.

Cooper was just old enough to suspect a crisis in the hearth, though she could never have fathomed the scope and complexity of the strife. She imagined her parents' fights as being grown-up versions of the spats she had with her sister, only more convoluted. Whereas she and Penny had specific causes—Penny using Cooper's nail polish, for example—her parents' disputes seemed to arise from mysterious sources, steady springs of discontent that could at any moment violently geyser.

That family frigidity, Mom and Dad not speaking, Penny breaking down in frequent sobs at the slightest of provocations—a missing doll, a lost button, anything (her misplaced response

to *something* being wrong, though she couldn't be sure what)—
Cooper would ignore it by putting on her headphones to kill the
hours until one of her friends' parents would drive her and the
friend out to their summer house.

Cooper hardened and Penny softened.

For Mark and Brooke, the sense of mutual discontent felt akin
to their omnipresent sense that they were depreciating, their real
estate wealth evaporating in the midst of the various investment-
bank failures and the bailing out of those who remained. Bankers
were unloading lofts in Tribeca; the writers, sculptors, playwrights,
even puppeteers had stopped moving in decades ago. It turned
out, for all their bohemian airs, as a community they were more
dependent on Wall Street, more *defined* by the financial services,
than they cared to admit. If those bankers, whom Mark had always
skirted in the school yard at drop-off, were really going bust, then
there went the whole neighborhood, their marriage included.

———

THREE DAYS AFTER Brooke departed, she called and said she
was returning, a ride to Portland, a bus from Portland to Boston,
a flight to LaGuardia. Mark was exhausted just thinking about it.

"Mommy," Penny shouted when she picked up the phone.
"Tell Virginia I'm getting a tattoo."

"No you're not!" Mark and Brooke both said, in unison.

4 1 6 El Medio

Brooke would surprise him by suggesting the move.

She said she liked it for the prosaic reasons: a fresh start, a new beginning in virgin land untainted by previous fuckups.

But it was also, for her, a way to let go of Ed. And Mark could function as well on that coast as this one. More television, films, and commercials being produced out there than here.

They could rent out their place, Mark said. Sumner had done it, and his loft wasn't as nice as theirs, and then rent something in Los Angeles. Penny didn't mind; Cooper objected, having built up a power base here in New York. She then reasoned that Los Angeles was where the entertainment industry was headquartered, making both Brooke and Mark wonder at whether they actually knew this little girl who was living with them.

It would cost over $17,000, more if you wanted the art reappraised before it was insured—and they did—to have professionals come to your loft, pack your stuff, load it into a truck, and then drive that truck down North Moore Street and out of sight to show up four weeks later in Los Angeles. The family moved to a hotel at the end of the block for two days before their flight to the West Coast. Mark put his manager in charge of booking the space—he would sell the space within eight months for $4 million—and the afternoon he walked out of the studio and back to the hotel suite, he felt a lightness and joy he hadn't felt in years, a freedom, a sense of possibility. Never mind that it was artificial, that perhaps he was on the cusp of huge mistakes and bad decisions and financial calamities, but what was exciting was that he was moving forward, looking ahead, persuaded, once again, of the structural soundness of his family. They were solid.

———

THE HOUSE, THE palisades, the beach, the white-capped ocean, it doesn't look like penance. How is he supposed to be offsetting malfeasance living in a place like this, where even during his walk to the curb to pick up the newspaper—he still reads newspapers—he is assaulted by the blue sky, gray-green sea, distant outlined Catalina Island? They didn't need this much space, the four bedrooms, three and a half baths, dining room, eat-in kitchen, but they could afford it after selling their loft and his share of the building. His daughters filled the rooms, his wife the other side of the bed. The rhythm of their mornings was different from Tribeca, both girls were driven to school, their lunches dutifully made at home, both dropped off on the street in front of the building. Cooper had mellowed with the move, her assimilation into the new cliques at the local public school forcing her into an uncharacteristic period of humility as she found the girls out here even meaner than her Tribeca friends. She began to cut out pictures from fashion magazines and tack them up on her wall. It took Brooke a few weeks to realize that the photos—actors, models, athletes—were all taken by Barnaby, Miro's dad.

Penny, on the other hand, seemed to have found an inner ruthlessness and suddenly seemed as dominant in her third-grade class

as Cooper had ever been in hers. Mark now recognized the symp-
toms and when another parent mentioned that Penny had said
her daughter was ugly, he immediately sat Penny down and told
her that was inappropriate. Perhaps it was a phase his kids went
through, Mark told Brooke, a sort of psychological growing pain.
They need to work through their mean period, before they could
mellow out a little.

"Sort of like adults," Brooke said.

Out here, Mark never even met the other fathers. Still, mornings like this, as he spooned oatmeal with blueberries, the distance
he had traveled, the travails their marriage had survived—could
leave him without appetite, spoon stuck in bowl, coffee cooling
in cup.

He would walk out to his Mini and drive to Sunset and Gower,
where he had a regular sound-editing gig on his friend's television show. His former coffee colleague, the disgraced memoirist
Rick, had also moved to Los Angeles and within six months—his
notoriety in another field actually gaining him entrée into this
one—had sold a pilot for a one-hour show, based on, of all things,
a Jewish mobster living in Tribeca. They'd had drinks when Mark
and Brooke were house-hunting. He realized now he had always
seen Tribeca as nothing more than an elaborate campsite, their vast
loft and show-off kitchen the urban tent and Coleman stove. Had
he tacitly assumed they would all come West together, to every
American's middle-age destiny: a lawn, a pool, the morning sun
in their faces?

Rick's bi-coastalism wasn't surprising. Marni, who had remarried, was living in the loft with her new husband, someone who
had made money from mortgages during the mortgage boom and
who had also left his spouse. And Rick's autistic son, Alex, now
lived with them. When Mark and Rick met up at a steak house
down in the Santa Monica Canyon for a drink, Rick said it wasn't
that bad, since it was hard to tell if Alex even missed him.

"It's a bitch, not knowing," Rick had said. "I mean, I fly back to New York every other week, but he doesn't seem to even notice I've been gone."

Tribe, now picked up for its second season, was what passed for a success these days, a few million viewers watched it on a cable channel, yet it was talked about and written about disproportionately, the Jewish subject-matter bringing out the yentas and pro-Israeli lobby, who were divided over whether the portrayal of a Jewish mobster was a step forward or a step backward in the evolution of Jewish characters in pop culture. (When the playwright Levi-Levy came out to write episode two of season two, he e-mailed Mark and asked if he wanted to have a drink. Mark never responded.)

Not surprisingly, Rick turned out to be nimble at making up stories—though his Jewish mobster, Mark noticed, as he sipped a martini and listened to Rick talk about his show, sounded like the most realistic thing he had ever written.

"I know," Rick said. "I'm finally in the make-believe business and I am writing the least fictional stuff of my life. Shhhhhhh." He put an index finger to his smiling lips.

It was easy for Rick to get Mark a job. Mark had plenty of credits, though in recent years he had made more money from rents than from jobs.

"You know where I've been going? Giancarlo's place out here. The place on Canon Drive? It's not as good as the Tribeca one," Rick said. "But it's like old times. Hey, his ex-wife? Beatrice? She ended up with Brick, of all people."

Mark tried to picture Beatrice, but kept on imagining Brick's wife, Ava.

"Let's have coffee sometime," Mark said.

They never did. Rick was too busy remaking himself, quickly emerging, in just two years, as more successful than he had ever been back in New York.

Mark was grateful to Rick for the steady work, well-paying, though without the proceeds from the Broadway studio he would never have been able to live as well as he did. He liked the house, the bluff just across the street, and in the late afternoon, like clock-work, an old man, he had to be in his eighties, would come riding by, towed on a skateboard by one of those Alaskan husky dogs.

"He must be one of the Beach Boys or something," said Brooke, who was stretching before she embarked on a run down the cliff. Since she had stopped smoking marijuana, she had become a zeal-ous runner.

"It must be fun," Mark said, "being pulled like that."

"Let's try it," said Brooke.

The man held fast to the leash, swerving as he went, never fall-ing off.

ACKNOWLEDGMENTS

————————

They helped: Billy Kingsland, Gail Winston, Maya Ziv, Jonathan Burnham, Barry Harbaugh, Christopher Cox, Nathaniel Rich, Archie Ferguson, Rhadika Jones, Terry Mcdonell, Phillip Gourevitch, John Podhoretz, Aaron Burch, Elizabeth Ellen, Ptolemy Tompkins, Sandow Birk and Benjamin Percy.
My father, Josh Greenfeld, earned his own line.
As did Bob Roe.
And of course
Silka
Esmee
Lola
Foumiko
(and Noah)

ABOUT THE AUTHOR

Karl Taro Greenfeld is the author of five previous books: the much-acclaimed memoir *Boy Alone*; *NowTrends*; *China Syndrome*; *Standard Deviations*; and *Speed Tribes*. His writing has appeared in *Harper's*, the *Paris Review, Playboy, One Story, Bloomberg Businessweek, Time, Sports Illustrated*, GQ, the *New York Times Magazine, Vogue, Best American Short Stories*, and *The PEN/O. Henry Prize Stories*. Born in Kobe, Japan, he has lived in Paris, Hong Kong, and Tokyo. He currently lives in Tribeca with his wife, Silka, and their daughters, Esmee and Lola.

www.karltarogreenfeld.com